THE COMEBACK

THE COMEBACK

by

Alex Cathcart

POLYGON
Edinburgh

First published in Great Britain in 1986
by Polygon, 48 Pleasance, Edinburgh EH8 9TJ.

The publisher acknowledges subsidy from the
Scottish Arts Council towards the publication of this volume.

Typeset by EUSPB, 48 Pleasance, Edinburgh, EH8 9TJ.
Printed by Bell and Bain Ltd., Glasgow.

British Library Cataloguing in Publication Data
Cathcart, Alexander
    The comeback.
    I. Title
    823'.914[F]   PR6053.A83/

    ISBN 0-948275-08-1
    ISBN 0-948275-11-1 Pbk

FOR KATHLEEN

EVEN before the split doors of the Clyde Vaults had come to rest behind him Gaffney was feasting on the fear: the fear produced by the fearful and paid in silent tribute to him, the lunatic fearless. He stood with his back touching an end wall of the narrow public house. A nod was aimed at the distorted face of the Hunchback pressed against the frosted glass of the doors in the opposite wall. The Thin Man snaked into position; quiet, staring, in line to the inch, impassive. The face at the window disappeared to take up the watch. Gaffney's head turned to take in the shamed; those supporting and being supported by the bar. The mix was the same as usual for an early Friday evening. The tired tradesmen, who hadn't made it up the flights to the tenement eyries, to the expectant wives and mothers perched there, waiting for the pay-in, these were recognised. Recognised by their oily and greasy boiler suits, and the strange shine pulsing from their faces as alcohol sweat mixed with the grease of the ships and machines they toiled over. The pub owner turned to his till. A customer made to go but saw the Thin Man and stayed. At the bend in the long wooden bar set in spittled sawdust, just in front of Gaffney, four young men craned their necks, exaggeratedly craned their necks, towards a television which sat on a shelf in the corner above Gaffney's shoulder. Gaffney looked at the screen. Four young men craned their necks, exaggeratedly craned their necks, towards a microphone which stood in the centre between hooked guitars. Tonight the four in the bar would probably get drunk. They would probably go to the dancing and pretend to young girls that the fabulous four were soon to be overtaken as yesterday's men.

Gaffney was annoyed. In Glasgow's docklands he was the most famous person. He reached up and turned down the volume as far as it would go. His eyes and head turned, scanning; studying the faces at the bar. Some faces equally studiously sipped at their solace, staring straight. Nervous faces smiled surrender. For what they wouldn't know. They knew Gaffney was here. Other faces

9

sought refuge in the eyes of a friend, to be embarrassed at what they saw there. They could not see that what was there, opposite, was reflected in their own. Gaffney could see. The pub owner pushed in the till drawer. Gaffney held the silence.

At the far end of the bar and behind it a skinny man in brown overalls repeatedly turned a domino through his fingers. A dart of annoyance once more pierced Gaffney. He felt aggression rising for the domino player. Yet there was no threat in his face, his stance, his action. The man looked really ordinary. A burst strap on the overalls was tied up with string and the toolbag in front of him was torn and patched. He was young. But his time was out. He was a tradesman. The spirit-level and the handle of the brace and bit stuck out from the bag shouting his trade. A joiner. A time-served joiner. Gaffney was angry. He shook these thoughts from his head. This silence had lasted long enough.

"I'm looking for Lord John," he said, loud enough to be heard all the length of the bar. No one moved, no one spoke, no answer came. No spoken answer was necessary. The ends of the line of men at the bar stretched like an accordion. Only a little enough to be enough. Near the centre a small space was left on either side of a stooped, slightly balding man of around fifty years. Gaffney stepped down the bar. The space increased, allowing him to fit in beside his quarry. "Did you hear me?" The question went un-answered. "Big Des says you're into him for a tenner and there's nothing forthcoming. You would not be at the fanny Lord John, would you?" The older man had turned white, accentuating the clipped brown-stained moustache that contributed to his ennoblement. His hand trembled around the base of his beer glass. Still he said nothing, his eyes riveted to the mirrored wall of the gantry. Gaffney addressed himself to the man's reflection. "Lost the tongue? I asked you a question."

The older man's head shook forward rapidly but still no sound passed his lips. The questioner scanned the mirrors. The others in the bar had edged towards the walls and the doors. The owner leaned his elbows on the drawer of the till and cupped his hands over his face. There was no danger from any of the remainder. Gaffney became more serious. "Maybe a wee drink will help you loosen your tongue. Here. Drink up. Lord John." He took the pint glass from Lord John's loosened hand and with his free hand grasped the other's gentlemanly jaw between forefinger and thumb, and began squeezing, and squeezing, squeezing till the mouth opened. Into the opening the beer was poured till the front of the mouth filled then spilled, overflowing up into the nostrils, finally running down the scrawny space between collar and fleshless neck. Gaffney eased his grip and replaced the pint glass on the bar. "Now, Lord John, have you anything for big Des?" Lord John's head was down, snot running from his nose, eyes clenched closed and top lip drawn tightly up and back. Gaffney remained. "You're still not talking much, Mister. Let's get down to it."

The debt collector laughed and kicked the debtor's legs wide apart. The man's head dropped violently. His nose entered the pint glass. The glass fell over and smashed. The man's head continued downward. His nose hit first, deflecting his head sideways onto the wet bar. Lord John slid to the floor, his hands to his face, cupping the blood which spurted from around the sliver of glass embedded in his left eye. From behind his hands came a scream mixed up with a plea to Gaffney to stop. The blood and scream meant nothing to Gaffney. At the sight of blood his emotions hardened even more. Screams like this meant he had won control over a human being. And those who heard would take note. He looked down dispassionately at the crumpled man. A boot was drawn back. There would be no money now. But the debt would have to be wiped out. Des would have to be satisfied.

"For Christ's sake, Gaffney, that's enough. Let him alone." Gaffney looked up into the bespectacled face of the Joiner who stood nervously gripping and regripping the handle of his toolbag.

"Who the fuck are you?"

"That's my old man," the Joiner answered. "I'm Hamish Creese." This information was given as if this was sufficient to warrant a stop. Gaffney pointed. "This old bastard? Are you weighing in for him then?"

"Not to you."

The words slapped into Gaffney's ears. This man was obviously so afraid he didn't know what he was saying. This was a challenge. Challenges could not go unanswered. Gaffney brought his foot up, burying it dead centre in the challenger's crotch. The young defender doubled over. Creese swung the toolbag weakly in front of himself, as much in defence as offence. Gaffney laughed and kicked the bag contemptuously to the side, stretched forward, grabbed the ears, cracking a rapid head butt onto the Joiner's nose. The man sunk to his knees. The next kick; speedy, up to the chin, knocking the body over. Thought was blanked out for Gaffney. He straddled the challenger's chest. Stretch the arms, dig the knees into the biceps. Maybe the Thin Man wanted a go.

"Your old boy, eh? Took you long enough to speak up for him. If it had been me I'd've been in there right away. You're a yellow bastard. That's right, Thin Man, dead right, isn't it?" The Thin Man looked down, and said nothing. "He's got my suit in a fucking mess, Thin Man. You think he'll pay for it? Fucking right he will."

The toolbag rested at Gaffney's hand. He rummaged in it bringing out a hammer. "Well. Look at this. How do you fancy this on the skull? No? What else've you got here?" Gaffney explored the depths of the bag. He withdrew a clutch of long nails. Hammer and nails were held high at the end of outstretched arms. "How's this suit you, Thin Man?" The Thin Man smiled and fell to his knees, gripping struggling ankles, smiling wider as the grip tightened. The palm was pulled round, the arm at right angles. The point of a nail was pushed into the centre of the Joiner's palm. Fear made the body tight. Gaffney hammered the nail, stopping only when the hand was pinned to the floor. Now the other. Round here, open, open, there we go, there, there there, there, through, you bastard. Now, get out of that. "Now the feet Thin Man, the feet." The Hunchback interrupted, shouting over the screams, pushing through the exodus.

"For Christ's sake Eddie. Leave it. Leave it."

Experience had taught Gaffney to obey his cop-watcher. He rose, giving a last grudging kick to the body. "I'll finish you;

sometime. Best to move on. Away." Gaffney hawked and spat into Creese's face. "Far away."

"I'll fucking get you, Gaffney. I'll get you. You'll get yours Gaffney."

Gaffney lifted the long leather toolbag above his head and let it fall of its own volition onto the face below. "Fuck off." Another screaming cry followed Gaffney out into the street: "You'll get yours. I'll make certain. I'll make certain. You'll get yours." Gaffney looked at his watch. Six minutes and nothing to show but a bloodied suit. Somebody would have to pay. He felt upset and hungry.

Creese lay alternately screaming and sobbing, feeling strangely relaxed, not wanting to rise. The screams were the repetition that Gaffney would get his. The sobs came from deep and were softer plaintive calls to his father, whom he could see huddled and crumpled at the base of the bar, uselessly trying to stem the flow of blood from his wounded eye. The owner left his till and scurried round to kneel beside the younger man.

"Hamish. You all right? Can you get up?"

Creese's head fell to his chest for a moment, then came up again. "Can you get these nails out?" His head was nodding forward now in exasperation. "There's a pair of pliers in the toolbag." He watched, still, curiously relaxed, as his helper ransacked through the bag till he found the pliers. The nose of the pliers were dug into the soft skin of his right palm. He felt them scrape on the nailhead. The pull was clean and came all in one draw. Creese tried to take the pliers but opening the hand proved too painful. The pub owner tried to repeat the extraction but the nail in this hand had been forced deeper. The pliers had to be pushed and screwed down to permit a secure grip. It took two two-handed tugs to free the nail from the floor. Creese sat up, looked at his palms, closed over them tightly with his fingers, and banged the inside of his fists against his head. He rose and hurried over to Lord John. "Da. Da. C'mon. Let's see it." The splinter of glass was a rounded piece of the pint jar which had hooked itself into the eyeball. "I'll have to get you to hospital. Any of you guys got a motor?" Hamish looked at the only man he knew to have a motor.

The man was not for volunteering. The till had to be watched. The car owner wiped his hands on his apron and spoke.

"Should he not get an ambulance?"

"Aye, maybe." Hamish closed his eyes. "An ambulance will take too long to come to a pub. And it would bring the bobbies into it."

The bar owner bunched more apron into his hands.

"I'll take you."

Hamish looked up to see the local coal delivery man. The man still wore his studded leather back guard clasped to his shoulders. The large man lifted up Lord John and took him through the door being held open by the publican. Between them Hamish and the coalman helped the moaning Lord John to the lorry parked nearby. The old man was crushed into the cabin between them, his head on a wet canvas coal bag which was draped over Hamish's lap. Hamish felt the damp through to his crotch and thighs. From the high cabin Hamish saw the domino game had restarted. The pub owner was squeezing a mop into a pail.

ALL the way to the hospital Hamish nursed his father's head in his lap. Even while standing answering the inane questions of the lanky man in the frayed suit who refused to get anxious, Hamish shooshed and rocked the shattered frail old man. Now he had made this guardian of the sanctuary angry; a piece of paper held high, the interceptionist was disappearing into the bowels of the infirmary. Hamish backed Lord John off to the seating area. The three or four individuals scattered over the enclosure did not move, did not look. They had enough pain of their own.

Hamish felt the pain for two. They slumped together forming a sad triangle with the bench.

Raw hurt tore out from his hands, forcing his eyes to close tight. The pain had to be fought, Lord John's had to be taken instead. Every sorrowing wail reminded he could not. Guilt and fear, guilt for fear, sorrow for guilt and fear, but mostly fear; pursuing answers in a mind jammed with untended, unrequited pain.

Gaffney would not rest content. The job was unfinished. Hadn't Gaffney said so? Yes, Gaffney would be back. Some dark night maybe. A knife, a boot; worse, a bottle. The shipyards and the docks, they were Gaffney's. He was unavoidable. A constant reminder of other men's fear of physical hurt. The old man would be all right. The injury for him was merely another degradation to be shrugged off come the next drink. There were no prizes in continuing to harass an old alcoholic. But Hamish Creese? Why Hamish Creese? Where to go? Why go? What was it he had done? For this? This pain's killing. These tears slipped out quietly. Curses; breathless; blaming the Lord John, his own skinny frame, Gaffney. Gaffney most of all, for stripping away the layers of humanity he had scraped around himself. Peel the veneer, reveal the slum upbringing. Now he was reduced to being the same as the wood he worked with; something to be nailed down and hammered. The eyes screwed up as even his mother came in for a curse. These were no help. These were attempts to avoid the knowledge that despite the hurt, the hate, despite the anger, Creese would not, could not, go after Gaffney. Nor would he wait for Gaffney to come to him. "No. No," he cried out involuntarily.

"Are you well, sir?"

A nurse addressed him without humour. Hamish looked at her blankly, needing a second to come out of his thoughts. "I'm all right," he answered, "but I think somebody should move quick to the old boy or he is going to lose that eye. I told Mournful Willie at the desk there." The nurse's cheeks flushed and she turned back quickly, to return with a man in a white coat. The man gestured to Hamish to bring his father forward. A penlight was shone into Lord John's eye.

"How did this happen?"

"He slipped on a pint glass."

"And you? You look as if you've been in the wars."

"I fell at work. Just before stopping time. I couldn't be bothered reporting it at that time."

Hamish kept one hand in his pocket and the other clenched upon an old rag he held against the wound in his palm. This was the Casualty. Hamish had never been here before, but he knew the rules. Everyone knew the rules. It didn't matter that he had never done anything wrong in his life, nothing was to be said to these people. They had seen the dirty overalls, the blood, smelled the drink, and guessed the rest. Boozer, pub brawler. His treatment would be less than the best. The stitches would be huge; marked for life. "It's not me I'm worried about. What about him?" The man in the white coat took Lord John away. The nurse with the pointed face gestured to him to take up his seat amongst the blank spaces and faces. Hamish took his seat without a word. He had sufficient faith in them to believe his old man would be all right with them. Underneath he'd never really believed those tales, but something kept nagging at him, egging him onto the defensive. An old woman near to him on the benches shrugged her shoulders in his direction and offered him a cigarette. Hamish Creese lifted his fistful of rag and held it out in the direction of the large sign which proclaimed 'NO SMOKING'. The old woman cast her eyes over him from head to foot. Quickly and jerkily she raised two fingers to the command.

Hamish closed his eyes. Red, green, purple flashes, lines, spots, dots burst and moved along and through the face of Gaffney. Jerking the eyes open only left the face suspended there, in the air, just above the head. Just a little back from the forehead. There, looking straight in front, laughing. A clutch at the scalp only made the face rise, to hang free, still; there. Scratch at the hair it stays, moving with the head, joined like an unwelcome alter ego come loose; dancing, declaring control from the outside. Oh Christ GO AWAY, go away. You're a bastard. Someday I'll get you. that's a promise. Easy, easy now, take it easy. He'll get his someday. Just wonder if these hands will be all right. Frightened to open them. "You're a yellow bastard." Oh you'll get yours. Come on. Concentrate. At least the fingers are OK. Young Bill had lost one. A hundred pound they gave him. Fifty pound a joint. Maybe it was just half of one. Now the feet, Thin Man, the feet. Tighten the stomach muscles. He's a pure bastard. Don't cry, no, no don't cry. Look. Look at these people. Wonder what is wrong with the old dear? Bronchitis likely, she's smoked non-stop. Even Gaffney would be scared of her. Sorry, the laugh was not at you. Oh come on where are they all? They're taking their bloody time.

The casualty waiting area was in dark, the benches lit only by what light escaped out from under the single shaded bulb which hung behind the reception desk. The long man in the frayed suit stood behind the desk: featureless in silhouette, shuffling papers from the ends of long arms, occasionally lifting his head and letting a loud sniff disturb the quiet. Hamish felt safe in the dark here. Crazy men had pursued wounded quarry into hospitals before now, but Gaffney was too clever to perform where witnesses were a different kind of people. Hospital people. They were. Them and the police. Different.

Lord John had almost been one of them. Almost. He'd lost that university scholarship for kicking a professor in the arse; kicked out to languish with the rest. A poetry-spouting misfit engineer whose only friend was anyone who needed a drink. Now here they both were. Son Hamish Creese was coming to much the same thing. Last night the yard had paid off the finishing trades with nothing on the stocks. God knows there hadn't been much for the shipbuilders this twelve-month. Nothing but a year of mergers that had squeezed men out like excess sauce on a sandwich. The old Clyde was dying. Now Gaffney had underlined his uselessness and solitariness. The pain had got through. Lifted up bent arms and clenched fists tried to push the chin through the chest. Air forced its way through teeth that seemed to be welded together. Hamish Creese felt alone. He was. Alone. The cry of the helpless could not be held back. "Why me? Why the fuck me? Bastard." The cry hadn't the energy of a curse. A body should feel ashamed of such a helpless-sounding sob.

The name seemed to float to him through the dark. At first the Hamish Creese sat still, wishing to see someone else respond to the call. There was no other Hamish Creese. On the third rising call of 'Mr Hamish Creese' he stumbled clumsily out of the darkened area towards the young nurse, who took his toolbag and gestured down a tight narrow corridor. The corridor opened out into a square room with green-curtained cubicles around the edges. The clean superior smell of disinfectant was attacking the competing smells that clung. That dirty smell of the pub floor, fighting with the almost sweet reek of nicotine, beer and whisky. The clean smell of wood on the overalls did not hide the pungency of the picked-up odour. He was dirty and unclean. He was more ashamed than embarrassed. There were only two other people being attended to. A fat woman in a faded floral dress was preparing to go, gingerly touching a white bandage which enveloped her head. There was no emotion in her bruised face. An old yellow-faced welder in a scuffed leather waistcoat was being treated for flash. He was enjoying his own crude jokes about his ability to manage sex while temporarily blinded. The nurse ushered Creese to a cubicle, seating him down opposite a half-moon tray of instruments. "Where did you put my tools?" he asked.

"I left them with Jack at the reception. You can pick them up when you go. Now let's look at you."

The accent was Highland. One of the northern refugees happier hiding in the hospitals. As she turned his head this way and that Hamish was shocked to feel little explosions of sexual attraction which had to be suppressed in his head and belly.

"Well, I don't think your nose is broken," she said, giving it the gentlest of tweeks, "but it will be a balloon tomorrow. You'll look like a Chad." She laughed at her own joke.

Tension eased as Hamish laughed too. Though he didn't know what a Chad looked like, he could imagine.

"That's better. Now what about these hands of yours?" She placed her fingers under his wrists and lifted the hands up and out in front of him. "You came in with the older man, didn't you?"

He nodded, feeling as though he could not stop his head.

"Were you fighting each other?"

His fingers flexed out involuntarily. His mouth opened. "Are you crackers or something? That was my old man I came in with."

"How did he come by his eye then?"

"He fell in a pub; right onto a pint glass."

"Are you sure no one brought the glass to him?"

Creese merely shook his head. The nice Highland girl had become like the rest. Questions that contained disapproval even in their asking. All the guilt for the asking by implication. Inferences, politely made. Everybody like him shared the guilt the questioners were sure belonged to others, but not themselves. Questions that always came from those with decent clothes and jobs to match. "He fell." Those kind always got short answers.

In silence both of them studied his hands. The holes in the back of the hand had become small clusters of dried crusty blood with red river traces which had flowed out, along and down, through between his fingers. She replaced them on his thighs then still without speaking applied an antiseptic to a square pad. Creese could not keep up the silence. The silence was his fault. He had told the lie. And in this silence he saw large stitches ahead. "Hope you're not for saying this is going to hurt you more than it will hurt me." The nurse smiled. She began to clean the wounds, along the back of the hands, the wrist, the side of the thumb. The probing antiseptic pad was poised to dab the palm. Creese prepared for pain. The wounds in the palms were ragged where the hammer head had burst the skin around the nail head. From the left hand a large gouge had been lifted where the pliers had been forced and screwed into the flesh to gain a grip. Under the strong light the wounds seemed huge, much larger than he had thought. The pain began to increase but here in the clear light he could not cry out.

A round red-faced doctor followed on a harsh rent of curtain rings. Without acknowledging Creese he picked up the hands and began forcing his thumb around the small bones. The pain was intense and the doctor's breath stank.

"Mr Creese, I'll have to have these X-rayed."

"Look, Doc, no offence but I'll be OK. Can I not make do with a bandage?"

"Mr Creese. These palms need stitching, but I do not intend to stitch them before ascertaining the full extent of the injury."

"Doctor, I know you mean well, but I have to get off. I'll be all right. Honest."

"Creese. This place is full of people like you on a Friday night. You've just rolled up earlier than most. We have to mend you, clean you up, stitch you up so you can go and do it all again. And while we're doing it we have to listen to your curses and mop up your vomit. Don't mess me about any more than you can't help. Nurse, get him to X-ray. Please."

With an aristocratic, theatrical parting of the curtains, the doctor swept out. Away. Fast. No time for Creese to protest. No use anyway. He couldn't explain. To blokes like that one he was branded simply by being in the pub. Creese looked at the nurse. She knew. She knew the shared guilt that people like Creese bore for those they were condemned to live with, who refused to feel any. It was in her eyes, and the feel for her fob-watch. Even she on the neutral ground of nursing still felt the guilt for the tongue-tied madmen, the escaping drunks, the plain ignorant.

"You must excuse him. A nurse was attacked right in here last month. It is the way things are just now. C'mon now. Follow me."

She led him out along close narrow corridors that seemed to

press in at the bottom and lean back at the top as though in distaste. He could only go along; follow. The X-ray room was cold; white-tiled from floor to ceiling. Rings of chrome and glass hung menacingly from the ceiling over unwelcoming metal beds. "Listen. Before you go. Can you find out for me how the old boy is? Please?" She smiled and nodded as if to a child.

She returned just as the anonymous white coat had finished placing his hands, turning his hands, and disappearing; till all he heard was a disembodied voice calling 'That's fine, Mr Creese'. Loneliness had begun shrinking him. Already he felt as if his clothes were on someone else's body. His nurse, guide and protector, ensconced him back in the cubicle.

"Your father will be all right. He may lose partial sight in one eye but he'll survive. He will now need glasses."

Creese had asked for the information but now he received it blankly. This should mean something, but right now the nurse seemed to be stating something that was of little interest. Sorry to hear this bloke might lose an eye, but that's the way it goes. Shame. The curtain rings rattled on the rail and the still red-faced medic returned to fill up the cubicle with the stink of his breath.

"Your X-ray is all clear. You have been extremely fortunate. No need to panic just yet. Time will tell. Nurse. Stitch him up and bandage his hands so they can't straighten and stretch the palm. Make them into a fist."

All this was said to mid-air without a look at Hamish Creese, who sat silent. Behind his eyeballs something was trying to push a way out. He needed his glasses, lost somewhere on the bar floor. All over he was tired, beginning to ache. It was time for home. Such as it was. Friday. The two through the wall would be full of wine and be watching and whooping at TV wrestling. Pass you in the close-mouth Monday to Thursday, only a nod. Friday, the blood was up, fuelled by wine and aggressive melodrama. 'Oh he's a bad bastard. Did you see that? Crack his skull son, crack his skull!' Inside he knew he was envious about something, something it made him sad not to have.

"Looks like you've been lucky."

"Aye. That's right. I've been lucky. They always say if you have got your health you are lucky."

He watched the stitching dispassionately, trying to judge the competence of the nurse as a way to blot out pain and painful reverie. Sweat was breaking out on his forehead making him aware he was alive. The concentration lapsed, the events re-ran, and his head twisted severely as he felt Gaffney's green spittle cover his top lip and run down into his mouth.

"Easy now. Relax. I am just finishing."

"It wasn't you. Sorry. It was me. Honest."

Voices echoed along the walls of the corridor. Loud, self-confident voices that bordered on the arrogant. Here they come. The police. Big black boots appeared in the gap between curtain and floor. Here we go. The cubicle became narrower. The nurse straightened, smiled, drew the curtain and squeezed herself out between the two policemen. Creese found himself looking at a broad scrubbed face, neckless, stuck onto the regulation blue shirt-collar. A hand pulled at an ear-lobe; this put the three stripes under Creese's nose. Behind him, skinnier, taller and darker, came a constable wrapped in a shapeless black tarpaulin with hands held down in the pockets. They insisted themselves into the square arena. Creese sat looking up the sergeant's silver buttons trying to focus on the wart on the broad forehead. The faces did not smile.

"What's your name, son?" asked the sergeant.

"Hamish Creese."

"That's right, son."

"I live at 66 Jubilation Street."

"That right? I know it well. What have you been up to then, son? They tell me your old man is in here too. Bad that. They tell me he is going to be blind. Bad that. I see that you've copped a right handful as well. What's the score?"

Sounds became sharper to Hamish. Instruments elsewhere clattered into pans; voices, words indistinguishable, seemed to beg his attention. It was time to be off, to be out to join in the sounds that passed over and through him.

"What happened tonight, son? We know it was not your fault.

You did not deserve that. You did not deserve to be . . . well, to get what you got. You did not deserve that, son."

Hamish sat quiet, scanning the two faces that peered down to overpower his mind. The gates of his memory had shut tight at the mouth.

"Would you not like to see him put away? That is the only way you will get him, son. Through us. The Law. Ignore us, he'll come back. And you are 'it' for the same again. Everywhere you see him you will have to dodge. In pubs I see you buying him drink for evermore. You'll never know freedom, son. Never. You will never be rid of him."

Hamish wondered what it meant to be free. What is that? To go in any pub, buy, or refuse drink for people. What is that? Is that it? Must be more than that. All through his life there had been Gaffneys, who for the most part took turns licking your face then beating it with their tongues. Others chained you with rules. These two wanted to do both.

"The Law is the only way for you, son. You won't ever get him yourself. Do you think for a minute you will be able to get him into a situation where you can do the same to him? Even if you did or got somebody to do it for you, he would come back and back. Him or that mad family of his. It would never finish, son."

A part of his mind was agreeing, even eager to agree out loud. Gaffney and his kind frightened him. Immediate revenge by himself was out of the question. Half of his own family lay pathetic somewhere, more worried about drink than revenge. The other half had troubles of her own. Angela. Sister and mother.

"Look at yourself, son. You will never be a fighting man. You look as if you need a good feeding. There is nothing you will be able to do." The younger policeman lifted his chin to speak, giving Creese a clear view of hair-filled nostrils.

"Maybe he thinks God will send all the baddies to the bad fire." Hamish considered the proposition. Maybe. The young constable would get a shovel with a short handle. The sergeant picked at his wart for a moment.

"What about your father, son? That eye is gone. He'll never get it back. You cannot get another one for him. At least we can put you-know-who away where he won't see much either. We can bang him up. If you charge him."

The cubicle had become very close; oppressive. Hamish wanted to dive out between them to the cooler air outside. He was starting to cry at his belly. But never. Never in front of these two. His head and hands pounded hurt. The friendly voice carried on.

"It, it is like this, son. We know you are not a rascal. You just want to get up in the morning, get out on the job, get your drink at the weekends. Match on a Saturday, dancing at night, and maybe knock it off with some bird. You're OK, son. You are not trouble. We are here to help people like you. But you have got to help us help you. Charge the bastard."

Hamish rolled his neck letting out sighs of exasperation. The whole body was tight. "Let me go. Will you let me go? I'm tired, I am sore. I just want to get to my bed."

The constable eased forward, drawing long fingers from the depth of a pocket and clamping them on Creese's head to stop the rolling.

"We could always charge you, you know."

Pretence was sucked out through the gap in the curtain, leaving them isolated in truthful vacuum. The game was finished. The sergeant spoke. Louder, angrier.

"He is a madman. Even when they get him to jail they will never do anything with him. He can never change. He's not like you and me, son, he needs to do what he's doing. It's like a drug. He eats people like you."

Hamish rose. On his feet he still remained dwarfed, hemmed in by the bulk of the policemen. So close together he felt they were well all getting ready for some highland dance. The sergeant looked puzzled at the smile.

"You have upset a dog that was feeding, Creese. This one is a mad terrier. He will never let you go."

Hamish slipped his way through the curtain. "I suppose I'd better get going."

"Going? If I were you I would emigrate. Son."

THE naked woman was silent as the curses filled every space
left between her and the frame of the window through which
she was being pushed. She stumbled out and tumbled herself into
a flimsy underskirt as loud anger was spat toward her by the
scruffy little man in the window. His hair spiked upward and
outward and between curses he pushed the stud of his collarless
shirt into his mouth. Bare feet pushing, she began to crawl up the
steep slope which led from the basement below to the pavement
above. From behind her, through the air above her, a pair of briefs
flew, coming to rest on a frost-bitten rose.

The knickers dangled from the rosebush; caught, suspended,
forlorn, resisting the attempts of the bare-breasted owner to pull
them free. The woman in her scramble slipped, and slipped again.
One hand clutched a skirt to her middle, the other wavered between
rescuing the caught pants and assisting in the clamber up the muddy
bank which once had served as a town garden. A grab for them made
her face meet the earth. Again, slower, she tried. This time they
ripped free. Almost dignified, she paused, cleared long stringy hair
from her sight, straightened her back, and sobbing, struggled up to
finally snatch and hold the railings which marked off the pavement
from the garden. She pushed her clothes through the base of the
rails then attempted to scale the fencing. A thrown shoe impaled
itself on the point of a railing. Another, thrown stronger, flew up high
over the rails to land in the road beyond the pavement, setting off
rings of reflected yellow lamplight from startled puddles. The curses
still followed her from the cruel face at the window below. Creese
stepped forward from the corner shadows.

"Don't you help that fucker. Keep away from that. Whore's
bastard. Just fucking leave her be."

Hamish hesitated. His hands were in pain. And bandaged. The little man was his sister's landlord. He stood, unsure. A scrawny hand shot out, wrenching his shirt. The woman forced him near. With a shove on his shoulders she pushed and slithered her way over the railings. She ignored Creese, wriggled into the skirt, collected her shoes and walked off, still bare-breasted, along the midnight empty street. The small window slammed, muting the curses.

Hamish climbed the front stairs and slowly opened the door. Workmanship in wood like this was gone now. Gone with the toffs who used to live in these buildings, left now to uncaring landlords or mysterious Indians with their blanket curtains at the windows. Inside, at the end of the main hall, a lavatory seat languished, raised up and resting against a long-suffering pipe at an angle of forty-five degrees. The dull and dark stairs which ran down to the basement rooms looked more frightened than frightening. There were four rooms on this floor. The door of the single room on the right closed quietly. Opposite, through the opaque glass panels of the door, the only light visible was that coming from flames in a fireplace. Hamish knocked anyway. With the youngster, Angela would not go far. Maybe they were all in bed. Someone was coming out of the adjacent room.

Hamish felt the smell before he saw Daft Lizzie. As usual Lizzie carried one bastard child in her arms while the other tugged at a dirty dress, peeping out from behind at the big people. The small boxroom was only seven feet square. From the room the combined smells of urine and rancid margarine and sweat and rotten vegetables rode out, as if the quarters were too bad even for them. Hamish's jaws were pumping. Sickness welled up in him. Lizzie opened her mouth to speak, drawing attention to the mis-applied lipstick which almost completely reddened the large prominent teeth.

"I don't know if she's in. If she's away you can come in here to wait."

The sickness needed stronger fighting. He felt disgust toward this helpless creature standing there, her stocking seams twisted around her frail legs; a female child dressing up like big women do. He struggled to find the compassion he knew he should be feeling. A guilty smile set on the mouth, above the belly still demanding to vomit in answer to the nostrils' call. The mouth remained closed; for the taste of the smell was worse than the smell of the smell. Angela's light came on and her door opened. Nodding a smile he waved in the general direction of the hiding child and pushed past his sister into the room.

"Christ, Angela. My God. That's awful. That lassie can't be fit to be a mother. What a guff." He dropped his toolbag to clutch his nose.

Angela was laughing. Hamish looked at her and began to laugh too. Angela. Always light. Fair, pale, bright with golden hair.

The wide dirty easy chair by the fireplace welcomed Hamish's tired body, altering its bumps and lumps to accommodate this latest body. Two blocks of thick wood sparked and burned in the fire, every now and again exploding a fiery small smoking splinter onto the bare linoleum floor. "I'll need to remember to bring you some more," he said, but realised he could not. There would be no joiner's shop for a while. "Anyway. Where's your man? And the wee chap?"

"Douglas is away at his mother's for a few days. You know she can't see enough of him and young Stewart."

"Aye. And she pays his father enough to bring him. That lot will take the boy away from you someday Angela. Mark my words. Could he not take you?"

"Look. You leave my family affairs to me. What on earth has happened to you?" The probe was turned.

"It's nothing much, honest. But I'd better tell you, Da is maybe going to lose an eye. They're not sure yet."

"What do you mean? What have you two been up to?"

Hamish told her about Lord John and Des and his own futile attempt to intervene with Gaffney. He lifted up his hands from the arms of the chair. Angela stood over him, between him and the heat of the fire. Hamish wasn't sure how she would take this news; the daughter-father relationship had been ripped apart years ago when drink had taken priority over payment of rent. She simply stood looking at the bandaged hands. Hamish was fidgety. "Don't get upset, Angela. These will mend, and they're not certain about his eye." Angela suddenly began to stomp the large room, her hands over her ears. She stopped, turned, tearful.

"Not you too. I thought you were keeping clear of this kind of stuff. Now you're in it as well. Just like the rest. Men, men, men. Fucking men. Playing at cowboys and we've to suffer in silence."

"Angela. I've never heard you swear before."

"So what? If you stay a little bit longer you'll hear some more. Do you know who was here tonight? Here, right here, talking to me. Des. That's who." She answered the question in Hamish's face. "Looking for Douglas. Here. He also just wanted to know if I had a family allowance book. Me. Kids' money. To pay him." Her head shook as if she still couldn't believe it. "Douglas apparently owes him money as well and he's been dodging him. He never told me. I thought he was getting it from his mother. Jesus. My mother, my father, and now Douglas and me. It all repeats. What do you get for trying?" Hamish said nothing. "Now you're dragged into it. Hamish Creese, pubfighter. You're all mad. Not a thought for women and kids. Just your bloody drink and your rotten guts." Angela had stomped her way round to Hamish. "You don't have to be like them, Hamish. Not you. I hoped you'd get clear of this muck."

The flames in the fire became an excuse for staring. Douglas and Des. Next move would be Gaffney and Douglas. If Gaffney found out that Angela was a Creese then there would be interest in the payment. It wouldn't be this week. There was always a week to scare the bad payers and drive them further into debt. Angela would be all right. The rules didn't allow women to pay for their men. Gaffney was only allowed to frighten her. Scare her because she had married a young prince who had turned out to be a pauper. An old pauper. Old before his time.

"Angela. I didn't know. I knew Douglas boozed a bit, but I never knew he was into big Des. How much does he owe him?"

"Oh, God knows. You tell me. Three shillings in the pound, on the pound if you miss, how the hell do I know? The fat bugger just seemed to be saying it was a lot." She knelt beside the chair, picking at the string on the arms which was exposed from the leather.

28

"I can get you some cash. You can take it and give me it back when you've got it. I can get it for Wednesday."

"It isn't the money. Pay this one, Douglas will come back for more. He'll have to pay properly eventually. You keep your money, you worked for it. By the looks of things you might be idle for a while."

A silence came between them. Hamish was uncomfortable. Not-so-deep down he would have grudged the money to Douglas. The man's company was worth a couple of pints. The stories he told. The jokes. Flattery. Bailing him out was a different matter, though if Angela had agreed, so be it. The room had turned cold. The bed along one wall, the broad, mirrored wardrobe, the huge black Welsh dresser of another age and the chair at the hearth, all seemed alien, lost and forgotten in this high-ceilinged room which dwarfed human occupants. Angela spoke first.

"Do you want a cup of tea?"

The discussion was over. Angela had looked into him, read his conflicts and miseries, remembered their origins, analysed their formulation and understood their outcome. Hamish Creese. She forgave him for not insisting on paying. "I'd love one thanks. Is it OK to go to the kitchen? I've just seen one of McCafferty's women come flying out his window."

"I know, I seen you watching. I was behind the curtain. There's a whisky boat in." That explained a lot. McCafferty was the tally man. "The woman hangs around The Three Wishes. She must have tried to do him, or something. Will you come down with me? That other cow down there has a real funny character staying with her just now, and I think they've got a customer in."

From a cupboard in the dresser Angela brought out a large teapot, its bottom black from being stuck on the fire. Down from the hall the stairs twisted to the right. They kept silent, keeping their backs half-turned to the damp wall. At the bottom, behind blackness, behind a door, voices softly celebrated the dark. Angela opened another door directly in front. Light came from a bed-lamp over a bed hidden in a recess. The small angry lover lay on top, his shirt tucked into dirty grey long underpants. A sock covered one foot. The mouth was wide open and air forced its way noisily down nose and throat. Hamish, following Angela, tiptoed over to the small scullery which housed the water and gas cooker for the whole household. Angela filled the pot and found matches.

"Damn. There's no gas. Have you got a shilling?"

They found it hard to suppress laughter as Hamish nodded and waved hands which could not go into his pockets. Angela fumbled through his pockets. A shilling was extracted from a palmful of silver. "Take two," said Hamish. Angela laughed. She retraced her steps up to the lavatory in the hall where the meter was housed and quickly returned, out of breath. In the closeness of the cramped scullery, lit by the warm blue flame which licked around the pot, Hamish felt safe; secure with Angela, where no one could see them. Here they could stay forever: hidden away forever from the oppressive world outside. Just remain here, cosy in the dark. Steam from the spout scalded his nostrils as he leaned over and down to check if the water had boiled.

Up in the room tea was shaken into the pot and stirred round with a pencil. Angela put on the last block of wood then poured the tea into mugs. Hamish stretched his legs in front of the fire. The walk from the hospital to Angela's had been long and damp. His own bed was warmer, but this seemed safer, wiser. Angela pulled a shilling from the pocket of her apron. Amused by the look on the face of Hamish she thrust it down the large flap on his overall. "You don't have to give me that back. I thought you didn't have one anyway?"

"Take it. The meter's burst. You put in the shilling, draw out the tin and there you are, it comes back to you." She moved on. "where are you going next, Hamish? There's not much work is there?"

"No, there's nothing doing, Angela. Not in the yards anyway. They're out to close us. Nothing surer. Some of the boys are talking about going to Australia. There's some contract job on in Whyalla. That's South Australia."

"What about Vietnam? I thought they were all coming back because of that. It was in the Sunday papers."

"I don't know. It's supposed to be a contract anyway. I really don't know, but they want them there quick." Angela listened. "Angela, do me a favour will you? Could you sort these bandages for me? I'm sure they put them this way just for badness. I can't use my fingers."

Angela placed her cup on the hearth and lifted his hand gently. The pin loosened, the bandages flowed from his hand to hers. Her hands worked like silent shuttles, lifting and rolling the bandage in one easy movement. The whole body relaxed. The pain was almost worth the mothering. He fought and suppressed the urge to lean over and kiss her hair. The room was disappearing. All life was being concentrated here; here in the corner, where an invisible ring kept out the forces which made him afraid. Peaceful. He remembered another night, by another fire, entranced, as his father had taught him his own favourite lines. He still knew them. Could still feel the man in the voice. There, side by side, in the dark, huddling for warmth.

> Is the night chilly and dark?
> The night is chilly, but not dark.
> The thin grey cloud is spread on high,
> It covers but not hides the sky.
> The moon is behind and at the full:
> And yet she looks both small and dull.
> The night is chill, the cloud is grey:
> 'Tis a month before the month of May,
> And the Spring comes slowly up this way.

"HEY. YOU. IN THERE. COME TO FUCK OUT HERE TILL I SEE YOU. OPEN THIS DOOR, BASTARD."

The screaming voice was accompanied by a kicking which made the glass panels of the door shake and the lock rattle. Hamish rose off the seat, came down, to remain on the edge, absolutely still; tense. The voice continued demanding, the kicks threatening. Gaffney. No. Not here. Now. The voice sounds began to splarge and splutter. This was McCafferty. Hamish waved his hand free of the last piece of bandage and hurried over to the door. The landlord stood; hair spiked, eyes bloodshot, lips purple dribbling saliva.

31

"Where's my shilling, you bastard?"

A shilling. What shilling? That shilling. His shilling. "You think I'm a mug, or what? She gets the gas and the bob, I get the fucking bill. Who is kidding who?"

Hamish looked at the pathetic figure, his mind still not taking it all in. One foot was still bare; a piece of shirt poked out from the fly of the greasy grey baggy-trousers. Daft Lizzie came out to view, the inevitable child in her arms; eyes wide, mouth wide. Hamish fumbled in the flap with his one free hand. "Here. There's your bloody shilling. Take it and fuck off."

"Don't tell me to fuck off. This place is mine. It's you that will fuck off. I'll go for the boys in blue. They'll be right round here."

"What for? A shilling? Do you want two? Here, take ten."

Daft Lizzie spoke from the side, addressing the landlord. "You did it first. You broke it. You always take the money. The meter is always empty."

The landlord turned his wild face to Daft Lizzie. A quick kick hit her on the leg, narrowly missing the peeking child. She began to withdraw into her room like a wounded animal.

"Get fucking in there you. Don't open your trap if nobody asks."

An unrestrained hand dug into the sides of the landlord's windpipe. Hamish ran him against the end wall. His head drew back. The head was back as far as it could go. Just beginning to take the shoulder along. A spring coiled from shoulder to neck to forehead. Now. Release.

"Don't. Don't, you bastard, don't. I'll get Gaffney on you. Gaffney'll sort you out. My boy knows him."

The hesitation became a freeze. The croaking bundle slid down the wall. Gaffney. Lord John. Angela. Himself. Puzzle pieces floating unfitted.

Angela pulled at his arm, pleading for him to go, go. She was right. The shilling was tossed into the face of the squealing pile. He turned away drawing a pound note from his pocket. "Here. Give that to the wee man when he gets back. Tell him it's from his Uncle Hamish." Angela was nervous, her hips bumping Hamish off balance as they made for the door together. At the door

Hamish stopped. "Look after my tools for me, will you? I'll collect them when this character has quietened down." Angela nodded, pushing him out the door. He went out, down still wet stairs, turning left at the bottom, not looking back, walking.

A shilling. A bloody shilling. What the fuck could you buy with a shilling? What could you get for a shilling? A cup of tea that was stewed black? Ah fuck it. No use arguing about it. The shilling was that little bastard's. It was his shilling because it was his meter. So he was due it. At least until the Gas Board came to empty the fucking thing. Angela. Jesus Angela. Thieving it to give it back to her wee brother. A miserable shilling. On a Friday as well, bloody pay night. This pay night in particular. The wallet was loaded with some of the cash they sold their jobs for. Anyway, Hamish Creese had never needed a shilling since they had cut Lord John off. A shilling. A fucking shilling. Who needs a shilling?

McCafferty was shouting from the top of the stairs: "Creese you bastard. You are done, done you fucker. You'll get what's coming to you, you shitebag. Just wait, wait. Your card's marked."

33

☆☆☆☆☆☆☆☆

S TEPPED-OVER lines between the flagstones of the pavement started to mark out an intuitive route: forward to square
corners, abrupt turns onto tarmacadam, merging at metalled
roads with water-filled holes the size of a foot. The inside of the
head had given up trying to arrange events, words, faces and
places into some sort of sequence. All that had happened today,
tonight, ran around this mind chased by pictures, voices of other
times, other people; a swirl of sounds and visions too painful to
stop and analyse. Best just to feel the wet, follow the feet.

Over a wall constructed of thin brick faced with white tile the
funnels of the small tramps for faraway places appeared straight,
solid, somehow superior. A young Hamish Creese with sad short
trousers and happy wonder had known all the great shipping lines
by the colour and markings of their flags and funnels. The
cargoes, routes and ports of call; an excited Hamish had known
them all. Rich imaginings were sparked and fuelled by Lord
John's tales of his times at sea. All doubtfully, hopefully, true.
Rudderless on the Cape, flooded en route to Valparaiso, fist-
fighting in Vancouver, jailed in San Francisco. A one-eyed drunk
in a hospital bed.

Big ships didn't call now; even for the human cargo bound for
Canada and Australia. Boy Creese had sat on top of this wall and
seen the hopeful, tearful crowds in their tight little groups;
hugging, crying, lifting then lowering suitcases for one last kiss.
Then he had considered them lucky. Now he considered them
lucky. Then it had been for the strange excitement of the travel to
these places; to cross the line, be heartily dipped by old Father
Neptune. Now, standing on tiptoe, looking at the empty basins
like parallel flooded graves, the mourning cranes petrified, their

ropes and hooks like stretched, frozen teardrops, now the deeper reasons for envy stood out. And now there were people like Gaffney.

The white tiles gave way to large solid blocks of red sandstone interrupted by thin high arched windows awesome as a cathedral. The Yard. The big solid door with polished brass handles, the same one Lord John had pushed him through to compete for the Apprenticeship. A little frightened, hesitating, overawed by two huge figures carved above the archway: Master and Tradesman, each with compass and square holding open the Plan. Lord John had explained it. Your wee brains and my big brains. Then he had pushed him in. That small ship sailed below clay feet over waves and the admonition 'LABOR OMNIA VINCIT'. Apprentice Creese had been laughed at because he had translated it for some of the lads, and defended it in the face of laughter. Uncertain fearful laughter to pillory a clever fool. Now he was idle and work wouldn't overcome the mess in his head, but the Victorian figures still impressed.

The doorway provided shelter from the drizzle, but stopping allowed the pain to dominate; running out from his hands to tighten up the forearms, the biceps, the shoulder blades, the belly, the thighs, the legs. Whimpers, groans, soft curses, amplified, echoing around the doorway, could only be heard by the stone figures in the tableau above. They were probably too engrossed in the grand Plan to care anyway. The belly was making demands as well. Friday. Clark's would be open. He worked all night every Friday to bake the weekend quota. The smell of newly baked bread filled the nostrils of the imagination and spurred the feet.

From the Yard the route to the bakery led along past the tenement rows. These were built long ago for the best tradesmen. Or the scarcest. Private landlords owned the blocks now. They collected the rents and left them to fall while people slept. The outside of the pavement was safest; away from the shop doorways and close-mouths where sudden hands could draw a passer-by up, and in, to be found in the morning by the milk-boy or the mailman. Odd rectangles of cream light created gaps of warmth on the cold black walls. The light that stirred envy in the outsider.

The cinema held its stars behind glass in still photographs, asking the onlooker to buy the ticket, make the dream come alive. Clark's bakery was this night's coming attraction; from here the smell was real.

The smell intensified as he passed into and through the narrow close-mouth out into the backyard. A light shone through wooden slats in a door set in the side of what had once been two boilerhouses for women to wash clothes in. The immigrant Pole had converted them, baked here, solitary through the night. Hamish thumped at the slats. A scuffling was followed by a drawing of reluctant bolts. The top half of the door opened and a long arm wiped along the bottom half which acted as a counter top. Only the flour in the black hair and on sunken cheeks was whiter than the complexion of the man, who stood, trying to judge his customer as trouble or no trouble. He stayed at the end of stretched arms, just looking, from shiny eyes set in black circles. "Have you anything for eating, George? I mean pies or that?"

"Sure, I've got pies. How many do you want?" Hamish came closer to the opening, pulled by the warmth. "Hey. You're Hamish. Hamish. You look a mess," the baker shouted, slackening off more bolts and opening the bottom door. "When I see you, you're all dressed up. You know, after you've been dancing. Fridays. You always look the part." He extended a stubby hairy-fingered hand from the light. "What is the matter tonight? Come in here. Come in, come."

The brightness of the inside hurt Hamish's eyes. He could not believe this. The tales he swapped with George had always seemed part of the selling spiel; football, women, the war. That post-war childish curiosity; a boy, crushed warm between fat bantering women who exposed black teeth as they mocked the virility of the hero from that night's pictures. From between them he had looked out, quiet, fascinated by the bustling man in the illuminated bakery. Hamish is here, inside. George is sitting Hamish down, being concerned. "We eat. You look bad, Hamish. Very bad." He fussed off to reappear with a teapot and two mugs, which he placed on the grey formica-topped table. Butter, milk, sugar were produced with a plate of hot bread rolls.

"Would you like a pie?" Hamish nodded. A plate with two pies was placed in front of him. Hamish held the pie steady with his one free hand, leaned over and nibbled the top off the crust. He felt like a small rodent. He managed to break open a roll and place the remainder of the pie inside. George poured tea, saying nothing. "George, you're a lifesaver," said Hamish, pretending hunger was worse than pain.

A newspaper was held up while Hamish ate, hiding half of the baker's profile. Remarks were made on somebody or something the newspaper thought interesting, but Hamish never replied as the half-profile never turned towards him. Pies were wolved and the painful hands thrust between secure gripping thighs. Only then did the questions come. How come the hands, how come the night walk, how come here? The answers were as much as Hamish Creese thought necessary, the words calling up pain; mental, physical.

"He is a bad one, that's for sure. Couple of years ago he come here, tried to take my pies without paying. And leave an order for more. I sent him away different."

"How did you do that?"

"Simple. I asked him if he knew how many Poles in this city. He said he did not know. I said, 'Three thousand, and we're all related'." George laughed, picking up his apron in his round hands and rubbing it with delight. "He never bothered me any more. You all think the Polish people are nuts, so that helps. Anyhow he knows the police come here in the middle of their shifts for tea and talk. They all know George." Hamish smiled. Three thousand. Some team. OK if you can command part of a team like that. Poles. Get them mad and they were nuts. To think about fighting men was painful.

"What would you have done if you hadn't been a Pole? You know, without Polish mates to call on?" George shrugged his shoulders.

"I would have waited my time. Time is plentiful and people forget. The wronged man does not forget. George does not forget. George waits for the time to pass." The shiny eyes focused on the bruised nose. Hamish scratched it. "Things happen in time. People look as if they have changed, but you don't change in here." He tapped his forehead. "Time gives everybody their chance, then you have to decide how to use it. If you want to. Today it's Gaffney; tomorrow, weeks, months, years, who knows, maybe Hamish will know his time." He angled his face over the table. "That's if you don't want to forgive and forget. Sometimes it is wiser to act as if we do."

George turned back to the ovens which demanded his attention, pulling out racks of bread, sniffing them, eyeing their colour then pushing the racks back in with an air of concern. The place was warm, as friendly as the personality of the man who moved easily from rack to rack, checking, muttering to himself, completely at one with his work. Hamish knew the feeling of the workman for the tricks, tools and product of his trade. To be lost in that separate world created by tools, material and mind in the search for perfection. George was in that separated world, lifted up, out of his immediate surroundings. Hamish did not exist at this moment, George was in search of the perfect piece of baking.

Hamish felt like staying; dry, warm, this was an ideal place to see off the worst of the night. Even if George received visitors breaking their shift for eats they would understand he must be a pal of George's. NO. These visitors would not be normal visitors. These would be policemen. Policemen looking at him, suspicious, asking questions, sarcastic, full of glee at each other's cleverness. Best to go. It hurt less to walk anyway.

Hamish stood up to go, jamming a pound note under the tea mug. "I'm off now George. Thanks for everything." George hurried over. Hamish sheepishly touched the pound note.

"Hey. You must keep that. Tonight I give you George, not the man in the bakery. Sometimes you get good things for nothing too. You stay if you like." The crumpled pound was pushed into the flap on the overall front as the guest moved away. Hamish stopped just as George was about to close the top hatch. "That wood is starting to rot there, George. If you get the material I'll fix it up for you. Might be as well to get a new door made." George held back the flap. He looked at the brown flakes of wood, silent for a moment. The silence brought a red flush to a transparent face. A white finger shook, rigid under a swollen nose.

"My young friend, you do not owe me for anything. You have nothing to pay me back for. Nothing. But thank you." George closed the flap.

The body demanded sleep, but the head ordered the feet on. The feet led on, down to the quays beside the oily brown river, past smooth redundant bollards to the ferry steps. A small grey shed with large glassless windows and flakes of brown paint dropping to a concrete floor stood in a pool of light. Light generously spread by a spotlight on a telegraph pole. No passengers sheltered in wait for the ferry, presently at rest at the foot of the steps of the other side. The feet were following a route from childhood. Over there, up beyond the tenements of the North side, the stores for the engineering works, the whisky warehouses and the doss houses, were the parks, museums and Botanical Gardens, of that other breed. That breed who dressed so well and spoke the same language in a different way. Miss Martin the primary teacher he had loved had lived there. Perhaps she still did. Miss Martin the jelly babies queen. Jelly baby for clean nails, jelly baby for clean teeth, jelly baby for clean shirt and jelly baby for clean shoes. Black ones for good readers. Those black ones would have to be bought especially for Hamish who read the Psalms so well.

"Keep getting as many little black ones as you do and you will go to the university. That is the big school for clever people up where I live." With a clean face he had wandered often, along wide terraces, along broad avenues, running breathless up wide staircases separating streets full of grand houses. All in the hope Miss Martin would look out a large window and wave him into tea. Just like George. From up there he had looked down at the spiked turrets of the grey big school and sensed he'd never get there. Not even if he had gutted himself with black jelly babies. Miss Martin never saw him. Not once. Never. No.

A drunk couple staggered through the light, tripping over the cobbles to stumble into the shed. The man pawed in eager nostalgia under the loose red coat which hung from the woman's narrow shoulders. The woman held up a grotesque tiny head and face, pushing a bent bottom lip under his raised chin. The man became impatient. He stepped outside and grabbed at the string hanging from the clapper of the large bell used to summon the ferry. The ringing signalled impatience. Hamish turned away. When these old Highland ferrymen deciphered impatience they sat tight at their whisky. In the night they were the masters of the river. They didn't have to run back and forth delivering people to the factory's hoot. In the night they decided when the runs would be. This had to be recognised. The couple had ruined his excuse for a solitary wait.

Back then, back, to brighter lit streets, past windows; windows of carpets, windows of beds, windows of dummies who didn't nod back. No thinking now. Only walking. Walking. Walking until the realisation, the Cross approached. Here at the Cross the coffee-stall stood. Hamish slowed down. A look. See.

Amongst the taxi-drivers, sobering drunks, pimps and their women, dossers with clasped hands round mugs of soup, were others. Better dressed, laughing loud in a place where most were content with their thoughts. Others like Gaffney; different districts, same occupation, watchfully neutral at the feeding hole. Gaffney might even be there. Somewhere. Some faces were in shadow, others, half-light, others stood out; moving nightmare faces that champed and chattered, spat and splattered in the stall's splayed light. Gaffney did not appear to be there, but this was no place to stop anyway. There was no newspaper seller on the corner opposite. It must be late; or early. Daylight wouldn't be long. Time for home; the call of the bed had to be answered. Hamish turned a corner abruptly.

Normal people appeared with the light; boilersuited workers, milkboys, housewives shuffling in slippers to dairies still not open. Hamish was glad to see them. He wanted to shout, to say hello to them all. The night had been long, but the morning brought this feeling of relief which almost made its trials worth it. This feeling of relief, this feeling of security just watching the early risers struggle to wakefulness. The night-black of the sandstone tenements was now grey turning silver. Little bluebirds flew up round a golden sun on pieces of stained glass decoration brightly set in painted tenement windows. This morning it appeared as if they really had somewhere to fly to. Past the curtains in his own ground-floor window the sugar bowl and the cornflake packet stood as if waiting upon the return of Hamish. Hamish came into the close confidently. The night was past. The door was open.

The small room seemed to be as he had left it; the objects still, lifeless. The Yale lock hung off, dangling from timber which had separated from the wall. They had come. Perhaps they had gone. Perhaps they had hoped to find him sleeping. Perhaps they had just gone away, deciding to leave it for another day. Perhaps. His foot kicked a tin box. He turned to the doorless cupboard to his left. A few shiny shillings littered the floor beneath the gas meter. No one was in this alcove. The radio. He carried on into the alcove. He lifted the lid from the bread-bin. No radio. A radio not completely paid for yet, bought on an impulse. There was no radio. No night-time companion.

The house was silent. The pain in the hands increased, fighting for a place of recognition in his mind, fighting for first place amongst his injuries. The meter, Miss Martin, McCafferty, Gaffney. A pool of wet was on the floor in front of his small fat wardrobe. He crossed the floor unsteadily. He stood over the wet. It was. It was piss. He pulled open the wardrobe door. The smell left no doubt. His extravagances, his good suits, the sports jacket, hung defenceless, displaying dark patches down the arms, down the fronts. Centre, the best silver-grey hung apologetically, soaked, the patch breast pocket darker than the rest. Below them wet shone from puddles inside his shoes. Sounds seeped out from the drained mind. Hamish fell to his knees. His hands hung helplessly at his side. Hamish cried.

☆
☆☆☆☆☆☆☆☆
☆

HAMISH laughed. The third hot pie was on its way to the mouth of the young man stretched opposite. No wonder the young hulk was built the way he was. If there was an archetypal white Australian, this bloke was it, surely. Hair blond, thick on the head; eyes clear, blue; thighs solid, set above muscular calves. But this one's tan was different. Not dark. Not even bronze. He glowed. What dim light there was in his corner of the hut seemed to emanate from his skin. Tight, tanned skin. Contrasted against the inevitable black vest, tucked into the faded black shorts turning grey. Muscles undulated like hills along the length of the leg, the light and shade thrown up by the angle of the sun which sliced through the door space. Even the hairs on the legs lit up. Entwined, almost alive, wrestling, the hairs were a miniature tropical rooftop hiding all sorts of life underneath. There was something obscene about those hairs. There was something about the square strength which proclaimed itself so loudly from one so young. Strength like that Hamish Creese should have had, fifteen years ago.

"I don't know where you put them, Adonis."

"That's the trouble with you Pommy wankers. You come over here half-starved and can't face a decent bit of tucker. And don't call me Adonis. That's a poofter's name."

Hamish laughed again, kicking one of the paper bags which littered the floor of the hut. The bag rolled out happily to sunlit fresh air.

"Hold it. Hold it now. I might have been half-starved but I never was a Pommy. I think I object to that."

42

"Yeh. Who wouldn't?" asked the pie-eater, picking a stray piece of carrot from the edge of his lips and licking it off his finger.

Hamish leaned forward on the bench and twirled his hard hat between his hands. Tiredness was creeping in, between the muscles and the bones; a weariness. Maybe this one should have been let go. It was a shit job anyway, might have been as well to move on, forget it. Maybe Gerry here would back off. He looked sideways at his quiet workmate. This one would be all right; he had decided the employer was a shithouse. That was it. That was all. That was enough.

Over and beyond the dust path chomped out by a digger's steel teeth, behind a bright white column with its crown of rust-red steel, Hamish could see the gaffer. Peeking out, unsure, lifting his hat, scratching his head; behind, in front; replacing the hat, biting a thumb and repeating it all again. It wouldn't be long now. Time was against him.

"Gerry, I think the gaffer is looking for us, or some inspiration." Gerry edged over and looked, but said nothing. The distant figure had begun walking toward their hut. Slow at first, then faster, then slow again as he made his approach. He stuck his head on a protective arm and leaned against the doorway, inclining towards them.

"I'm looking for you two. Are you for working this afternoon or what?"

Creese shrugged his shoulders, up and outwards around the ragged edges of his sleeveless shirt. "The boss man going to square us up what he owes us?"

"That's nothing to do with me. I'm just the gaffer here. I told him on the phone again this morning. I can't do any more than that. Look, I just want the job done."

"Plus your finishing bonus when we all finish it. Sorry, mate, no offence, but my young friend and I have just decided we're on strike." The head came up sharply from the protective arm.

"What are you giving us you're on strike? Who says? There's only the two of you. Everybody else is working OK. Come on, don't give us your bullshit. Two of you can't go on strike. Come on; out, out you come." Creese tried to push his ear down to the

43

base of his probing pinkie. He studied the blob of wax that came out stuck to the end of the finger.

"You're hearing us alright. We are on strike. As of now. We're chippies, mate. The only two on this site. We're fully paid up members of the Australian Woodworkers and Federated Trades. The total membership here has called a meeting and now we're calling ourselves out on strike. We're staying here till the bossman pays up."

The gaffer removed his hat and began to scratch again. Hamish wiped his glasses on a red handkerchief and settled them back on his nose. Gerry crossed his legs at the ankle, placed his palms together and thrust them between his thighs. The air in the small hut was becoming warm. The gaffer spoke.

"Creese, I don't know who you are, or where you've come from, but you don't get away with these tricks here. Here we work. You two are the only real chippies I've got. I've ordered the concrete and I need those columns lined up before it gets here. Don't make a monkey out of me Creese. I'm too old for it."

"I wasn't even trying. Just get on the blower to Scrooge. Tell him Creese wants his cash. Please."

"And me too," reminded Gerry.

The three pulled on the silence. Gerry bowed his head as though in elongated prayer. Hamish felt the challenge of the gaffer's stare. The man was pitiful and so not to be pitied. No sense getting emotional. That's how they beat you. This guy didn't even have the sense to realise he was being screwed as well. You had to admit his knowledge. He was the key man; the boss could never have organised this lot. Too bad.

The gaffer wiped the flaked bottom lip with his wrist. He bent down, stretching an arm under the small table in the centre of the hut.

"Give me the tools and I'll do the bloody job myself." His hand gripped round the handle of the toolbag. Hamish fell to his knees. Two strong hands swung out forcefully from his side. Grasping hands reached in under the table and grabbed the gaffer by the collar, pulling him through the space. The head was jammed by the neck between the knuckles of angry fists and the under-edge of the table. The face turned white, then red, then white again. The eyes rolled.

"Touch those tools and I'll split you. No one touches these tools." The voice quiet, definite. "No one." No one. No one touched these tools. These were the tools of Hamish Creese. Once before somebody had been given them. These tools were nearly lost to a dirty grubby pawnbroker. Those tools; the passport, the road out, lying there somewhere. Hamish Creese had to watch, plead, worried, stuck in a wooden stall, counter up to the nipples, listen to the whiner, watch the eyes shifting from the ticket then back. Hamish Creese is the name. The initials are on the tools. What? What do you mean? What do you mean I am not a woman. Fuck what's on the ticket. You're right I'll shout.

"Have you ever seen a woman carpenter you bastard?"

The table had slid down the gaffer's back, pinning his legs. Gerry leapt over to remove it, one hand reaching out to try and force the release of the gaffer's neck. He kicked the table over and away shouting louder.

"Ease up. Ease up, for Christ's sake ease up. You'll kill him." The hands of Hamish Creese were pulled free. The gaffer knelt clutching his neck, wide-eyed, alarmed, face white, mouth open, lips pulled back over old yellow teeth. Hamish fell back to the corner, his legs straight out, toe-caps turned up straight pointing to the ceiling, face telling the mind was far away. The gaffer mixed some words with some saliva.

"You're mad. That's what you are. Mad. I seen madmen before and you're one. You're cracked."

He backed away. Creese looked up and drew a breath which forced his chest out. "Just you tell him we want our cash." The gaffer hesitated in his nursing then turned and walked away spitting curses towards his feet.

Hamish went out around to the tap and ran water into his mouth, allowing it to spill up and out over his face. He stripped off his shirt and splashed the cooling water over his chest. Gerry stood looking at him, saying nothing. "What are you looking at? I eat hot pies too you know." He flexed his biceps playfully till the large vein stood out. "Maybe you are a poofter. Fancy a bit of Scotch beef do you?"

"Liable to get a prickful of thistles, mate. You Scotsmen come over here and all of a sudden thistles start sprouting out of every bloody hole in your body; your mouth, your ears, and your arse. Christ half of you bastards haven't seen your own country, you're fifty dollar tourists that don't want to go home. No, you keep your Scotch beef old fella, judging by your performance there I think you're going off. Did he call you something or what?"

Hamish squeezed water from the tail of the shirt, slipped it back on, ignoring the feel of the wet on his skin, using the buttoning process to buy time to consider a reply. Something had made him go over the top with the oldster. There had been a man there, squeezing, wanting to see pain; but somewhere he heard a voice questioning, alarmed, demanding release. A voice not heard for years but owed a listen, due deference for reasons long forgotten. Three men had been there under the table in the fight for the throat of the gaffer. One to choke, one to free, and one watching. "Scotch beef never goes off. It only gets tougher. But I'm no tourist, son. I've been here a long time. A long time."

"Yeh, alright maybe so. But you can't go reducing the population. We're supposed to have you jokers over here to boost it. You were just a touch crazy trying to croak him like that."

"OK. It's just these little shithouse jobs, they always give money problems. There's always somebody trying to screw you for that extra few bob. A man's got to fight for what he's owed, or they'll have you working for nothing."

"Fair enough, Hamish, but the gaffer's not your man. He just gets paid like you and me. Personally, I'm satisfied with giving them a punch in the mouth. As far as I'm concerned that's what gaffers get paid for, taking the punches."

Hamish picked at his teeth with a broken fingernail, watching Gerry lift the table out onto the path. The table stood askew; incongruous on the dirt track, naked without chairs to cover the space between the shiny tubular steel legs. Gerry lifted out his own tools. He bent down to remove the battered leather portmanteau which served Hamish. Gerry straightened up, pointing an exaggerated open palm towards the bag. "Piss off," said Hamish. Tin cans and screwed-up paper bags were shifted to litter the

46

ground around the hut. Hamish followed Gerry back into the cleaner hut, out of the sun. To wait. Over on the site he could see the brickies and their helpers watching; watching while waiting, whispering, wondering. A little slower with the bricks now, but staying clear, leaving the two mavericks to it, hoping for their failure, to confirm their own rightness in passivity.

"Are you for this piss-up tonight at Port Noarlunga?" asked Gerry.

"Oh I'll be there all right. I worked with old Conroy, you know. When I came to Adelaide for the first time, I was just down from the Yards at Whyalla. I'd never worked in construction before. The first job I went on they teamed me up with Jacky. He gave me all his knowledge." All of it. Including how to beat the bosses with one big union. "In fact, I stayed with him and his missus for a while till I got fixed up. He's a great old bloke."

"Have you seen him since you got back?"

That question hurt; reasons, excuses, lies; all chased around inside the head while the belly felt suddenly empty and the muscles weak, surrendering to sudden acknowledged guilt. "No, I haven't. I'll surprise him tonight." Nobody knew Hamish Creese was back in Adelaide. So what? What did it matter anyway? "Be alright if we can get our cash today, Gerry boy, then we can have a right good night."

"Too right. I think we might need it. I do, that's for sure." Gerry was not pursuing his original question.

No air exchange now; hot outside, hot inside. Dust particles dancing in the beam of sun which had now shifted nearer the door as if giving up on the attempts to bring light to this hut. Hamish watched the specks in their suspension, moving as lazily as the heat itself. Gerry was quiet, hairy arms folded over his chest, legs out, head down, hard hat pulled down over his eyes. Time to wait and see. Time to conserve energy. Cancelled concrete would make some people angry. But this was just a shit job. No need for dramatics.

"Where are you headed after this one Gerry?"

"After today you mean? Don't think I'm sure. Maybe I'll just go home to Victoria. I was for going back at the harvest time to see

47

Mum and Dad anyway. I've been away too long. What you gawking at?"

"Nothing, nothing. I just never heard you talk about your folks before. I thought you were like me: footloose and fancy free."

"Oh, I've got folks alright, but I'll tell you something. You're not fancy free. Australia's your prison, mate. You've worked your way round it, up and down, across, but there's nothing here for you. You've had a lot of time to stop and try to fit in somewhere but you just keep running; the next job, the next state. I don't know where you belong Hamish, but I don't think it's Australia."

"You got a sister, Gerry?"

"Bloody right I have, but she's too young to fancy you."

"That's not why I was asking. I was just wondering, that's all."

A squeal, intimidating, breaking out of a cloud of dust, was the signal to snap out of the reverie and analysis. A white utility truck with yellow streaks down the side stopped just beyond the hut. Doors slammed and the boss approached, the gaffer behind. The suit was sharp; khaki with a pocketful of protruding shiny pens sticking out over each breast. The value of an expensive coiffure was lost by ears which stuck out. The boss twiddled the truck keys, hesitating outside the hut door. A sarcastic knock was rapped upon the side of the hut. He entered and sat down, his thigh touching the thigh of Gerry. Gerry slid over. The gaffer remained outside.

"What is your problem, Mr Creese?"

"You know the problem. You owe us cash."

"But I pay the basic union rate, Mr Creese."

"My arse you do. You pay basic without the Construction Industry Allowance. Don't give us any bullshit. By now you owe every man on this site one hundred dollars. Each. Me and my mate here we don't care too much about those spineless bastards out there, but we want ours."

The bossman brought up his bottom lip to almost touch his nostrils. He scratched under a smooth hairless chin.

"Mr Creese. I need you. I need you both. More importantly, I need your tools. I will give you both twenty-five cents an hour extra as of today."

"Like fuck you will. That's something I'd forgotten. You owe us two dollars a week for wear and tear on our tools. You've got fuck all here. How did you get into this game?"

The boss jumped to his feet pointing the truck keys at Creese. "I will give you and your friend here fifty dollars, here, in your hand, and the extra on the rate."

"No thanks. All or nothing."

"You have assaulted my foreman Mr Creese. You are finished. Get back to work or get off the site. Or I will call the police."

Gerry spoke now. "Better start dialling now, mate, there's nobody moving."

Powerful silence met impotent silence. The boss turned and hurried away, the gaffer at his heels. Hamish spat out the door then tried a second spit to see if it would go further. He noticed Gerry had the tobacco tin out so he watched, as always a mixture of curiosity and awe. The papers were licked, placed together with no fuss; the shag teased out with the tips of the fingers which nibbled at the strands. And now the cannabis itself. Gerry's face was always a study in expectation as the last lip of paper was licked. Gerry laughed at Hamish's interest.

"I always keep a piece of potato in the tin. I reckon it keeps the shag damp. You know people reckon my rolls are just a little bit better. Don't see it myself. Must be the potato; they're not used to it."

He took a wheezy drag and offered it to Hamish. Hamish declined; he had tried it in the Bush but it had done nothing for him. He was as confused with it as without it. So he abstained; but he felt this had more to do with a Miss Martin who didn't like him to enjoy playing with his willie and wouldn't let him suck his jelly babies till playtime and work was over. Alcohol was to be preferred. Alcohol brought oblivion, refused entry to the bad black dreams, some of which included Miss Martin.

Gerry rose to kneel and push the tin under the hut.

"You never know with these bastards."

They just sat, fidgeting; legs on the bench, legs off the bench; feet on the table, feet off the table. The sun quit the hut to spread its rays elsewhere. It grew no cooler. The hairs on the legs of the young Adonis had turned creamy white in the dullness, but the overall tan still glowed, incandescent. Hamish became aware of Gerry looking at him, puzzling the stare.

"Hamish. Are you a poofter?"

"No. Nonononono." The denial struggled out. "What makes you ask that?"

"Oh, just the way you never talk about settling down, getting yourself a woman."

"That's pretty conventional stuff, coming from an Aussie. Especially one as young as you."

"Yeh, but we're not talking about me. I've listened to you; underneath you're not so tough. I don't think. You're just one of these conventional Pommies — sorry, Scotch guys. Yet I never hear you talk about women. Sometimes I get the feeling you'd like a shot at me."

Hamish scratched his head with all of his fingers, shaking his head at the same time. "No. Don't be stupid. That's daft."

"Have you got a girl somewhere?"

"Not exactly. No. I haven't. But you can relax."

The other site workers had gathered into a loose knot; by the direction of their heads something was up and coming up.

"Judging by their jabbering, young Gerry, this must be the law. I think we should meet them outside. It's too cramped in here. They'll fill the place up and we've just cleaned it."

The two officers stopped short as the two workers came out of the hut together. Hamish noticed they had left their caps behind. He put on his hard hat. Gerry did the same. The four stopped, stood, each selecting one to stare at. The boss shuffled in behind the police, rolling his truck keys around in his palm.

"Which one of you is Hamish Creese?" said an officer.

"I am," said Creese, making a point of looking at the sweat stain at his interrogator's armpit.

"Your employer, he reckons you assaulted his foreman. He says if you want to go off the site quietly he won't charge you." Creese drew his heel in the dust as though bothered by some itch. The officers kept their eyes on the steel toecaps.

"We are on strike here, officer. We are in pursuance of a

legitimate claim. The police have no remit in industrial matters unless the State government order you to become involved. As for the assault, well my young friend here is witness that this foreman you're talking about made a lunge at me. Dead set, he was. He came on really heavy. In fact, I may just charge him."

The boss brought his left shoulder out from behind the protective back of an officer of the law and placed his hand and arm almost against Creese's nose. A drop of sweat had rolled down a long straight nose but was somehow defying gravity.

"Attack you? Attack you? You Scotchman bastard, you don't care what you do. What about my concrete?"

Hamish leapt back hands held high in the air. "Hey. You blokes see what I mean? I'm the one under threat here."

One officer pulled his lips looking for the wisdom that sometimes goes with the gesture. The sweaty one tensed and stretched one arm, wiping the other one under his armpit.

"Which union you two in?" Wisdom was beginning to take the form of expedience.

"AWFT."

"Right. I'll radio for an organiser to be sent out here. Keep your eye on them, Ben." Ben switched to wiping his other arm as his colleague walked to the car and spoke into the microphone.

Upon his return he was wearing his cap and held out one to Ben. The policemen asked each of them the story in turn; sucking on pens, pausing for effective thought, looking at watches; unmoved by jokes or pleas. Just as the scribblers were scratching around for questions to pad out the time a long red car drove up behind them. The officers kept their heads parallel with their pens making a point of not looking up. Hamish and Gerry looked at the man emerging from the car.

The figure backed out, pulling a briefcase from the far seat, turned, and stood tapping his fingers on the door handle. That figure was more portly now but it was still the same Paul. Made-up blue flag of the Southern Cross stuck on his red hard hat set square above silver-black reflector sunglasses made to repel sunlight. Now coming over; pushing himself off the car, swaggering toward them, the incongruous fat briefcase leading the way; a figure which frightened the workers as much as any boss. At the group the pathmaker briefcase was given a rest on the ground between spread feet.

Hamish smiled toward the place where the eyes were usually situated. If a smile came back to Creese it was only a twitch of tight lips. The officer who had put out the call pulled his own reflector glasses from a breast pocket, settled them on his nose and began to explain the situation. Nobody interrupted. Hamish bent his head, angling the top of his hard hat into the group and aiming facial expressions toward his crotch. Gerry walked over to the tap and noisily slurped some water. The truck keys continued a dance from long nervous fingers. Paul listened to the policeman. Brickies and labourers came to the edge of unfinished floors and mimed the act of work, furtively harvesting the scene which would be rehashed later as the fruitiest piece of that day's labour.

The policeman finished. Paul tapped on Hamish's hard hat and thrust a questioning chin at the upraised face. Hamish gave his side of the story. Gerry nodded from start to finish. The boss dropped his truck keys. Four pairs of eyes watched him bend and pick them up. When he straightened up Paul spoke.

"You're in the wrong here, mate." He held up a hand to silence a mouth about to protest. "I don't want to hear about any assault, that's between you and these jokers." The briefcase was picked up and swung easily into the boss's chest. "You owe my members their money. If you want to stay in the building game in this State you'd better come across. You pay them and we will leave immediately. Unless you want them to stay. Is that right boys? All right with you?"

Gerry shrugged his shoulders and nodded at the same time. Hamish nodded. At least tonight would be a good piss-up. "Any chance of the cash today?"

"Give him a break," said Paul. He turned to the defaulter. "You send the money to the union offices in Adelaide, or hand it in, these two can pick it up there." Paul pointed the briefcase out, up toward Creese. "Maybe you'll square up your dues when you're in." A hand grasped part of the case handle, a quick twist and the

52

case now rested in Hamish's hand, at the end of an arm held up straight, firm. He turned the case around ninety degrees using only his fingers. "That's always been my way, Paul." Paul took back his briefcase, turning to the boss.

"Don't mess us about or you'll never build so much as a mud hut in Australia. Right mate?"

"But my concrete. Today there was no pour."

"Tough shit." Paul jerked his head in the general direction of the site. "Those blokes all getting the rate?" The boss dropped his truck keys again. The group dispersed.

Paul followed Gerry and Hamish back to the hut. The hard hats were flung in the corner. Hamish fussed over his tools saying nothing, content to let Paul make any running in conversation. Gerry retrieved his tobacco tin and settled himself in the corner to wait until Hamish was ready.

"When did you get back to Adelaide, Hamish?"

"About three weeks ago. I've been meaning to come in and see you but, well, you know how it is. I would've come for my card once I made a few bob."

"Never thought I'd hear you say that sort of thing. No one stepped on any site you were on unless they had a card."

"Aye. Changed days right enough. How's things at the branch anyway? I hear Bernard is still running the show. Has he found a chair to fit his big arse yet?" Reference to Bernard's girth provoked no laughter.

"It's still much the same as when you left. We made Dudley the new organiser."

Dudley. Dudley McKenna. Don't let on he's got through. "You gave it to who?"

"Dudley McKenna."

Dudley. Organiser. The job that was Hamish Creese's. Or so the boys on the sites said. Organiser. Come on temporary till the boys get used to you. Then be permanent. No fuss. No voting, no advertising, no applications. Non-members of the Cohort cannot enquire. Selection by tap on the shoulder; singled out as one safe to maintain the ways of the Cohorts. Unsound Hamish Creese. Definitely unsound. Only individuals went walkabout. So Dudley gets it. The Aborigine with the Scots grandfather. Must say something about Scotsmen. Dudley. Never attended a meeting of the branch in his puff; except those three-in-a-row occasions when Bernard had looked to be in mathematical bother. And mathematics is the language of politics. He was there; with the other strangers.

Gerry lit his smoke. "Is that the guy that was the footie player?"

"That's the one," said Hamish. "Guess he must have been a chippie too. That right, Paul?" Paul never answered but led them out of the hut down toward the car. The Southern Cross flag hung limply from the radio aerial.

"You blokes want a lift into Adelaide?"

"No thanks Paul. We'll have a few beers at the Flagstaff then we're off home for a wash. It's old Jacky Conroy's do tonight."

"Is it? Maybe I'll manage in for a few. Well, if I don't, I'll see you when you come for your cash. I don't suppose this joker will want you to collect it from him. Personally."

"OK. See you mate."

Paul entered the car, placing his hard hat so that the sticker pointed out of the rear window. The car seats threatened to envelop him at the shoulder. With a wave he was off in a scatter of dust. Hamish and Gerry brushed it defensively from their nostrils and mouth. Together they walked off down the truck road, down past the gaffer's face looking from his long hut window. The site workers turned back to their day's work. The bonus had to be made up.

THE Bay Hotel: a piece of English Empire stuck out onto the beach; white painted wood and wrought iron running around supporting a straight planked balcony set below a steeply angled red tiled roof, looking outwards to its place of birth in someone's faraway nostalgic fantasy. Hamish and Gerry entered the bar together and pushed through the Friday night crowd to the private room at the rear. Three faces looked up from their beer. Hamish knew two of them. The man nearest slid off his stool and came over, grinning, laughing. Hamish felt the slap on the back. This felt good. Hamish was smartly dressed, good comfortable shoes, fresh shirt and amongst mates.

"Hamish. For goodness sake man. I never expected to see you here." Two pints were called. "How've you been? Where have you been?"

"Not bad Danny. Yourself? Have you not made your first million yet?" Danny. Danny Fairweather. Always grinning, always laughing. Daft Danny. Daft Danny been buying and selling houses since he landed from Liverpool. Daft Danny the labourer; house like a mansion and MG sports car imported from England.

The beer came up and introductions were made all round. Broken conversation began, to find ground for a common verbal meet. Remember that job, you did know him, what about the time; trusted beginnings to relate unrelated incidents and people, all interspersed with silent sips at the beer, hiding lack of knowledge with a gulp and a nod, egging the beer on to render a common link irrelevant. The room filled, with people, with smoke and with chatter, but each time the door swung open all heads rose to seek the guest of honour.

A shout went up when he came in. A shout which forced the man to stop at the door. Embarrassment made all his extremities move. His feet shuffled, his head tried to force its way down between his shoulders and his hands and arms moved up and down, out and in, till finally a triangular salute was made and held above his head. Faces and mouths of all shapes and sizes sang: for he's a jolly good fellow, in accents of all sounds and origins. Jacky Conroy was in the right room.

Hamish found his way to the corner at the junction of the bar and the wall. He stood with his back to the wall, watching the old man, seeing his pleasure. Feeling no joy. There was only a room here. Only a noisy bunch of men shouting for some other man. Look at them. Stand back and look at them. Jacky Conroy has retired. Jacky Conroy was not a bad old bloke.

Jacky Conroy, now retired, held his hands up, open. The room went quiet. "Where's the bloody beer?" he yelled. Two barmen kept the amber liquid in supply as Danny Fairweather passed out the orders and the money from the kitty. A game of darts started up, one blunt dart continually falling out and down to the floor. A knockout competition was organised. The man was here. It was time to get pissed. A dark European came in, selling watches. Danny haggled. Two for the price of one or fuck off. Two were bought as prizes for the darts tourney. Names were called. Cigarettes were rejected for cigars. The barman took off his dicky bow and loosened his collar. Jacky smiled his way around to Hamish.

"Hamish Creese. I thought that was you. I don't believe it. Liz and I were just talking about you just before I came out this evening. Will you come to see us? Wait till I tell her you were here. Will you come Sunday?"

"Too right I will Jacky. You know I will. Give Liz an excuse to make another roast."

"As if she needed one. Who's your mate?"

"Jacky, meet Gerry. A true blue dinkum Aussie from Victoria."
Jacky and Gerry lifted their glasses to one another. Jacky asked

about Victoria as Hamish studied him. The old work-horse was visibly older; face fatter, more relaxed but puffed under the eyes. The hair is receding, black, with individual white hairs threatening to consolidate and take over, even on the moustache. The moustache is all grey now. A beer belly's there; starting to stick out over the belt; the struggle is finished; age and beer have won it. The fingers told the story. Stumpy, broad, the whorls and folds of skin around the knuckles cracked and rough and corrugated, the tinier cracks in the folds of the skin becoming lost in the fat of old age. Those whorls talked. The fingerprint of a working man's life. Hamish Creese has whorls, but they're not the fingerprint of Hamish Creese. Not really. The work life is there, folding up over spread knuckles. In a fist they're smooth, telling little. Even Jacky's fingers did not seem to fit his looks or personality.

"You dreaming or something?" Gerry pulled him back into the company. "Jacky here reckons there's nothing doing just now. Looks like you might have to go back out the Bush."

"That so? Tonight I don't care. C'mon Conroy, this is supposed to be a piss-up not a flaming job exchange."

The beer was kept on the go. Danny and a couple of helpers kept a supply run open to those hemmed in away from the bar. Smoke ran in a circuit overhead plugged into each pointless conversation. Spilled beer was at their feet, on the floor, on the tables. The spoken word was now shouted and yelled. Good jokes were listened to and bad ones mocked or helped along by interjection. The chief guest was away mingling and mixing, pretending to know of them all, but genuine with the smiles and the nods.

"He's a happy man, Hamish. It's quite a turnout for him," said Gerry. "Reckon you'll see as many when you turn it in?"

"Me? Reckon not mate. They'd have to go on a bloody Cook's tour to find me for a start."

"Don't you keep in touch with anyone? I mean don't you get letters, or anything?"

"To get letters they'd have to know where I was. I gave it up."

One of the men was banging a glass on a table and yelling for order. He removed a man from his chair and climbed awkwardly up. The request for silence was rippling its way out from the centre to the edges. Quiet was already on the way. He placed two fingers in his mouth and whistled. The whistle was loud.

"OK, OK. Listen you obnoxious bastards. We've got ourselves a darts final. Now since these lads are playing for a piece of magnificent Swiss Oriental jewellery, let's have some shoosh around here. OK? Now, before you settle down the barman has asked us to pass over any empty glasses that are lying around. OK?"

"Who's the master of ceremonies?" asked Gerry.

"Peter Ray. He was a dogman in the days when they used to fly around like Captain Marvel. Broke his bloody hip just before they banned the flying."

"What'd he do?"

"Well, he stuck his foot on the hook and waggled the other one at the crane driver. The lift just started. He was only fifteen feet up when somebody threw him an apple."

"What happened?"

"The silly bastard tried to catch it with both hands." Gerry spluttered a laugh into his beer.

The decibels in the room had come down with the totals of the darts players. Shouts were staccato now between throws. Peter Ray scratched the latest scores on the small black piece of board. The scratching could be heard. One man needed double twenty to win. The other to throw. Treble nineteen. Fifty-seven. Sixty-three to go. A try for treble seventeen. Seventeen hit. Forty-six left. Keep it even. Go for twenty, leave double thirteen. Five hit. That's a long walk to pull out the darts stuck in the board under a spotlight. The opponent weighed the darts in his fingers. All quiet. He threw. A mile wide! Easy. This time. Oh. Nearly. Just a little up. Couldn't be closer. This one, this time. The dart is there. Beauty. No. It's bounced out. The flight's in that puddle of beer. Him again. Quick, this time. Double seventeen. Not clever. Five. Smack in the centre. Double one to win. The barman has stopped, his hands around a glass in the wash-basin. And thud, it's in. The double one. Cheers all round. The finalists hugged

58

and made their way through the shouting assembly. Peter Ray stood on the chair.

"OK fellas. It really didn't matter who won, because both of them have won a watch." He handed down the watches from his height. He continued. "I'm not one for making speeches but you all know what we're here for. Some of us at the PN site have had a whip-round for the old bastard and we've got him a little memento to remind him he's a chippie." The labourers gave lighthearted jeers. "Any of you who missed the whip-round can put it in the hat now."

Jacky was pushed and clapped forward. The lump in his throat was moving.

Peter came down from the chair and pointed to it. Jacky climbed up on it. He turned around. Peter knelt on the floor, head bowed, his arms held up, straight. In his hands was the memento. A brass hammer, set on a plinth, head down, the claw facing upward. Jacky took the gift. Tears struggled in his eyes. He held it up, out, hugged it to his stomach before kissing the inscription plate.

"I'm beat fellas. I don't know what to say. I never had any cause to make a speech in my life. I won't forget this, if any of you want a bookcase, well, I've got the time to do it." The full room laughed. Hamish smiled. Jacky went on. "Maybe you haven't done me such a good turn, when Mother sees this she'll think I've just brought her something else to polish."

"You'll do the polishing now, mate," shouted a voice. Again the laughter came. "I can only say thanks again." He stood on the chair as the men clapped, shouted and whistled. The cheering subsided. Hamish called out. "What about one of your poems, old-timer?"

The request was taken up. Peter Ray cleared the table and assisted Jacky to stand on it. On the sites, at lunch or smoke-o, people came to hear old Conroy, the chippie, spouting off the Australian poets. Rained off, Jacky could make the time pass quickly, acting out the ballads of drovers and bushrangers. Immigrants and Aussies hearing of an Australia they would have loved to have known.

A cotton sun hat was passed up to Jacky. He pushed it down on his head, hitched his trousers and prepared to soliloquise.

"Right, here we go. This is the tale of Bluey Brink and the firewater that's about the same as the stuff you get in this place." The barman didn't laugh. Two flat, broad thumbs were stuck into a thin black belt.

> "There once was a shearer, by name Bluey Brink,
> A devil for work and a devil for drink;
> He could shear his two hundred a day without fear,
> And drink without winking four gallons of beer."

The hat was off now, clutched, almost totally hidden in his hand. A melodramatic finger wagged at the barman.

> "Now Jimmy the Barman who served out the drink
> He hated the sight of this here Bluey Brink,
> Who stayed much too late, and came much too soon;
> At evening, at morning, at night and at noon."

The audience was held. The table became the reciter's stage. Exaggerated movements of face, foot and finger; he was Bluey the shearer larger than life; or Jimmy the Barman, feeling the strife, making sulphuric acid the pint for his drinker. Hat and sad face off and on with the verses. Large men all gaping, nudged fellow listeners with encouraging elbows. By the final two verses Jacky Conroy filled the room.

> "Says Jimmy, and how did you find the new stuff?
> Says Bluey, it's fine, but I've not had enough.
> It gives me great courage to shear and to fight
> But why does that stuff set my whiskers alight?

> "I thought I knew drink, but I must have been wrong,
> For what you just gave me was proper and strong;
> It set me to coughing and you know I'm no liar,
> And every cough set my whiskers on fire."

The old trouper made a low bow to applause and calls for an encore. The barman called him over. A pint was theatrically poured and pushed over to him. Conroy was still in melodrama. He held the glass high, turning it round and viewing it suspiciously. The glass was lifted to his lips and sniffed at. He gulped the beer. The glass was replaced on the bar. Jacky-as-Bluey gave a satisfied smack of the lips. The old actor frowned. He leaned forward and entered his nose into the glass; sniffed. His head hit the bar. Old Conroy slid to the floor, cupping his hands to his face. A scream came from his mouth.

The audience cheered. Danny Fairweather helped the performer to rise, dusting him down. The act was over. Reality was back. Hamish resumed drinking. The noise level increased. Beer and Bluey the Brink had brought babble. Hamish stood looking at Jacky over the top of an emptying pint pot. Claps on the back followed Jacky over.

"Good knockabout stuff, Jacky. You can't beat the old stuff."

"Well at least they can follow it, more than you can say for the Coleridge you spout."

That act had made the ruddy face red and little drops of sweat appear. Hamish put his arm around Jacky's shoulder. "Take it easy, take it easy. But tell the truth now, you're just a frustrated old ham. Let me see your new hammer." Jack passed over the brass hammer. "I thought at least they would've made it a Scotch claw," said Hamish.

"Trust you to say that. But you're right you know. I reckon that Edinburgh's the best type ever made. Mind you, I don't think they need all the bloody polishing you give yours. First thing I noticed about you on the sites, the way you looked after that hammer in particular. Have you seen him at it Gerry? He's worse than a bloody woman at her furniture."

"Or something else."

"Piss off," said Hamish. "That hammer was one my Da gave me when I started my time. It was out of his box; he never used it much."

All around there was a cheer. The beer had worked. Conversation now would not be remembered later. A great night; sufficient to know one had been there. Peter Ray was on the chair again, whistling and bawling for quiet.

Several lads had decided to carry the night on down to the strip clubs off Hindley Street. All welcome. More cheers.

"Never been to one of those places in my life," said Jacky. "And now I don't need it."

"You're not past it yet," said Gerry. "Anyway, you'll see enough to stir the old memory box."

TAXI doors opened to spill out the happy cargo who tripped over pavements, abused each other and laughed. Jacky was in difficulty. He held the brass hammer in both hands. Hamish and Gerry stuck in the door as each tried to help him. The taxi-driver leaned over and pushed him free of the back seat. They followed the others to the narrow entrance which was jammed by three bouncers. Two moved; the third remained, leaning against the wall, hands behind his back, legs angled out in front. His head was down, his eyes on his crotch.

"Do you think he's fascinated by his own prick, Gerry?" asked Hamish.

"More likely he's wondering if he's got one."

The narrow entrance forced them all into tight single file to be compressed past the bouncers and the kiosk, pushing their money under the space in the glass.

Inside it was dark. Danny and Peter were arguing with a man in a shiny black suit. The man looked somewhere off to the back. He gave a sharp nod to the two protesters. Peter and Danny signalled for help. Four smaller tables became one larger table running down to the front of the stage area. The thirteen who had made it crushed themselves around after cheering Jacky into the seat at the top, with the brass sculpture in front of him. The place filled; some happy, reluctant to end the night; some hiding; some curious men come to watch the reaction of the curious women with them, some men just curious about women. The kitty was called for. Jacky insisted on piling in fifty dollars. The final bundle was pushed over to Danny Fairweather. Danny gave the order for drink. Two anonymous waitresses brought over small cans on tin trays. Danny queried the cost. His voice rose. Other heads at other tables rose. The voices at the long table began to sing: Why are we waiting. Danny laughed and paid up, all the while explaining the competitive cost of beer from the pub. "I thought it was Scotsmen who were supposed to be miserable," shouted Jacky.

The dim light grew dimmer. A small spotlight below each front corner lit up curtains which looked maroon. From somewhere the music played loud through speakers. The tune wobbled then became clearer. A polite choir of voices was singing that a pretty girl was like a melody. The near-maroon curtains pulled open. Six women in different dress draped themselves in a semi-circle at the back of the small brightly lit stage against a backdrop of violent red. A small bald man in a loud white and brown check jacket minced onto the stage.

"Christ that's some jacket," said Jacky. "You could bloody play draughts on it."

"Don't laugh," said Hamish, "I used to have one just like it. A long time ago."

The link man was introducing the women with asides and double entendre, with winks and evil leers. But first on would be a firebrand fire juggler all the way from the jungles of Borneo. Hamish watched. The act was good. This bloke was in excellent shape. The stomach muscles were tight corrugations, the spaces rippling silver against the smooth black skin as the fire whirled around him, over him, under him. The pace of the man increased, dancing round fast, faster. The flames became a single light as he and the torches twirled around. He slowed down, dousing the torches as he did so. He stopped. The jungle man turned his back to the audience. The speakers blared out a roll on jungle tom-toms. At the peak of the roll the grass tutu he was wearing was pulled off and thrown to the side. Two tight buttocks were moved to the beat, a booming mixed-up jumble of sounds. He jumped around to face the audience. Jubilant arms were held aloft. From his crotch a fire torch dangled. He stamped his feet on the floor. The fire torch was made to dance up and down, up and down. The body half-turned, the torch aimed at a giggling lady near the front. Jungle cries came from his mouth. The lights went off on

64

stage. In the dark there was only the flames going up and down, up and down. A voice cautioned him to beware of burning his balls. A woman's voice. The curtains closed. More beer was called for.

The next act was introduced as 'the woman that makes Kama Sutra possible'. A lean woman in a black leotard entwined her arms and legs and body in and around each other. There was no giggling and little whistling. Only jokes about giving it to her this way or that way and the impossibility of getting the Missus to recreate those positions. At the end of her act Hamish clapped politely. He felt sorry for her. More beer was called for. The strippers were due.

The first stripper danced her way on, skipping round the stage to an upbeat version of *There Is Nothing Like A Dame*. She was tall: a maybe young woman; maybe looking older than her age, or maybe just the age she looked. She wore a riding skirt, brown boots and carried a large stock-whip. On her head was a swagman's hat, the bobbling corks swinging to the moves and pouts of her head. Between shakes of her body she caressed the handle of the whip, stroking it, kissing it; curling it round her neck as she undid her khaki blouse. The blouse was swung ritually overhead then was released to wrap itself round the face of the man in the shiny black suit. Some people laughed.

"Christ. Do you see the shoulders on her?" asked Jacky. "Wouldn't fancy her giving me a right cross."

"Bloody right you wouldn't," said Gerry, "she's probably a man."

"What do you mean?"

"They're all fellas, old-timer. They've got it all taped up under."

"You mean we're paying our money just to watch a bunch of galloping poofters? Jesus Christ. I think I want my money back."

Everyone in earshot laughed. The stock-girl was down to her boots, pants and the whip. The corks still swung from the hat. She strutted to the front of the stage. She crouched on her haunches sticking out a hip towards the men at the bottom of Hamish's table. A young blond man was pushed forward by reaching, pushing hands. Just as his fingers settled on the bow she was up, off and away. The young man was left stranded, half out of his seat, his body stretched over the front of the stage. "You're too bloody slow, Gino. That's why you're still pulling yourself." The cans came again, Danny extracting dollars from the decreasing spread.

The next woman on was a repeat of the format. This time unzipping herself from a space-suit. Hamish was bored. Jacky kept quizzing Gerry on the sex of the strippers, trying to puzzle it out. Gerry egged him on, telling him to get down on the floor and peek up. The music changed from disco drumming to a hoarse male singing *Maggie May*. A woman trying to look like a nineteenth-century prostitute was divesting herself too slowly for the crowd, whose blood was fired by alcohol and who were eager to be titillated. Behind her a sleeping head poked out from under a blanket on a camp bed. Danny Fairweather was singing the song into his beer can.

"Hey Danny," Hamish shouted across, "you're getting a bit maudlin there."

"I don't know about your modelling but there's more life in a dead budgie than there is in this number."

He slammed his can on the table, walked to the end of the table and climbed on the stage. Danny ignored the woman who was trying to put her right breast into the sleeper's ear.

"This song's a great song," he shouted to the audience. "C'mon, let's hear you all sing it. Oh Maggie Maggie May, they have taken her away, and she'll never cruise down Lime Street any more. Oh she robbed so many . . ." Two men bounced onto the stage, one from each side. Danny shrugged the first off and tried to continue singing. "Oh Maggie Maggie May . . ." He was bundled in the back and pulled from the front, off sideways down the stage, up through the tables; only visible when his face passed under a small light. His face was angry.

At the long table some laughed, others wanted to scrap. Others looked around, saying nothing. Hamish watched the bouncer who had been contemplating his bump move nearer the table. Figures shuffled in the dark to the rear. Peter Ray stood up. "OK fellas, settle down. This mob is quite heavy. Let's not be stupid. Danny will be OK."

The black-suited manager came forward. "Your friend has only been put out," he said. "Please. No trouble."

"No trouble? He wasn't no trouble." Jacky spoke, standing up and shouting across Peter. "He was only up there to sing a song. He wasn't interested in your bloody women. They're a shower of poofs anyway."

The bouncer laid his hand on Jacky's shoulder. "C'mon. Do as your mate says. Settle down, there's a good old bloke."

"Who the hell are you? Creeping about there like a bloody dingo. Why couldn't you have let him back in amongst his mates?"

The music blared louder. Jacky shouted louder; Jacky shouted louder. The fingers tightened on his shoulder. Jacky pushed him away. The figures at the back shuffled forward out of the dark. The bouncer gripped on Jacky's bicep; squeezing, squeezing and squeezing till Jacky's mouth opened with pain.

"That's enough. Let him alone," said Hamish. The bouncer held on and lifted his free arm straight up, signalling with his hand. His nose cracked as Hamish butted the bridge. Jacky's arm was freed. Gerry thrust the statuette into Jacky's belly.

"Head for the door old son. Go for your life," he shouted, pushing him away. The bouncer's jacket was pulled up over his head. Hamish pulled on the jacket, forcing the head inside down. A knee crunched into the bouncer's mouth. Gerry saw the other bouncers move in from the back. He pushed the manager in their general direction. Gerry pulled at Hamish, calling him away. Hamish let the jacket go, moved away, stopped, turned and kicked the bent bouncer. The kick landed in the ribs. The man fell over. The two pushed and punched their way to the narrow exit. Hamish and Gerry were blocked off. Two large men stood between them and the passageway. Hamish lifted a flower vase and broke it on the edge of a table. The thin jagged neck was held out in front. He gestured to them to move away. A hand shot out to punch. Glass tore at the knuckles, ripping right across. The exit was clear, at this end. "Back to back here, Gerry." Gerry faced in. Hamish felt Gerry's back on his own; warm. He moved forward through the tight passage, past the kiosk, toward the light. The street was there, out, just past this last man, right in front, filling the space. Blooded glass was held out. Hamish held it straight out, up. The man stood still. Hamish was pushed forward by Gerry at his back. The glass was in line with his eyes. Hamish screamed. He threw the glass over the man's shoulder.

That movement, dodging the glass, that's enough. Grab the lapels. Tighten. Let the bastard have it. Swing him round. Against the wall. Head. Again. Head. Again. Head. Again. Again again again again.

"For Christ's sake, Hamish. Leave it. Leave it."

Gerry dragged him away. They were out. On the street. Danny Fairweather stepped forward. "Run you guys. Run." Hamish and Gerry ran with him.

"Where's Jacky?" asked Hamish.

"He's all right. He's in a taxi. Peter's got him."

Hamish ran easily. The familiar streets now just streets, just pavements anywhere, of rushing air, cutting off the other two. The old man had been stood up for. He was all right.

"Was he?" he shouted to Danny.

"Was who what?"

"Was the old man OK?"

"Sure. Just keep running."

☆
☆☆☆☆☆☆☆☆
☆

M ISS Martin is coming. Miss Martin's coming; strands of black hair above the white neck, fringed over those black eyes. Miss Martin, she's coming up; there, out in the water, forward through the waves of the sea. She's coming up, forward out toward the beach; white frilled blouse between perpendicular edges cut sharp on that black jacket. The one that never quite hid the handle of the big big leather belt. She's coming up, lips tight, head shaking the sharp nose forward in small jerky movements. She's coming up, that black skirt still collapsed into that mysterious long hollow between her thighs. She's still dry, on top of the water, dry. Miss Martin is coming. She's coming for Hamish Creese. YEH, YEH YEH, YEH YEAH YEH. Hamish Creese you better run, she's going to give you the belt. Run. Run. Up up up the beach. Run. The sand is slipping beneath the sandshoes. Polished flat, no grip. Those are not white. They're grey. Dirty, dirty grey. Run. The sand is slipping, oblong pits spreading, nothing solid to push on. Miss Martin is coming. Miss Martin is going to belt Hamish for looking at lasses' knickers. Here it comes. Don't take it Hamish. Grab it, grab it. Miss Martin it's sore. Don't pull Miss, mind the hands, stop; the strap's a steel hawser. Don't pull Miss the hawser's splintered, the sharp bits are pushing into the bleeding palms. Hamish is falling. Don't pull please. The sand is scraping. All along the tummy it's jaggy sore. Hamish will drown in the water. The sand, the sand is choking. Hamish must vomit. Hamish is vomiting Miss, vomiting all the black jelly babies. Must vomit, vomit.

Hamish vomited and woke up. The vomit was mostly fluid. Deep retches, sore on the stomach muscles. There was no one else on the beach. There was no one in the sea. The sea was empty, stretching flat, out across the gulf, nothing in sight. No islands, nothing. Just Hamish Creese on the beach. It was early enough to be still cold. A crust of sand had formed, stuck to the vomit on the side of his mouth. Hamish wiped it away and sat up. All the way to the cliffs of the south, nothing. The rocks interrupted the view north. Some people had filmed about Jesus in a cave there. The crew had set up their gear leaving Jesus to meditate on his big part. Nobody noticed the tide cutting him off. Poor bastard couldn't even swim. Nobody there now. Only sand. And sea. Water to the reef quarter of a mile out, then more water. Deep all the way round; nibbling the whole continent, throwing flotsam and jetsam and pretty shells on the shore, defying the pieces to struggle and slip away back on the next tide. Hamish pulled his knees up. The classical pose of the weary. Knees up, head down resting on the back of protective arms. The pose didn't help. The sickness was still there. Hamish felt little heat from the new sun. The shirt for a night's carousing was no use for this early morning air. Hamish stood up, brushed himself down and moved along the beach to the jetty which led from the esplanade to the reef.

Jacky's house was only just over the esplanade from this pier. Over and up the hill. Maybe it was too early. Maybe it would be best to start heading toward Adelaide, although here this distance it might be as well to find out how the old fellow had survived the night. Maybe Hamish Creese just wanted somebody to talk to. A line of porpoises jumped out in the gulf; a straight perforated line. All jumping the same way. One after the other. Wonderful. To watch. He washed his glasses at the water tap for the nippers and dried them on his shirt-tail.

The little shop which had sold greasy fish suppers and chips was gone. The whole place was changed. The red and brown brick consumer palace declared itself. A shopping mall. Here. In Port Noarlunga. Big brick boxes spread out under home-made flags of no nations. The front of the pier where the kids ran flicking towels defiantly at red-faced mothers. In shadow. The big store signs were up and above square yards for automobiles. In

Port Noarlunga. The fishing place, Noarlunga; that's what the Abos called it. That must have been a long time ago. The sandy-grass pavements down past the house with the broken-down Mark Twain fence. Disappeared. Hamish felt dizzy. Hamish Creesc had lost his bearings last night. In daylight the changes still confused. He turned and walked up the esplanade toward Jacky's home.

The wooden holiday homes, once for city folk then the hippies then the defiant wanderers, were down. Rebuilt. Brick veneer with brick garden walls. Brick from top to bottom. No passage for air underneath. Air conditioning does the job. At least Jacky's old place looked the same, squatting there right on the top of the hill. Seventy-two steps from the beach. The two round stone pillars still there; still incongruous, running up at the corners to hold up a tin roof. Not tin now. Tile. Conroy has tiled the roof. The house was a pink-white crab which had wandered up from the beach and solidified.

Hamish sat on the garden wall. Still the water. Flat. Green now turning blue. Not even a sail to be seen. No ships' funnels in the distance cutting geometrically between two points. The sea was empty, suiting the mood of Hamish Creese. A flat board of a sea with nothing to inspire. He swung off the wall and moved up the side of the house, past the motor launch which lay displaying brown patches under a careless green tarpaulin. Hamish raised a fist to knock at the door. The hand stopped in mid-air. It was too early. Liz would still be sleeping. Best to go back to Adelaide. Back to the flat. Back to the grey brick walls kept apart by other bare brick walls and a fridge full of beer.

Hamish knocked. Three single raps on the door. A dog over the next door's fence barked. Hamish rubbed the vomit stain on his collar. He knocked again, a little harder. A key was making noises on the lock.

"Who is it?"

"Hamish, Liz, Hamish Creese. Your old lodger."

The key made more noise. The door opened. Through the gauze of the fly-screen Hamish looked at Liz, plump round Liz, the pads of the same purple housecoat flattened now and shiny.

"Will I come in?"

"You'd better; or you'll be standing there gawking all day."

Hamish followed Liz in, past the kitchen into the living-room. Liz picked up a man's shoe from the floor and another from the well of an armchair.

"Don't have to tell you whose these are," she said.

Hamish grinned and took a chair. Henry Lawson's portrait still looked down. The poet who told Australians who they were. According to Jacky Conroy. Below the portrait, on the top of the walnut bookcase, sat the brass claw hammer.

"You look bloody awful Hamish Creese. Where've you been? Were you in that taxi that dropped him off last night? Bloody old fool. Drunk and giggling like a teenager. What happened to your forehead? Have you had breakfast yet?"

The last one was the most important to be answered. Liz hadn't changed much. By the sound of it Jacky was OK.

"No, not yet. The shops aren't opened yet. I really just came by to see if Jacky made it home."

"Of course he did. Did you? He'd make it home with the beer flowing out of his ears. Bloody old fool. But at least he slept in his own bed last night. Where've you been?"

"Nowhere really. I fell asleep on the beach last night."

"You're a bit out of season for sleeping on the beach, aren't you?"

"Do you mean me or the time of year?"

"Bloody both, you bloody crackpot."

Liz rose and left the room to return with two towels. She threw them over. "Here, go and take a look at yourself. I'll make you a fry-up."

"Thanks Liz. But can I ask you a favour? Is there a beer in the fridge?"

Liz fetched a can of cola. "That'll do you."

Hamish went round the back of the house to the shower-house. Stripped under the blunt pencils of water he opened the can. Coke for a hangover. Makes no difference. It's not the coke, or the beer, it's the gas bubbling up from the belly till a burp shows the channel to the guts is clear. The showering water is good.

Move the head around, feel it. The solitude of the shower is sensual; for cleaning out the body. Sing in the shower; the tiles are stone deaf and the echoes drown out thought.

The mirror showed one large bruise. On the forehead, puffed, yellow and brown below the perfect imprint of a tooth. Black shadows now, under eyes that did not shine. A finger-end of toothpaste, a shot of male deodorant from a dusty bottle on a dusty shelf and Hamish Creese was ready again. One last rub at the black semi-circles of tiredness. The cooking smelt good.

Hamish's place was set in the kitchen. Liz had pulled on a frock. The dainty flowers on the black material stretched, attempting to rise over the hummocks of fat which fell away from her middle. Liz's hair was all grey now. Hamish acknowledged her smile. The plate was placed down, full, one egg slapping over the edge of the plate. Hamish felt a protest raised by a belly that was not hungry for bacon and beans. Liz sat down opposite. Hamish began to eat as she poured tea.

"Jacky not wakened yet?" he asked.

"Hamish, it's a miracle you're looking for. With that grog in him he'd sleep till tomorrow if I let him."

Hamish ate and sipped the tea, answering Liz's questions in between mouthfuls of respite. Most of the time Liz shook her head. Hamish fiddled with the last bites. Perhaps there were more questions to come.

"You should have stayed here you know, Hamish."

"Well, you know what it was like at that time Liz. There was no work for me here in Adelaide. Anyway, I wanted to see the place."

"So, what's to see? Why couldn't you be like the rest of us and see it on holiday? It was that bloody old fool up there putting ideas into your head about 'the Bush' and all that stuff. It's an Australia you'll never find Hamish. You'd be as well going back to Scotland and looking for bloody Brigadoon. Anyhow, you're back now. What's next? There's a lot less work now than there was when you left. Have you been in to see the union?"

These questions slid off the plate. Time to chew. The union. Bernard, Paul. And the Cohort.

Liz took the dishes to the sink. Hamish followed and picked up the towel to dry.

"That's what I liked about you when you came here. You never minded working in the kitchen, making the beds or stuff like that. Bushranger Ben through there would never have done it," she said, her hands hidden under the suds. "He does it now though; Hamish, I'm getting heavy and old. All I want to do now is sit on the porch and look at the Gulf. It's easier now; with the shopping mall here I can just toddle down and come back. No travelling, just a nice little walk. Those stores have everything, Hamish, you'll have to go see it."

"Is the two-dollar library and the old theatre still there?"

"Oh, it's still there, but nobody bothers much about it except us old ones. Old Charlie Murray died a few years ago. Mrs Murray still tries but, well, it's all different now."

Charlie Murray dead. A craftsman with wood. He had re-boarded that stage all by himself. Not a nail on top. Taught Hamish Creese to french polish while they made props for a production.

"Hamish. Wake up Hamish. The city is pushing south, Hamish. All right down the coast. The young people need all the new stuff and they get it."

"Only when they pay for it in advance."

"Oh Hamish, don't start your stuff. It's just the way of the world now. Things are changing. Times are changing. No wonder you and that old fool get on so well."

They walked back through to the living-room. Hamish sat down, stretching his legs and knitting his fingers together across his chest. Liz handed him an envelope.

"This arrived for you about a year ago. I meant to return it but I kept forgetting and, well, I kept hoping you'd come and collect it yourself. Bloody old fool that I am."

"I'm glad you did."

From Glasgow. Could only be Angela. Angela. She had never written before. Now this, when her brother had stopped writing years ago, just gradually, finally, accepting no replies would ever be sent. Angela was there, somewhere, Hamish Creese was here, somewhere. Alive, probably; dead, perhaps.

Liz moved away into the kitchen. Hamish read the letter. Hamish read the letter again. Douglas was dead. Angela had wanted to write and tell him that. Her husband was dead of the cancer. Hamish had to know he died slowly. Now she was on her own with two children. Hamish Creese is uncle to a girl who looks like her mother. That hoodlum Gaffney might be getting out of jail. Angela was still Hamish's sister and sent all her love, her best wishes were always with him. Hamish read again. That bastard might be getting out of jail. No mention of Lord John. Not a mention. She wrote Gaffney might be getting out as though he would be interested. Hamish Creese in Australia did not even know Gaffney was inside. All this time. Here, Hamish Creese, in Australia, and Gaffney was in jail. The bastard. Who was he over this time and space to make a man's belly tighten and tears fill up these pouches under the eyes? Fuck Gaffney. Maybe the bastard has rotted. Why did Liz have to put him in the first letter from home. Home? Scotland? Was it? Or was it Brigadoon? Fuck Brigadoon. Fuck Gaffney.

"You can come in now, I've read it," he shouted. Liz re-appeared.

"Good news, I hope?" Hamish folded the letter and pushed it tight down into his back pocket.

"It was from my sister. She wanted to tell me she's a widow."

"Oh. Poor dear. Is she young?"

"Just a little older than me, Liz."

"Well at least you can get in touch. You'd better write." Hamish closed his eyes. The mind was upset. The brain refused to function. Liz spoke from somewhere. "I'm off to the shops while it's quiet. You'll wait and see Jacky won't you, and have some dinner. I'll make a roast." A laugh came involuntarily. Liz came over and grabbed an ear. The guest had to stand up. She pulled him over to the sofa. "Lie down here," she commanded. Hamish Creese obeyed. Liz fetched a blanket and wafted it over him, tucking it behind his back and under his chin. "You'll have my roast and like it. Now sleep." The spectacles were gently slid from the face and Hamish Creese fell asleep.

Hamish rubbed his eyes. The air was hot. It was hotter under the blanket.

"You back in the land of the living?" Jacky's voice. Hamish put on his glasses. There he was, sitting in his chair, reading glasses at the end of that flat Aussie nose, paper on his knees.

"I'm not sure. How's yourself?"

"I'm bearing up. I think I'm maybe a little too old for too many of these shenanigans. Do you want a beer?" A beer was fetched and thrown and caught. "What happened to your head? You been banging it against a wall?" Conroy hadn't seen the scrap. Just as well.

"I fell. Liz was telling me Charlie Murray is dead. You'll miss him." The beer was cold. "I never saw anyone treat wood the way that man did. A craftsman. That's what he was, not many of us left."

"Too true, Hamish." Jacky had accepted the change of subject. "I reckon you and I are the last of a dying breed."

"You can bloody say that again," shouted Liz from her kitchen.

"They don't make them like us anymore." Jacky was shouting deliberately loud. "Pioneer stock, that's what we are. True pioneer stock. Turn our hands to anything." Liz accepted the bait. She came to the kitchen door, potato and knife suspended.

"Oh sure, we know, we know. 'With these hands I created something out of nothing'. I suppose you'd have liked it if we had lived in an old gum tree like the Herbigs? Us women having babies between night walks to market. Is that right?"

"Too right Mother. That's the stuff. Maybe that family lived in a gum tree but those Germans battled through in the end. They worked bloody hard at everything."

"And what did they get for it? Come the bloody war they get thrown in jail, that's what. Couldn't even call themselves German. You don't fool me with your stories."

"But Liz sweetheart that happened all over the world."

"But this wasn't all over the world. This was your bloody Australia. The home for all aliens, remember?"

A beer can seemed a safe place to hide in but a difficult place to laugh in. "What're you laughing at? You're an alien too, aren't you?" Jacky leaned back in his chair. Hamish was the target now. Liz lifted a finger. "Oh, I forgot. You're a bloody Scotsman, so you're always at home where there's a dollar to be made. Mind you, you don't look too prosperous to me." Hamish held out his arms in supplication.

> "For I am a ramble-eer, a rollicking ramble-eer,
>   I'm a roving rake of poverty and a son-of-a-gun
>   for beer."

Liz and Jacky both laughed. The way someone used to do when young Hamish Creese said clever mature things.

"Well," said Liz, "you must be Irish like this old fool. The Irish came here to sing songs to each other while you lot made the money. You Scots were clever enough not to believe your own nonsense outside of a whisky bottle. Hamish Creese you are a let-down to the breed."

"What makes you think I haven't any money?"

"Oh? Holding out on us are you?" asked Jacky.

"No, not really, but look, it's not money Scots emigrate for. Scots emigrate in answer to nagging voices in their head, prodding away at them to get on, don't be poor, pecking away at your brain till there is only one solution: get up and go or forever feel guilty, for there is no one to blame but yourself. Emigrants just hear the voices louder, that's all."

"Is that why you came?" asked Jacky. "Did you hear voices?"

"Me?" Lord John Miss Martin Angela Gaffney . . . where's mother? Hamish has been pissed on. "No. It's best just to say I was booted out."

"You're a strange one Hamish Creese," said Liz. "Why haven't you tried to 'get on' as you call it?"

"I'm a bit like Jacky there Liz, I need an audience. An audience that knows me. There's nobody here to see how well I've done. That's why a lot of them go home from time to time."

"To show off?"

"No. To wallow in Schadenfreude."

"What the bloody hell is that?" asked Jacky.

Hamish rattled the ring top around inside the can. Why had this come out now? Was this Hamish Creese? The words were sound evidence. He knew them. Knocking around Australia watching them, listening to them compare the value of the pound against the dollar, the day's temperature in Edinburgh and Sydney, the rainfall. Can you wear shorts in Glasgow in October? Always seeking confirmation. "Schadenfreude is the clap in the back they give themselves when a mate is having a bad run."

Jacky lifted a lower lip over an upper, looked over his glasses and shook his head.

"Hamish, do you believe that?"

"I'm one of them, Jacky. I've been away, but I know them. I've heard them rejoicing in their own smartness at getting out and piously feeling sorry for the ones they left behind. They're smug, Jacky, but underneath they need constant reassurance that the one big decision they made in their lives was the right one. That's what they want from home."

"Well you should know," said Liz, "you made the same big decision yourself." Liz freed herself from Jacky's arm which held her secure on the arm of the chair. She went to the kitchen.

"Want a fresh one?" asked Jacky. Hamish declined. No more beer just yet. He walked over and picked up the brass claw hammer from the bookcase.

"That was really good of these guys getting this for you, Jacky."

"I thought so, Hamish. You know construction: one job finished you're moving off, on to the next one that pays a dollar; moving on till you're too old to follow the money. Or else your fingers seize up on you. Nobody usually lasts long enough to get anything from anyone. I was lucky, I reckon."

Hamish read the plate. "TO A DINKUM AUSSIE." A dinkum Aussie. A lucky bloke in a lucky country. A chippie who made it without his hands giving out on him. "The bosses give you anything?"

"Not me Hamish, are you joshing? They gave me the cheese-board I would have got at Christmas. Can't moan too much. Bollerone gave me the job in the yard." In the yard; pottering and giving off knowledge that was disappearing. Kept in reserve. Just in case.

"Didn't you give them some stick in the old days?"

"No more than the rest. But that was a long time ago, Hamish.

I've quietened right down now. Old age even gets to old wobblies like me. The last of the Kellys is past it Hamish. I just watch and listen and have a good spit, then rest content I'm nearer my end than my beginning. The game's over Hamish." Hamish gave the inscription plate a rub and replaced the statuette on the mantle. "Hamish; Liz and me, we've done our share. I just want to make sure that Liz enjoys what's left of the Australia we grew up in. She's due that at least." Jacky Conroy, former International Worker of the World, now retired.

"Never thought I'd hear you talk like this Jacky."

"Well, that's the way it is, Hamish. Half the unions want to collaborate. Consensus they call it. The other half are split between Moscow and Peking. And then arguing about the road to whichever solution. The arguing is all they do now, Hamish. They're organisation men, pure and simple. Even fat-arsed Bernard; he's resting on his laurels from the Green campaign." Jacky took a gulp of beer. "Look at the kids Hamish. They know more about the Sundance Kid than they do about Ben Hall. The game's over. Have a beer."

Jacky left for the beer. Hamish heard a slap. Liz shouted at her bloody old fool. Hamish stretched out on the chair. Hamish Creese wasn't quite sure whether he was ready for a beer or not.

☆ ☆
☆ ☆ ☆ ☆ ☆ ☆
☆ ☆

CHAIRMAN Mao was gone. Lenin still looked over the shoulder of Engels, staring out over the fallen figure of Marx. The red felt in the space left by Marx was cleaner than the rest. The white busts had odd yellow stains; like tea stains, but lighter. The books in the window looked the same as always: *Toward Revolution in the Seventies* was now *Toward Revolution in the Eighties*. The others all looked the same as always. Nothing appeared to have changed. It all looked the same. Just the same. Framed in the space left by the fallen Marx, past the books, beyond the statuettes on their raised dais, inside the shop, there was the bookman. Feather duster in hand, still in the same grey clothes, crescent-shaped white face; suspended in time, pulling out and pushing in these books of Marx and Lenin, shuffling around dusting them off. Eager, younger, Hamish Creese had complained about the lack of poetry for working men. The bookman had sold the enthusiastic face a volume of the songs of the wobblies. 'Hallelujah, I'm a Bum' waiting for 'Pie in the Sky'. The bookshop owners didn't rely on pie in the sky. This whole building was theirs, and the union paid to lease the offices above. The bookman doubled as a rentman. Solidarity Forever. Hamish looked away, down the street. Gerry was there.

Gerry was there at the corner standing free amongst the lunchtime paraders and shoppers criss-crossing to the light's command. Gerry made them all look lost; an intense herd hurrying unconsciously in a pre-set pretended ramble. Gerry had made it. Hamish Creese was relieved. It would not be so bad seeing Bernard again with Gerry there. The talk would have to be kept light. Question and answer could be kept to shallow catechism. Gerry was moving up through the red-brick streets past the fake Victorian street lamps and natural-looking square brick shrubberies, turning his head to look at the short-skirted girls from city centre offices who used the mall as a temporary stage to be strutted.

"Some people never change. Are you fit?"

"Depends what for. Nothing wrong a few dollars won't cure."

"Did you recover from the piss-up?"

"I've no worries, mate, but I think you made an arse of yourself. I think you've made a right blue with your mate Danny."

"Jesus, no, you're joking."

"Only too right, mate. You'll have to square yourself up there, and with his missus. They were only trying to stop you leaving his place for your own good, but you kept rabbiting on about checking out the old fella."

The night came back. Danny holding his arm, beer spilling over a snooker table and Maggie Fairweather stumbling back, falling, caught by the chair. And crying. Oh no. No no no no. NO.

"It was me that pushed you out the door for your own good. You've definitely made a right blue there."

"I'll go round and see them and make it right. Could've been doing without it, though."

Especially now Liz and Jacky hadn't seemed too happy with the Hamish Creese who babbled on, took their dinner but refused a bed. Maybe they're just getting old. "C'mon, we're going up here."

The narrow tiled entrance which led along and up to the offices was cool. The stair-rail was polished by many hands, the brass fixings shiny in the dull close. Hamish pushed at the glass-panelled door. The sign said PULL. Gerry stretched his hand over and pulled it open.

Behind the long wooden counter, over in the corner, a woman was speaking into the two-way radio. Paul was wanted; somebody, somewhere was acting up. Employer or employees, it didn't matter, Paul would sort them out. No worries. She turned her head to acknowledge their wait with rapid noddings of her head which threw her hair over her face. Paul crackled in to learn that the boys at the railway job were refusing to work because the subbie had refused to install a pie warmer. Yes it was past smoke-o time and the steward's name was Paddy Reid. Paul would attend. The clerkess laid down the microphone and switched off. This was the same one. No tousled hair, no faded denims, no badges declaring her loyalty to the union. Now it was the white blouse and the pencil black skirt. Now she had grown up to fit into the uniform. She was a woman now. An office woman. When Hamish Creese had signed on she was only new, a fresh start straight from school. She came over. She didn't recognise Hamish Creese. How long since he left Adelaide? Seven years? She smiled at Gerry. "Can I help?"

Gerry held out his palm toward Hamish. "We were on a job at Flinders. We expected some money to be left for us."

"Oh yes, sure. It's a Mr Creese and Mr Thomas, isn't it?" Gerry was nodding like a child who had been invited to an ice-cream. "Sure," she continued, "the money is here. Excuse me." A key was drawn from a dress pocket, a drawer released and two envelopes withdrawn. She brought them over. "The man who left the money was quite agitated. I don't think he wanted to part with it." Hamish began counting the money.

"That's the impression we got," said Gerry. She laughed at the crack.

Hamish spoke. "Is Bernard in? I'd like to see him, if that's possible. Tell him it's Hamish Creese."

The woman did not respond to the full name. "I can see if he's free. Could you hold on please?" She disappeared through the door set in the partition. Through to the meeting room. She would be breathing in, past the chairs, touching the green leather backs, polishing the brass studs with the palm of her hand. Up along the row to Bernard's door. The voices mumbled and did not carry, but he was coming. A door, to the left, right next to Hamish, was opened. Bernard stood there, looking, trying to take them both in, friendly. Bernard hadn't changed much. The hair had always fought a losing battle over the plain front of his head, above that ploughed field of a forehead.

"Hamish. Hamish. How y'goin'? Come in." Hamish hesitated. "Bring your mate. Who is he anyway?" The hands that pulled and pumped and slapped at his back were still strong. There was still a lot of strength in the big man yet. "Paul said you'd be in. Glad I was here." Hamish palmed Bernard off on to Gerry, turned back and fetched in the extra chair he knew would be needed.

Bernard's office was small; the sides of the desk just failed to touch the wall. The jumble of paper lay scattered, as if Bernard was a man careless with words. Behind the desk was the black leather swivel armchair. Bernard's new chair. It was a wide one. The woman came up behind and asked about coffee. Bernard wound himself down into his chair. Hamish and Gerry scraped their chairs around to accommodate each other. Bernard was asking all the usual questions. Hamish Creese answered. Hamish Creese was becoming bored with his own employment history.

These questions weren't quite usual. There was knowledge behind them. Bernard knew the answers. Bernard knew. Bernard knew where Hamish had come from, where he'd been. He knew about Queensland, Darwin and Iron Knob; the geography and the history. The woman brought in the coffee on a tray with milk and sugar and little teaspoons and a saucer of digestive biscuits. While they performed the ritual Hamish bent his head into the coffee cup. Bernard probed away at Gerry. Gerry didn't say much; covering his answers with jokes. Bernard would have to reserve his judgement there. Bernard sat back in his chair. Another question was coming.

"You look really comfortable in that chair, Bernard," said Hamish.

"Too right. That's the first thing I did after I was elected, got myself a new chair. Paul fancied his backside in it but he can get one of his own now. He's off to Canberra."

Canberra. "That's new territory for this union, isn't it? We don't have enough members there to justify a branch, do we?"

"Now we do. Paul is going over to help them become established."

Paul off to Canberra. In at the top. Getting established would probably take years. "That'll be good," said Hamish.

"I wish you'd stayed," said Bernard. "There would've been a job for you to do there. Paul could have made something there for you."

"Sure." An organiser's job maybe? Just like Dudley? Somebody's kidding.

Bernard changed the subject. Now it was time for tales from the old days. Tales about Hamish Creese, the Green hero, rousing up the neighbourhood groups to fight for their old parks and buildings. Keep Los Angeles in America. The land of the Southern Cross can be the green and pleasant land, the lucky country for lucky people, only if Australia builds what Australians need. Always the good finisher.

"Do you remember that dame with the plastic mac, Hamish? You never saw anything like it, Gerry. Real top-drawer stuff she was." Hamish Creese remembered. "Hamish here had just made a speech and everyone was cheering him off the platform, when up jumps this sheila and stops him in the passage. What was it she said Hamish? 'You should be rewarded for what you are doing for Australia', then she flings open her coat and there she was, stark bollock naked. Christ that was funny."

"What did you do there, mate?"

Hamish smiled tightly and picked at the green leather desk-top with a fingernail. Bernard slapped the desk. "He just blew her a kiss from off the back of his hand then he turns and walks back up the steps to the platform and sits in his seat till the place emptied. Christ that was some do."

Gerry was mocking a frown and looking sideways, quizzically, at Hamish Creese. "Fucking hell," was all he managed.

Bernard prattled on, reliving the days of the Green Australia campaign. Hamish listened. It was time for Hamish Creese to have the ego massage. Bernard was making it appear as if there was no one like Hamish Creese for haranguing builders, shaming white ants and holding strikers solid. But he wasn't telling the young man of the struggle to free the union from the mobs. Free elections. Free elections for Bernard to get elected. Free elections for organisers that were only appointed temporarily by Bernard. Hamish preferred not to think about it. Gerry was looking bored.

84

"So where's all the work, Bernard?" asked Hamish.

"Ooof. That's asking something. There's really nothing doing. Except for the one that Bollerone have got at Happy Rock. But everybody and his brother are trying to get on that one."

"Happy Rock," said Hamish, "never heard of it."

"It's a dead-and-alive little hole, close to nowhere and far from anywhere," said Gerry. "It's a small fishing place about three hundred miles down the Bight. What does anybody want to put down there?"

"We're not quite sure, well, we've got a bloody good idea. It's really two jobs. At the shore they're building some kind of cracker plant, but the real big one is further along the coast. They're digging into the cliffs and we reckon it must be some sort of military complex. Nobody is quite sure."

Nobody is quite sure. That means nobody wants to know for sure. The men on the dole need the wages and the unions need the subscriptions. Ten years ago this would have been one for the campaign. "How long will it last?" asked Hamish.

"Oh, a couple of years at least."

Two years. That would be another couple of thousand dollars anyway. "What's the accommodation?"

"They're letting wives go, giving the married blokes fancy caravans. Taking a chance there, I reckon, with blokes like young Gerry here stomping around." Women. Women. On a bush job. No no. Surely no?

"And what's for the bears?"

"Barracks. At the other end of town."

"Oh Christ." Barracks. Not Whyalla over again. Hamish Creese, new over to build ships, lying there in the dark, listening to the Turks and the Greeks scuffling between the rows of beds, stabbing till screaming curses came. Curses that conveyed the hate. No need to know the language. Hamish Creese was in Australia. Alone. "Ah Jesus."

"What's the matter?" asked Gerry. "You getting too old for it now?"

"Could be. What's the chance of getting on there?"

"For both of us," reminded Gerry.

85

Bernard reached down to a drawer and brought out two large forms. He passed them over. Hamish and Gerry took one each.

"What's this?" asked Hamish.

Gerry laughed as he turned through the pages. "Hey, look at this, I'm famous; they want to know my experience and achievements. Does that mean all of them? I started when I was still at school. Really early." Hamish didn't laugh.

"C'mon Bernard, somebody has got to be joking. Is this to help the blacklist?"

"Sorry; these are it, mate. I agree with you, I agree. And you can blame one of your Scottish countrymen for this." Hamish moved him on, chin up. "Bollerone brought over a guy called Seaton from the car industry in Melbourne and the first thing he does is start hitting the lads with these things. Now every bloody builder in the Masters Federation is doing the same thing. They've even stuck a bloody computer in Hiram House and they're all bloody plugged into it. They're trying their best."

Everybody on tape. Four pages of questions. Name and Date of Birth? Nationality? Is that Australian or Scottish? How long have you lived in Australia? Too long maybe? Put the answers into little boxes. List your experience and achievements. List your experience and achievements. "A load of bullshit," said Hamish. "I think it's maybe time I was going back for the harvest."

Bernard laughed. "Don't worry, mate, we've seen his type before. It's all ambition with them so they don't make friends even in their own camp. This one reckons he'll be an Industrial Commissioner in next to no time."

"But where does this put Gerry and me?"

Bernard shifted paper; both hands at once, broad lumpy fingers compressing a thick pile to thin. "I'm not sure. It's been a long time since you worked in the State, maybe your name won't be on the computer. Does Gerry have your record?"

Gerry laughed. "Not yet, but if I keep working with him I might end up just as nutty. But what gets me is half of the blokes on the sites are Italians and Yugoslavs, how do they read this stuff? Never mind answer it."

Bernard shrugged his shoulders. The telephone rang. Bernard

picked it up and began nodding his head forward and back, muttering and pursing his lips. Hamish looked at his watch. Thirty minutes. Old habits die hard. He signalled Gerry to stand up and prepare to go. Bernard replaced the telephone.

"Sorry about that boys. It's been one of those days." Bernard leaned over and shook Gerry's hand. Hamish picked up his chair to replace it. He pushed it back under the conference table, pausing, remembering, picking out the seat which everyone left for him. The one which allowed him to see the door at either end. Bernard called him back in. "Are you doing anything tonight, Hamish?" Here it was. Maybe he hadn't moved fast enough. No. He had hoped this call would come. It was bargaining time. The union still had some power. If Hamish Creese wanted to go to Happy Rock he would need them. Bernard could stop him with just a word in the right ear.

"Not really, no, why?"

"Oh, just some friends of yours are meeting tonight for a few beers. You know the kind of thing, little bit of beer, little bit of political discussion. Thought you might fancy coming. They'd love to see you."

The Cohort. "What time and where?"

"Do you remember Molly's house? We're meeting there; eight o'clock."

Old Molly. Unkempt Molly, fag ash permanently flowing down her clothes. "Sure. I'll be there. Look forward to it."

Hamish went out to the long counter. Gerry was watching the woman. She was seated in front of a black screen that glowed green letters and words, and numbers. The keys made slight clicks under her fingers. Hamish Creese watched gerry thomas appear on the screen.

"What's your address, Mr Thomas?"

"I haven't got one. I live in my van."

"Oh."

"Do you want the licence number?"

"No thank you. Where do you live, Mr Creese?"

"I'm staying at 34 Miara, Edwardstown."

She clicked it up on to the screen beside Gerry's name and

beside his number. She turned her head while clicking away and smiled at Hamish. "Are you paying for the year or the quarter, Mr Creese?"

"Three-quarters. Do you want my card from Queensland?"

"No. That's all right. In fact I think I've still got you listed in our dead file." She crossed the room and bent to the bottom drawer of a grey filing cabinet. Gerry made an approving face. Hamish hit him on the back of the neck. The woman returned with the card which she tore in two and threw into a bin before resuming her place at the machine.

"What's all this for anyway?" asked Hamish.

"This is our computer. It helps us keep a check on who is up to date or not. If Paul or Dudley phone in with a query I just press the buttons and there you are, it's all in front of me."

"So you've got all the answers on tab?"

"That's right. And next year we're hoping to link up with Melbourne and Sydney."

Hamish took his receipt. Gerry followed him out, along, down to the cool tile corridor. They came to the same door as they had come in. Hamish pulled at the glass-panelled door. The sign said PUSH. Gerry pushed it open. Out they went.

THE long spout of the small green watering-can was pointed on a line parallel to the cigarette which was forced upwards by a protruding bottom lip. Molly moved along the porch; between stops her matted hair merged with the moss which poked out from the wire of the hanging baskets. Molly was pretending, pretending to be lost in the act of looking after her plants, while Hamish Creese stood on the path. The plants were failing. The water arched out to be sucked up by the dry plants. Hamish stood, waited. He stood to be recognised. Molly moved among the floral creels. The contest was in silence, fought by silence. Hamish Creese could remain quiet as long as anyone. Molly weaved her way along the porch, in and out of the wet, dry, baskets. The dustcoat she wore had a black and red rose motif. She looked as if she had wrapped herself into a roll of wallpaper from the forties. That pattern had been all the go in the tenements. Molly moved. Hamish waited. The fly-screen flung open. A thinnish gentleman in a silver-grey suit appeared, wine glass in hand. A draw would have to be declared; for now. The wine glass was being raised up and out.

"Hamish Creese. Bernard told me you were coming and I had to just hurry over. Immediately, you understand."

"That was nice of you, Professor. How have you been? Read any good books lately?"

"Ah, if only you knew, Hamish. The students nowadays are actually demanding I teach them something about Literature. Just enough to pass exams you understand; so I set them to looking for shiny new symbols and rusty old ironies while I write eulogies on

89

them for the Public Service. Between the worriers and the bureaucracy of it all now I hardly have a chance to read anything at all. Ah me; changed days, changed days. Molly, don't be rude and come and say hello to our long lost chum."

"I'll be in. Take him in and give him a beer."

Hamish went to the kitchen. The pots were piled high, the top one full of water. The fridge was jammed full of beer and wine. A full turnout being supplied for. Hamish took a can through to the living-room. A girl in a brown dress with her feet tied into thick leather sandals sat alone. Black socks covered the feet and lower portion of her legs. She looked up to Hamish from the floor. "Hi." American; on tour: Australia today, home tomorrow. Save Australia from Capitalism first though. What is shits for General Motors is shits for Holden cars. But Hamish Creese from Scotland looked the same. Anyway, capitalism is international, always touring the world and following on in the luggage of the immigrant.

"Hello," said Hamish, sitting down on a lumpy settee. This settee had no definable shape. The front, back, top, bottom, left arm, right arm, all the parts, were trying to break away from each other and failing. The cabinetmaker had defied all known physical laws. Or had longer nails than anyone else. The Professor sat on a chair opposite.

"Are you still writing poetry, Hamish?"

"Not so you'd notice."

The Professor laughed. He turned to the girl. "Hamish has a talent for poetry, you know. Rhymes fit to start a revolution. All good radical stuff, you understand. What was that one I liked Hamish? Ah, yes,

> How many Eurekas happen every day?
> Not the kind that needs trooper and gun
> To try and destroy a pride that's new won,
> Or blood to spill out in defence of fair play.
> But human decisions, sometimes made alone,
> To stand and declare: My mind is my own."

The girl smiled without showing teeth.

"Hamish used to tack them on to the inside of the lavatory doors on the building sites. Didn't you Hamish? I think they went down rather well. Ah, if only he'd received an education." The beer was cold.

"Isn't it about time Molly did something about the light in here?" The girl's response had been stopped. "We're caught between pitch black and gloom. Ah, gloom, gloom. I love that word Hamish. It rhymes with doom. It also rhymes with this bloody room."

People were coming in. The narrow door made them come in all in single file. Paul, still with his glasses; Bernard, fingers spread, waving hands in front; and Dudley, pulling at the lobe of his ear; and another man. A man with long straight blond hair down to his shoulders, framing a white face. A moustache and new beard adorned the pale face. The man was a walking sculpture of Jesus. He was introduced to Hamish: Paddy from Ireland. Dudley and Paul sat on either side of Hamish. The routine began anew.

Hamish concentrated on Dudley. "How are you fitting in as organiser?"

Dudley was off. The question was enough. Dudley recounted the tales; how he had shown the bosses a thing or two or three. As he spoke more people came in; edging in, pushing in, loud hellos, soft responses, sitting, standing, conversing, dreaming. Hamish Creese was losing count. They were all around. There were a lot of strangers here. They were filling the room. Cross-legged on the floor, hunched on the arms of baggy chairs, flopped inside them. Others sat straight-backed, silent, watching from stools. Some faces were known, but most were younger, new, unknown. The men in the suits sat. From years ago Hamish Creese had never got to know them. Never heard them speak. Another two squeezed in; just standing, looking down. The voices had become a hum. Dudley was underlining his hands with some speech. Hamish Creese was hearing nothing. "I'm off for a beer." Through the door Molly stood. She backed herself against a wall. Hamish faced her to slide past. Smudges of ash rubbed off on his shirt.

The kitchen was cooler and smoke free, but it didn't smell any cleaner. Hamish selected a can of beer. He wanted to respond to the ssshsh and clack of the ring-pull, to answer it back, thank it for its conversation. Hamish hung on to the fridge door, keeping it open, feeling the waft of cold air on his neck, watching the light, just looking at the illuminated cans of beer and the sparkling wine.

"You coming in, mate?" It was Bernard. Hamish lifted out another can.

"Sure. I just came through for some beer. No offence, but I get a little thirsty while the talking is going on."

Bernard sat on a tiny chair which poked out from the kitchen table. He balanced on one buttock, the backside of one trouser-leg a billow between waist and knee. A beer can was hidden by his fingers. "Tell the truth Hamish, you never did care very much for the meetings. You always pushed yourself into a corner, especially if the Professor was in one of his moods."

"Ach, maybe so, but really, I thought they were OK. I think I'm just getting too old for them now. Some of these youngsters here tonight make me feel like Old Man River."

Bernard laughed and leaned forward onto his thighs, rolling the can between his palms. "I know how you feel. By the way, is your mate a union man?"

"Gerry? Yeah, I suppose so. He knows what's what. Why?"

"Known him long?"

"Since Queensland." Since Queensland. Bernard would know when that was. He would know all right. "We teamed up there and just seemed to knock it off. I was the brains and he was the muscles."

"You're not in such bad shape yourself, and from what I heard you've been doing a bit of scrapping yourself. You and him. But is he sound?"

"I told you, he knows what's what. You're asking a lot of questions Bernard." The beer can was up. The gulp was a long one, moving the Adam's apple. Bernard was drinking it all in. "You're an old fox, Bernard. What's the score? You don't ask questions for nothing. What's the interest in Gerry?"

"Oh, it's just in case a job comes up."

"Take it from me, he's OK."

"Nobody said otherwise."

Bernard stood up, crossed over and closed the door of the gurgling fridge, cutting off the yellow light. The kitchen was as dark as the living-room. In silhouette against the window pane the handles of the pots and pans ran round and round, spiralling like the skeleton of a staircase. Round, round, round and up like the railings running up under the banister playful Hamish Creese slid down, knees up, elbows in. Like the railings playful Hamish Creese had cowped the cat over and down as a check to see if it had nine lives. Or at least more than one. Like the railings curious Hamish Creese had crept against to keek down at the screaming lassies around the cat in the stairwell below. The cat had only the one. No one saw and Jimmy Gunn got the blame and the tanking from his Da's black belt.

The door of the kitchen opened. The long nails and hand appeared around the door edge; tight skin, pale, with speckles of black dots around the knuckles. Molly's face appeared. The gurgling in the fridge cut out. She looked long at Bernard. Bernard's can blipped as he pressed too hard. The cigarette disappeared part-way into her mouth, then was brought out again to point at its angle up past the tip of her nose. She removed the cigarette and blew smoke.

"You and our Shelley of the shithouse coming through?"

Shelley of the shithouse. A poetic alliteration. And Molly would know; for she was the Witch of Atlas. The bad one. But Hamish Creese was not here to be an invisible Pan. Hamish Creese was alive and well and sipping beer. Right here. Hamish Creese was here to be seen and heard. Tell her.

"We shall be right through, Molly. Bernard and I were just catching up on all the gossip. And we wouldn't want to miss the start." Or the middle. Or the finish. Particularly the finish.

Molly left. The curls of smoke remained in a vaporised outline of her head. Bernard let the can fall from two hands into a full waste basket. Back through a man with a face full of beard stopped talking as they entered. Hamish wedged himself into a space on the floor between the side of an armchair and a pair of brown leather shoes. Expensive shoes. Bernard sat near Molly. The man began again. The accent was South African. Hamish wished he had gone for a pee.

"To be ready for our rôle in the revolution to come it is agreed we must do certain things. We must keep ourselves educated in the writings of Marx and Lenin. We must seek to educate others, not just in the literal sense, but by example. We must take and practise effective leadership in community groups, the workplaces, the trade unions and our student bodies. There must be no difference between commitment in a play-group and a campus, or a factory. We must use our positions to advance our comrades to positions of power. We must organise ourselves into cohorts all over the continent and be sure that our cohorts are skilled and ready to take over the apparatus of capital and use our knowledge of that apparatus for the furtherance of revolutionary socialism, and leadership of the masses. The question I am here to discuss tonight is how a member gains a position of effective leadership, and where we must aim to have our leaders. First, let me leave to one side the bourgeois notion of charisma . . ."

"Didn't Lenin have charisma?" The American girl's voice was quiet.

"I wouldn't know, since I don't recognise the concept. Comrade."

A few titters ran round the room. Molly smiled. The man continued.

His lecture was good. He knew his stuff. But it was old stuff. Familiar. Hamish remembered Molly speaking the same story; quietly, in the kitchen, keeping the new convert entranced, quiet, till she had come near, close, and pulled at his privates. Hamish gulped at the beer. Probably this guy was better at it anyway. Hamish Creese could never have put his heart into it.

This was a new bit. Now he was suggesting that computer experts be recruited into the Cohorts as a matter of urgency. The proper person in the proper function could cause enough havoc to ease the way of the revolution and allow it to take its traditional path. Traditional. What tradition? Whose tradition?

Hamish sipped quietly from the can. If they had any bloody foresight the experts would be in place already.

The speaker stopped. The silent gap broadcast that his audience were not aware the end had come. It took time before the usual first question was asked. "What do you envisage as the role for these communications experts?" The lecture began again. Hamish opened the other can. The froth spilled over into the shoe at his side. Hamish looked up. The man was either sleeping, or engrossed; or rigidly disciplined. Bernard stood up.

"Right. Thanks, comrade. Before you all go splashing through for a beer, you might like to know our newspaper reached a circulation of 1,909 last week; which isn't so bad when you consider we only moved to our new address two weeks ago. If we can keep the law away maybe we'll break the 2,000 mark this summer. Remember, if you've anything for putting in see Rory here." The South African smiled. Some people clapped him on the shoulder as they made their way through to the beer.

Hamish eased and stretched his legs forward. This room was getting darker. Gloomier. The thin window looked redundant. From this position on the floor it appeared as a white rectangle. Nothing framed in it; no view; only a rectangle of white. Not sky. Just white. Molly sat waiting for the others. The lecturer for this evening sat on the floor with his shoulder tucked into her thigh. Molly's hand rested on his shoulder. The brown leather shoes returned and took up the place at Hamish's side.

The Professor was the last to come back. He stood in the centre of the room, turning his head, looking at them all, in no particular order. "As you know, my comrades, it is necessary for members of the Cohort to know themselves thoroughly; in order that we understand exactly what that tool is, which is to be placed into the service of the people. For only by understanding ourselves can we, as members, understand those forces at work upon the people as a whole. Only by understanding can members overcome these forces; and further, lead others into an understanding of how these forces — ideological, material — are the very essence of their subjugation."

Hamish decided to leave the remainder of the beer in the can. Bernard calling him back, the big turnout, the big speech. He placed the can between the feet of the standing man and crossed his legs over to wait. Hamish Creese was on next. Nothing was surer.

"So it is that we have our sessions aimed at the understanding of the self. Tonight we have back with us a comrade from other parts. We know the role he has played, before, and we know he still has a leader's role to play. BUT, but . . ." There it was. Voice up, hold it, hold it, space out the next four . . . "we are not sure he understands his present motivations. We are sure, however, that he knows we are always here to help him back on to the road towards a deeper understanding. Hamish. Will you come forward please?"

Hamish was helped up by the man in the brown shoes. He stepped forward to the centre of the round raggedy carpet. A hand pushed out a stool to him. Hamish sat down. He faced the window. There was still no view. His hands gripped the edge of the stool from between his thighs. It was getting dark outside. Darker inside. The faces were dark on dark. Except for Paddy from Ireland. A red cigarette tip glowed. Fag ash making its way down Molly's chest.

"Begin in the usual way Hamish, please, for the benefit of those who only know you on the surface." The Professor merged somewhere into the black back of the room.

On the surface Hamish keep it on the surface don't let this mob in. They only want to probe around in somebody else's midden keep it easy. Keep it easy give them the usual this is a jamboree for these cunts wine in the fridge and somebody else's bones to pick over juicy stuff. It was always going to happen Bernard knew the score are you doing anything tonight Hamish? Fly old bastard. They've done the once a year clean out to each other full of bullshit now they fancy somebody different. Hamish Creese? Chap left the Cohort left the path don't think he's had any critical help for years hasn't really had a chance I hear he's been up Bush for years that's no excuse. Don't need to see their mouths move to hear them and Molly's just waiting. Maybe no maybe she's all right doubt it. Don't fancy the young Springbok one iota. Talk more talk Hamish but keep it at the surface. Gie them the bosses and the shipyards that goes down well thrown out with nothing to do but emigrate an industrial gypsy no a bad wee turn o phrase that. Easy now never mind Gaffney they don't want to know about Gaffney oh chap was wrong but merely a victim of his environment just as you were before your political enlightenment thanks for enlightening me. That'll be fucking right. Fuck Gaffney. It's dark in here. Whyalla. Whyalla. Working men of different cultures all fighting like fuck. Don't swear use their language don't swear keep it cool like their bloody language. Bernard and the Green campaign bum him up a bit organising Adelaide. Wonder why Angela wrote after all this time Bernard the stalwart comrade. The hospital strike that was a good one cheapskate bosses meet solidarity fuck better bum-up the branch the support from the Cohort then. The Professor good guide and teacher opening windows the right books the books the thirst for knowledge and help and Hamish Creese wrote an article the unions and ecology. They must know that maybe the young people don't might impress them scare them off a bit not likely. Don't mention the elections no don't what's next what's next.

"Well, I think that's as far as it goes."

"And it is all right as far as it goes, but you have avoided any analysis of your actions. No analysis Hamish. No whys, no wherefores."

Where was the face? Hamish Creese could not see the face.

"You went away rather suddenly, didn't you?"

That came from the brown shoes.

"Not really. I'm sure everybody knew I was restless, I wanted to travel, see Aussie."

"Ah, but you did not tell your trade union comrades when you were leaving. Or us."

The Professor was leading from the back. In there, somewhere, in there.

"It was just a sudden decision. I can't really remember."

"Do you remember your rôle? To tour the sites with Comrade Paul and spread the good news and recruit members. Do you remember? Is that how you saw it?"

"Yes. We impressed on the members their union was now an honest union."

97

"You didn't impress upon them that you should be their new organiser?"

"No. That would have been unfair. Anyway, I didn't stand for any office."

"But you left when all the publicity was finished and the cheering was finished."

"That was coincidence. I was going anyway. I suppose I could have done more.

Hamish Creese had been in it, but not of it. The trade union comrades had never allowed it. Too much support among the bears. Charisma maybe. Paul is asking something.

"Eventually you didn't stand. You forget I was with you comrade."

"I don't follow you."

"You did want to be an organiser. Even without an election. You thought you should just get it. You thought you were due it, didn't you? All you wanted was the position that would allow you to play the folk-hero."

"Ah. Is that what you wanted, comrade, position and fame?"

Position and fame. No, it wasn't that. No. It was just the way things were at the time. It was; it was the way elections for the job were not to take place. And who was Dudley anyway?

"I was willing to do my bit anywhere, in any capacity."

"But you went away."

The brown shoes again. The suit is grey, but the face is in shadow. Paul is getting excited, his arm is up as if he is holding that case.

"You wanted to do your own thing, take the route of the individual. In fact you rejected the discipline of the Cohort. That is why you were not considered for the post of organiser. Your tendency was always to disobey instructions and give pride of place to your own opinions."

That's it, Paul. Selected works, volume two, pages thirty-one and thirty-two. Chairman Mao will never die.

"I am not aware that is my tendency, comrade. And if it was at that time it was your duty to inform me."

Page thirty-three page thirty-three page thirty-three. Paul should know that.

"Paul, by not informing me of this you have harmed the organisation and me." That red glow was moving. Molly's for a piece.

"Why did you not contact other Cohorts in other places?"

"The places I went to were all up-country. There was no organisation as far as I could tell."

"You did not try to organise?"

"Not in the sense of getting new members for the Cohorts, but I did recruit for the union."

This circle is getting smaller. The stool of repentance is a fucking hard seat. Hamish Creese needed a rest. Up there, down here. That glow, arching, becoming brighter.

"But other comrades who worked with you have told us that when they approached you for guidance, for learning, you rebuked them. Why do you reject comrades?"

Who was she talking about? Rebuke? What kind of word is that? Rhymes with puke.

"If I have failed in that direction I'll apologise to any comrade offended. But even though I was away I still fought the bosses for conditions and the right cash."

Over there. In Molly's corner. He's straining at the leash. Molly's running dog wants to trap. The dog has been shown the rabbit.

"Not correct, comrade. To confine the struggle to these workplace issues is to fall into the trap of the bosses. It is not enough merely to struggle for cash."

Merely to struggle for cash. Merely. Merely get your head kicked fighting blacklegs. Merely get the shit jobs, grovelling in the muck and the mud while gaffers laughed. This is a merely not in his dictionary. Molly's lifted her hand. He's out from under, coming closer. His teeth are white. Listen to him. What the fuck does he know? How canst thou hear ?

"For example, comrade, I go amongst my students and take the message to them, to fight for their rights, study the system and generally raise their consciousness. I help them inquire into them-selves and study their own attitudes to questions of the day. Through this some have come to be here tonight. To argue for money only demonstrates that you have fallen into the trap of the cash nexus."

A university man. And a do-it-by-the-little-red-book man. Try raising the consciousness of men struggling to form words in a foreign language.

"One thing, mate; on site it is the union working, not me. We just hope that when we do something for the blokes they remember. Sometimes they do, sometimes they don't. But they know whose side we're on."

How canst thou hear who knowest not the language of the dead?

"But you, you have no plan, no direction. You are dealing with these issues on an ad hoc basis. Furthermore, I suspect you have fallen into the ways of liberalism. Do you know what I have here?"

The American girl had her hand up, just like a schoolgirl.

"May I come in here?"

"No. I have not finished. Do you know what this is?"

He's waving it round everybody. The ones at the back have crept forward, craning their necks to see. A newspaper? A newspaper.

"The Townsville Telegraph. This is the edition which published your poem. This poem is no more than a piece of pretentious nonsense, which, when analysed, displays all your liberal leanings."

That poem was a good poem. It was. It was a good poem. Jacky Conroy had framed the cutting. It wasn't terrific. But it was good. Who is this cunt?

"Ah, Rory. One should not take so seriously the amateurish writings of a comrade who comes from a land famed for its hedgerow poets. The poem is of no consequence here tonight."

Amateurish. Of no consequence. But that was why Hamish Creese had joined in the first place. Paul had said it. The Professor at university had liked his poetry. Come and meet him. No surely not? But the poetry was good. Of no consequence. Does the Professor mean that it has nothing to do with this circle of crows? Crammed around, impatient, chaffing for the dumb crambo to begin. Give them a rhyme, give them a clue. Then they'll know who Hamish Creese might be. A rhyme and a puzzle, a riddle-me-ree. Perhaps they'll guess it quick. All these clever people. The students; her with the sandals, she looks brainy. The Professor, he's studied the stuff, he'll make sense of the rhyme. Molly. She knows already. Hamish Creese; a man of no consequence. He's insisting.

"I disagree, Professor. A critical structuralist analysis reveals the writer to be reactionary. I am not talking about the style, which I agree is amateurish, but on the content. The man reveals himself through it an idle romantic reactionary."

Hamish Creese was no longer here. Now hamish creese was a concept, like the working class. Why didn't they ask Hamish Creese about it? Why ask a carpenter about the structure of a poem? Of no consequence.

"Comrade, do you wish to read your poem?"

"No."

"Quite wise. But I shall save you from being Maevius, I shall read it."

Maevius. Who is Maevius? A joke had been made at the expense of Hamish Creese.

"Listen, all of you, listen to this:

> Black frangipani with ash grey flowers
> That fall in my beer jug
> Gently
> Blind Koalas munching softly
> While the tail-less kangaroo rolls over
> Gently
> I."

Who was Maevius? This guy was not reading the poem right. No no, the pauses were too long the inflection too heavy Miss Martin said the inflection in a poem was the zephyr on the cheek scarcely noticed but softly there. This guy is up and down like a yo-yo. He's sending it up.

The feet were shuffling, the faces laughing. Someone leaving the room. Another splutter covered another laugh.

"YOU'RE NOT READING IT RIGHT."

The poem was waved higher, the voice was raised to follow it. hamish creese leapt up and was quickly over to throttle off the voice from the throat. Fingers and thumb perfected an arc into the windpipe and held the face up to watch the slow descending fist that came and connected with a crack. "That's style you bastard, that's style. Now go back to your concrete cave in your university. Tell the weans you met style. Style." The front of the fist met the jaw on its way back.

Four hands pulled Hamish off. They pulled him away. Bernard threw a thick arm around and turned him to the door. "It's all right. I'll take him. I'll take him. He'll be all right." The man in the brown shoes stood aside to let them pass. Bernard took Hamish along the lobby and out to the porch. The sky was there. Right across; the sky. Hamish Creese had been the frog in the well. Bernard sat down beside him on the verandah. "You feeling better, Hamish? Don't worry about that bullshit artist too much, he's had it coming for a while. Molly's got him by the balls and winds him right up. He thinks he runs everything. Truly, don't worry." A drip fell from a hanging basket onto Hamish's head. The wood underneath him was wet. Hamish felt a damp through to his crotch and thighs. Bernard was speaking.

"You bleed awful easy these days, mate. You were always a bit of a hard case but this is definitely not your style." Bernard knit his hands together letting them hang down between his legs like a stray bunch of bananas. "Maybe it's your change of life. You reckon?"

"Bullshit." Menopause. Pause from Meno? What does Meno mean? What does Maevius mean? "I don't know what happened Bernard, but that guy was definitely taking the piss. Sometimes these intellectuals give me the shits."

"Half of your bother is you want to be like them and belong to their little tiny circles. You get all screwed up if you think some joker's got a paper medal. That's screwy, mate."

A face was looking at them through the fly-screen. Paddy from Ireland. Hamish stared. Paddy from Ireland disappeared back inside.

"Look Hamish, your place is with the blokes. Really."

"Seems I've been with them an awful long time, Bernard."

"Aw Hamish, you know I would fit you in if I could."

A second drip fell on Hamish's head. He wiped the wet away with his palm. Another drip fell. "I didn't mean it that way. What is on your mind? What's the score Bernard?"

Bernard leaned forward, picked up a stone, and chipped it down the path. "Bollerone has been getting things all their own way in the State since this Seaton arrived. We're taking a bit of a pounding. Just enough to make the builders cocky. We need something to remind them we're here. We reckon the job at Happy Rock is ready made for us."

"How's that?"

"They've got a team down there who think they are the original men who built Australia. As soon as we've paid a visit they're pushing and pushing the blokes. The manager's a young guy, he's breaking every rule in the book. Hamish; we want you to do a job for us down at Happy Rock."

Another drip fell. Hamish moved his head and it splashed on his shoulder.

"Anybody I know down there?"

"Aristotle's the main man, you've worked with him before."

"Sure. OK Bernard. I'll see what the situation is. I take it we're hitting them on safety?

"Anything you say."

"Will Bollerone give yours truly a start?"

"Doubt it. We can get you on the site with one of the subbies who owes us a few. That's about it. Now you can go home."

"What about Gerry? Can you fix him up?"

"Always looking for the quid pro quo. We'll see what can be done. Now will you go home?"

☆
☆☆☆
☆☆☆☆☆ ☆ ☆
☆☆☆☆☆
☆☆☆ ☆☆

AN erect army of steel props stood; up and down; set in lines across; braced to hold up the wood which formed the shape of the floor overhead. Scaffolding tubes, shackled and tied, tube to prop, tightened and tensioned, bound them all steady, bracing them to absorb the shocks that came when the stuff was poured down onto the structure from above. Jammed between dirt ground and the formwork of the floor they supported; they should be ready, aye ready, to stand fast. They should not move. Not this way, nor that, but remain.

"They will move, Gerry. Some of these props have no packer plates under them."

"I've seen worse; I think. That box beam looks as if it could do with another prop under the centre. That's some weight of concrete that's going in there." Hamish looked up. An edge of one of the squares of plywood had been sawed rough, but it would be OK. But the centre might sag.

"I think you might be right, mate. Two's not enough. What's the mix?"

"Not sure. 1:2:5, I should imagine."

1:2:5 at 10lbs per square foot, plus live load of a total 40 to 50lbs per square foot, plus extraneous matter — a ton weight anyway.

"It needs another prop, Gerry."

"That's what I said, you wanker."

Rattles; stone chips on wood; aggregate knocking its way into the wooden box above.

"Christ. Stoker's started the pour. Is he fucking daft?"

"Well here's one observer who's standing well clear."

"Bastard. You're bloody right. Jesus, Gerry, this is going to be touch and go."

The vibrator ground on, grating on the criss-cross of small steel rods that were to reinforce the floor, sending its groans and knocks through to the watchers below. The vibrator man would be bullying the concrete into the crannies of the formwork and rattling it round the heavier reinforcing bars of red iron. Underneath, green slurry slipped between plywood, tin plate and timber.

"Who's on the vibrator?"

"Your drinking partner. Billy Irons."

"Oh. Him. Well he might be a nutter, but he knows what he's about."

A thump thumped.

"Christ. Who's up there?"

"I think your old mate Peter Ray is doing his Captain Marvel act on the skip."

"Fuck. He's a real bampot."

Aggregate hammered its way into the hollow beam on a staccato burst of scrapes and knocks. The steel trellis above rapped on the wood of the floor around the beam. Four men up there, maybe five, maybe six, maybe one too many. Gerry stood looking up. His eyes were on a timber which ran as a support all along the length of the beam.

"Hamish mate, come and cast your expert eye over this, will you?"

Hamish scrambled through, lifting his legs over the bottom tubes and bending his back over the next up and weaving through the upright props.

"What's the matter?"

Gerry scratched under his hard hat. "I may be wrong, but have a dekko at that timber. Look at the grain."

The timber had a large knot of three inches diameter right on its edge, below the knot the grain dipped and flowed away in a sudden change of direction.

Gerry was scratching faster. "It's probably brittle hearted as well; it looks as dry as a bone."

"Shit. A blind man could see that."

"Thanks a lot."

"Well, you know what I mean. Who put this lot up?"

"It started with our boss and the boy but Stoker came down with his hurry-up act. Shirtsleeves up to the armpit, arse up, head down, frightening them to death. The man's cracked."

"At least it's on the outside edge, it'll only be taking about half the strain."

Another thump thumped. A prop shook.

"Whit the fuck was that?"

"Concrete on the floor, mate. He must be doing the floor at the same time as the beam."

"Both ways. Both ways. The strain is pulling both ways. There's too much weight pulling on the centres. Gerry, this lot will go."

"So? Stand back and let it. It's not our fault."

"Gerry your mates are up there. They can't see what we can see."

"I was only joking mate. I'll check the one that rattled.."

Hamish Creese had to get off, up top. It was a struggle through the forest of steel tubes and props and loose shackles on the ground, hard hat hitting the props, till out, in the air, out, to the ladder. Hamish ran at it, climbed it, scaled it till his trunk and head stuck over the edge of the floor on top. Peter Ray stood on the rim of the skip, suspended with the concrete load, one hand on the cable, one foot poised to kick down and open the jaws of the skip.

"Hold it, Superman. What do you think you're on?"

"I'm on the skip, mate."

The labourers sniggered and had a lean on their shovels. A good excuse for a rest had come up. Peter Ray was nodding and shaking a mournful face around the group. "What's yourrr prrroblem? Misterrr Crrreese?"

"Smart arse. You're dumping the stuff. The timber is shonky and some bright sod made an arse of putting it up. Get off that fucking skip anyway. You of all people should know better."

"I put it up."

Stoker's eyes were staring wider than usual. Big blue dartboards; black bulllseyes.

"Well you've made an arse of it."

"Creese, you get back down there and observe. You will observe that this pour will be perfect."

"I'm telling you there is far too much strain on that beam. If you're for pouring the floor and the beam at the same time, the fucking lot'll go."

"I'll say what goes here Creese. Get down there."

Peter Ray muttered into the walkie-talkie strapped to his chest. The crane began to lift the skip. "That's the stuff, Boss." The skip, the concrete, Peter Ray, rose away slowly. "Here y'are mates. No worries." Ray's foot kicked the bar.

Concrete flumped.

Shakes ran through the floor.

Banging and crashing came from below. The concrete squad scattered. Props under the beam buckled, separating, teetering away from the steel trellis-work. A corner completely collapsed from under the grid. Stoker lost balance and fell face first on to the sloping, sliding steel. The box beam finished its fall. Stoker's legs dangled over the edge into space. That corner dipped. Stoker held on, the edges of the steel lace ripping his shirt. Wet green concrete was sliding from its mound down the slope towards him, covering his head, filling his mouth. Hamish Creese was up the ladder, lying flat, crawling to him, scrabbling away at the concrete. Concrete continued slipping. It got into the ears, the eyes and choked up the nostrils. Hamish put himself between the stuff and Stoker. "Get that fucking hook back here." More props were crashing down. Hamish Creese needed somebody to hear. "Where's the hook?" Hamish lay on his side; a human dam against the concrete, which pushed and weighed against the spine. He dug big boots into small gaps in the trellis and turned the head up, round, anywhere to see the hook.

The hook came. Slow. Slowly descending, cable splattering grease, inching down. Hamish wrestled with the hook, trying to hold back the pulley with his shoulder, till the smooth lump of curled steel slipped into a gap. An index finger, and then the whole hand, waved up, up.

The hook rose. Slower. The grid of reinforcing was pulled up. More props fell from below. Hamish Creese rose with the grid. Stoker rose. A clutch with one hand attached him to Hamish Creese. As Hamish rose, Stoker rose. The total floor below gave way, creaking to a crash that left it all a sad jumbled mess of wood, steel tubes and redundant props. Stoker was slipping. Hamish quickly took one hand away, leaned over and held him by the belt of his trousers. Helpers waited to control the wobble and swing of the crane's load and assist to terra firma.

"Was Gerry under there?" The crowd moved.

"You think we country boys are silly? No way, mate. Only the good die young."

"Creese." Stoker. Trying to dust off rivers of concrete from his body.

"Yes, my old son?"

"What were you and Thomas doing under there?"

"Don't follow Stoker."

"I built that formwork with your boss. There was nothing wrong with it."

Men were moving back. Was a circle something instinctive?

"It was poor, Stoker. Bloody poor."

"If we'd kept you on 'B' site fussing with that office panelling it would've been all right."

Enlarging the circle; was that in hope of someone else's anger?

Creese stepped over to Stoker pressing body to body, face to face, until drips of wet slurry ran down the bridges and joined two men at the tips of their noses.

"Stoker. I'm not one of your shuttering cowboys. I'm proud of my work. I've never sabotaged a job in my life, but I could be persuaded to sabotage your face."

But don't. Don't. Don't be persuaded. Hamish Creese has them by the testicles. Reduce this to a one to one situation and they'll win. Good old Hamish if Creese wins. Big red face if Creese gets thrashed. And everybody goes back to work. They had their fight, man to man, and we're all men in a man's world. Not this time.

"Where's Aristotle and Billy Irons?"

Two came forward. "Get your men out. We're going to a meeting."

☆ ☆ ☆ ☆ ☆

S OME put shovels back in the store, most did not. Down stairs not complete, down ladders and scaffolds, off staging and up from the basement: Labourer, Scaffolder, Rigger, Fitter, Plumber and Spark, all came in answer to the call, grouping first to confirm the news then marching, sauntering, ambling, swaggering off the site to learn the score, following Hamish Creese to hear. Gerry cut through a group to walk with his mate.

"Hey, Hamish, here's your hat, where's your hurry?"

Hamish took the hat from him, saying nothing.

"Hamish, old son, this is me; I was there too you know."

"Sorry, Gerry, but you don't expect me to be splitting my sides when I'm covered in this stuff do you?"

"She'll be right once you get a shower."

The track to the church at Happy Rock passed the site and led upwards, up to the cliff and the church. Hamish discarded the shirt on an acacia, doing it slowly to allow Gerry the push at the door. The door opened. The door of the church was always open. People at Happy Rock had built the church on the high edge where the rock split and water flowed from the fissure. Vicars could not live by holy water alone; the parish was unpriested. Gerry pushed at a door that was always open, for anyone who needed something. The union needed a meeting.

Feet scraped, echoed; some men dipped a knee, crossed themselves; others wandered down the aisles open mouthed, heads revolving. Construction workers at a loss in the House the Lord built. They sat, shoved up, shuffled their feet and shook their shag out; borrowed a light and blew forth the smoke. Hamish Creese sat in the front pew, staring ahead, pushing the front of his forehead with his hands till the muscles in his neck moved.

Gerry pushed up beside. Irons the Labourers' man slid along. Higgins of the Plumbers and Electricals sat in the centre apart from Irons and pushed a thin roll of rice paper and some tobacco into a hole somewhere between the upturned collar of his boilersuit and the brim of his battered grey hat. Aristotle the Greek came down the far aisle, spindly legs making the shorts flap.

"Hamish. 'B' site is coming off too. We must wait for a few minutes. How do you wish to approach this one?"

"You're the steward here, Ari."

"I did not wish to pretend about it. I shall ask for Mr Thomas and yourself to speak and any of the other stewards should they so desire."

"Let us not pretend, Ari. It's a strike we're after. Right?"

"Yes. At least until we obtain some guarantees on safety on these sites."

"Don't bullshit me, Ari. You mean until we've created enough stink to embarrass Bollerone, and that means Mr Seaton."

"As far as I am concerned it is a straightforward safety issue."

"Who's pulling your wires, Ari boy? You were sent down here to bottle it up and you don't have the bottle for Stoker. So don't give me any 'straightforward issue' bull."

The 'B' team were in; not so many, not so loud. Aristotle stood on the altar steps and held up his arms. The congregation quietened down to the last echo. Aristotle waved a long crooked finger up the centre aisle. The door boomed shut.

Aristotle explained the day's proceedings three times: once in English, once in Italian, once in Greek.

"Streuth," whispered Gerry.

"There's four more he can do it in."

"Big deal. He bored me with the first one."

Aristotle avoided rhetoric. At least in the English. He presented the facts and tried to set them against the background of unrest upon the site.

A check along the faces; listening hard, just a bit bored, fed up; with Aristotle going on; with the site; with Stoker; with Happy Rock. A lid of boredom on a tight spring of energy. Peter Ray's face was not there. That face was not there. Aristotle finished. He was calling upon Gerry. Gerry came forward. "I was under most of the time. That was the worst piece of formwork I've seen for a long time. If I'd stayed there I would've died for Stoker." He began back-tracking, wise-cracking his way through it; beginning with Stoker kicking in the door of the kazzie and ordering him below. Gerry warmed to it. His hard hat punched the air around his cracks.

"So I told Mr Bloody Stoker don't go calling me out of the thunderbox if all you want me to do is go on the job and shit in me pants."

The lads listening laughed. Higgins leaned forward as Gerry waved himself away.

"There's no business like showbusiness, son, eh?"

Gerry had inherited an audience whose ears had been dulled in three different languages and turned them into a band with something in common: somebody to laugh at. Stoker. Aristotle introduced Hamish Creese to speak. The difference could be felt. Hamish Creese felt it, felt for these men, the bears.

"There is more to this than working safe. You blokes know it as well as me."

"Speak up."

"Can't hear you, mate."

The loud voice, to hear. They had asked to hear.

"I'm sorry, mates. There is more to this than plain safety. More to this than me and my young mate spoiling our trousers. What is at stake is: who says a job is safe? The man that works on it, or the man that needs it finished? What do they mean by safe? Safe for who? Me? You? Or safe and cheap for the boss? Bosses can buy cheaper nuts, and bolts, pipes, wires, bricks and mortar. But they cannot buy cheaper safety and the client just wants the cheapest job, the boss his profit, and Stoker his finishing bonus."

The louder voice had kept them on the boil. The questions were being answered; in nods into shirts, into pipe bowls, into neighbours and face up to Hamish Creese.

"Our safety is as much our business as theirs. That's what they tell us isn't it? Put your boots on, John. Where's your goggles,

Frank?" Blokes were looking at the two well-known offenders, and laughing. "But always: who knows best? Us? They are right, you know. Safety is our business. These are our legs, our arms, our hands, and our fingers. Not theirs. Ours. And it's our wives and families who suffer. Wives and families who only want to be lucky enough to share their lives with the men who build this lucky country."

There was a quiet now, wives, families, even sisters, were far away.

"Did we come to Happy Rock to be killed? Did we? Let's take our safety back into our own hands. All we need is the right to elect our own safety reps. Men who know what they're about, trained men, safe men. And men who will be trained in a First Aid that's more than knowing how to open a tin of Elastoplast. Would Elastoplast have saved Gerry today?"

Put the voice lower now. The men are waiting for the voice of Hamish Creese. "I say here, Stoker must go. Stoker must go, and all the madmen that work with him. Stoker must go."

Feet at the front, they're all stamping; fists banging on the pews. Stoker was unpopular; now he was personally responsible, a man to be stamped out.

"Good on you mate."

"Bene. Bene."

"You said it, china."

"Good old Hamish. That's the stuff."

A voice shouted into a gap in the praise.

"We can't hear what you're saying, mate." The men at the back didn't want to be left out.

A look in the direction of the voice, the hesitation, a turn, and a run to take the steps of the pulpit two at a time. Hamish Creese was in the pulpit, looking round, at his congregation. They were waiting on the word. Two arms were thrust in the air, the hard hat held high. They were waiting.

"Can you hear me now? Can you hear me?"

"Yes."

"If I say, no more death traps; can you hear me?"

"Yes."

"IF I SAY, STOKER MUST GO; CAN YOU HEAR ME?"

"YES."

"IF I SAY, STRIKE! CAN YOU HEAR ME?"

"YES YES."

The bears at Happy Rock were on strike.

☆

☆ ☆☆

A SCURRY of men stumbling and jostling past each other with mock curses and happy slaps woke Hamish from a sleep which had come late. He unloosed his arms from across his chest and freed his fankled feet from each other. It was light; early light; moving in and up from the side windows, through the air, to highlight the underside of the thirty-eight straps of truss and reflect as silver from the dark main beam they all supported. Except for beam number seventeen; the gap in the mitre joint was at least a whole inch. That beam gave no support. No tradesman had cut that at that angle. Or he must have been drunk.

Coughers coughed, doors slammed, plastic thongs flapped, and cotton towels cracked at unprotected tender bits. The bears were early on the prowl this morning. The spectacles were on top of the Shelley under the bed. A stretch and grope of the left arm found them. Gerry's bunk was empty. Empty. Empty. Gerry was on the fishing roster for today. The voices were pitched high, nervous. Something was on. Another diversion from the tedium of the strike had been found; another childish wheeze. Best to let them get clear. Their spirits were high. Today could be the last day of the strike. Hamish lay on his back. Today would be the last day of the strike.

The gap on that mitre looked bigger this morning. Today would be the last day of the strike. There was nothing surer. Hamish Creese knew. The big boys were flying in today, like sky heroes. Bernard; and Eagleson of the congress; and the smaller heroes of the ancillary trades. No doubt they had struck a deal with Bollerone; in Sydney. Bollerone knew what they were doing, taking it away from the State to the Commonwealth Commission;

get the Chiefs away, leave the Indians sitting in the desert. Particularly Hamish Creese. Two weeks ago it should've finished. Back to work boys, you've done as much as you can do. As much as they wanted them to do; enough to embarrass Seaton and make sure he didn't become Industrial Commissioner. At least not this year. The lads had done the business, but for nothing. Last meeting Bernard had stood up and said it was all over; Seaton had cut the legs off him; he had nothing to stand on. They were beat. The site was safe.

Hamish Creese followed. The faces were there, unbelieving, looking up, anxious. Sick. They were being sold down the crowded industrial shit river. From the Clyde, the Murray; they always finished up down the Swannee. It was there: in the eyes and the crush, crack and split of plastic cups. What chance did they have? First the site was unsafe to work on, now it was safe. Surgeon Hamish Creese is here; to sew your legs back on Bernard. Nobody goes back till we have been paid for every day we have been on strike. Bernard walked out okay. Now they were all flying back. The deal had been cooked. Or maybe surrender.

A face came into focus, mouth first. "The fuzz have come for Josiah's women. They're at the caravans now clearing them out. Looks like they've tumbled him."

Josiah Reedy's women. The bears' recreation. All bookings taken at Josiah's sports shop in the main street. The stock is constantly renewed from Adelaide by the men in the flash safari suits. Orders taken if enough want the same games. Hamish swung out of bed. It was time for a wash.

Hamish washed, shaved, taking up a basin between two small men who continued jawing across the flat of his stomach. The soap and razor and toothbrush and toothpaste were replaced in the cabinet beside the bed, and the towel hung neatly over the bed-end. Sleepy-headed dreamers anxious to catch up pushed past him as he made his way up the central aisle to the door. The Reader still lay in his bed perusing his dictionary. Outside, Happy Rock hung as it had grown, lay as it had fallen. Hamish looked down past the accumulation of wilted wood and angles of crinkling tin, through the spaces between the aluminium shells that made home for some; out to the beach, where the waves of the Bight rose up, fell over and ran rushing down, foaming flat, spreading wide, till fizzing spent, they curled up backwards and ran bubbling back; to come again.

Ripples of red corrugated iron ran on, roof after roof, over arthritic structures which had already quit the true vertical to follow leanings toward a more horizontal posting. Happy Rock had been laid in a drunken straight line, taking its marker from the jetty where the fishing boats tied up. All except for the church and the jail. The jail was set in another drunken straight line fifty yards from the back door of the hotel. The church sat on its cliff and had been built at a strategic slope to allow the congregation to keep a weather eye on the sea behind the vicar. The fishermen had supplied the gold boom, when men had poked about the holes in the cliffs which lay to the west. The gold had been a tease and Port Lincoln had made the fishing trade its own. Happy Rock set to die a dusty death, but respired when deranged tourists came to film the fantastic shark which never bothered the locals but objected to being peered at from a cage under the water. In deference to the danger lovers, the Happy Rock Hotel was renamed the Shark Bite Hotel. Now the bears were here, but the name remained the same.

All good blokes, come to build the concrete and iron, put in the tanks and the cylinders and the plush offices that would make Happy Rock rich and modern and civilised. Happy Rock rallied for real.

The Coca-Cola sign was dusted off and the Shark Bite Hotel installed a bigger freezer all the way from the brewers in Adelaide. Benny the barber opened his shop on Tuesdays again, now only closing on Fridays, Saturdays, Sundays and Mondays. Miss McCimley made over part of her father's ironmongery to the sale of high fashion, sent for by the wives of the trailers so that they might be properly dressed when visiting each other's caravan, or when fighting flies at beachside barbecues.

The caravans lay to the east of the jetty, just above the beach. Aluminium boxes, set at all angles to allow the maximum of privacy which was the minimum anyone required. From a pole the flag of Eire flew. A woman was already hanging out a washing;

perhaps to be ready when all the wives herded the children down to the beach then lay back and gossiped, sat up, gossiped, swam and gossiped, gossiped and sipped Marsala with the declaration that this was the life. Josiah's women would be in the gossip. Maybe Hamish Creese and their men's long strike from an unsafe site was in there too.

The tailfin of a black and white automobile could just be seen jutting out from behind the giant dune which separated Josiah Reedy's quartet of caravans from the more moral majority. Someone was sitting down with his back against a sand wall. Two others appeared to be conversing, one waving an arm down the gap to where Josiah had parked his trailers to form Happy Rock's red light district. On blue days the dunes around were as active as army manoeuvres: men left, men approached, others watched till all was clear, and most tried unsuccessfully to find a new private entry and exit, in and out of the happy gulch. All human life was here. Hamish Creese was here.

Men were passing down the track from the huts to the town. Hamish followed, eyes down, lips held tight against teeth, nodding here, acknowledging there. Ahead the thirsty vanguard grouped, under the window of the owner of the pub where they yelled at a figure, who hung out and yelled back. It was time for the tavern door to be opened: tomorrow was here. The bears said so. The window was closed and the doors opened by the bare-chested, brown-nippled Banjo Dilley. Banjo bent over and pulled at the bolts as the questions were shouted in his ears. The bears wanted to know about his early morning sex life with Mrs Banjo Dilley. Banjo shook his head at Hamish Creese; the knowing shake which seeks an ally. Hamish Creese cocked the chin up, the eyes up, and dared Banjo to articulate the complaint. Banjo ran behind the bar to help his wife with the beer. The queue was long, slow, and noisy; a frantic Banjo marking up the series of blackboard slates laid out under the bar as Mrs Banjo Dilley slid the beer out and along the line of grasping hands. Hamish caught his beer, paid cash, and made for the long corner seat. An old aborigine in a long dirty raincoat and crumpled baggy trousers smiled through his beard, slid off the seat and scuttled off to a stool at the bar. Hamish gave him the thumbs up. The aborigine waggled his toes in reply.

Two men joined Hamish, one of them placing a jug of beer in the centre of the table. Hamish moved over to make sure his view of the door was not blocked by Billy Irons or Bruce Higgins.

"What do you make of this carry-on, Hamish old son?" asked Billy. "If this is what they get up to after nine weeks on the street what will the bastards be like if we go in six months?"

Billy used the Glasgow form of 'bastard'. Hamish Creese heard and acknowledged it as his own; the spit of the first syllable, the hiss of the second and the clip of the last that made it all a bastirt.

Higgins spoke. "Take it from an old hand like me, Billy boy, those girls won't be away long. Those wowsers in Adelaide just have to be satisfied for a while. They'll be back, no worries." Higgins was right. The snappy dressers with the Volkswagen campers would bring a refill for the caravans when the time was right. "Anyway, from what I hear he'll still have The Snowy. He's claiming she's his live-in but he doesn't want to know about the others, claims they just happen to be his neighbours." Higgins' tongue finished on a cigarette paper.

"Aye," said Billy, "he won't let the Albino go. She must turn over some cash for him." Billy was looking at Hamish Creese, grinning. "If you'll excuse the expression, Hamish."

"What are you getting at, Irons?"

"Oh, we've seen you giving her the wee smiles when you think nobody's looking."

"Piss off and don't be a big wean."

Higgins separated his tongue from the gum. "Billy boy that doesn't mean anything. Hamish smiles at old McGuire over there." Higgins jerked a finger at the black man on the stool. "It's a matter of kindred spirits, Billy boy. Creese the loner and his people. All colours, black and white." Hamish Creese needed a retort.

"Bullshit. You both talk a lot of bullshit. Anyway, here's the chairman."

Aristotle came edging through and placed another jug between them, then removed the empty to another table. Aristotle the Greek filled his glass from the jug and brought them to the business of the day. Irons drew figures of eight in the wet on the table, Higgins rubbed an index finger in the non-existent cleft of his chin. Hamish Creese was listening behind and between sips of beer which flowed from habit; from the table to the mouth, from the glass to the throat. "So this time they want to settle with us. Last time they nearly had us, last time we'd have been back if Hamish hadn't turned the blokes round. Back with lots of words and nothing much more." Higgins changed to a rub behind his ear. "What are we likely to be offered, or bloody told more like?"

"The subbies have been telling them not to pay up on the wages we are claiming for our strike time. I don't think we'll get it, but we'll probably be allowed to elect our own safety man. And maybes they'll boot this team of wild men managers back to Adelaide." Billy Irons drew faster; flat-bottomed blobs of circles.

"What's our position?"

"It is hard to say. The men want to win the cash, the fishermen will still lend us their boats, but some blokes are drifting back to Port Lincoln and some to Adelaide. It is perhaps in the lap of the gods. I think we may have to settle." Higgins rubbed his right eye red to match his chin and ear. "What do you reckon, Hamish?" Three filled their schooners, one after another, after another.

"We must hold out for the cash, and repeat: every day we're out, they have to pay. It's a payment for their negligence. They broke the rules, they've got to pay."

Irons wiped the wet beer across the table with the side of a fist. "That's the game, that's smashing, bloody smashing. Hamish, the guys are getting fed up being stuck out here, watching out for scabs that'll never come. The wives are acting up. And that's not to mention these bastards coming for the women." Billy boy was angry. But he had a point. The men were faltering. Maybe this time the bears wouldn't follow, follow. Maybe Bollerone would put it to the test.

"OK Billy, I accept that. Let's just play it by ear for now. OK?"

Aristotle decided no decision was a friendly decision and sent Higgins for more beer. The talk turned to the fishing catch, the food distribution, Josiah's women. And the latest evacuations.

"Droopy Daniels and his missus are off," said Bruce, shifting his scratch to a four-fingered tear at his chest. "The sheila just opened her caravan door and yelled for Droopy. Droopy, she shouts, what the bloody hell am I doing here? So, they're off." Aristotle smiled across. No one smiled back.

"A lot of people are like that. Sometimes they are so homesick they empty inside and cannot throw it off." Hamish watched the tracing finger in the wet beer slow down, and the hand reach across, slowly, deliberately, for the jug. Billy's big tale was coming: Billy Irons walking out on his wife in Glasgow. Billy still bothered, until, one year, in Brisbane, at Hogmanay, Irons gets drunk, sentimental, takes a flight, then a taxi, up the three storeys, pitch black on the stair, and knocks on the door. It was time for Hamish Creese to go for a pee.

The pee didn't take long enough. Billy had delayed the ending for his return.

"So there she was rubbing away at this dish towel and looking at me."

Aristotle responded on cue. "What did she say?"

"BUGGER, OFF. I jumped on the first flight home and I've been as happy as a pig among shit ever since, no worries. Y'see I just had to know if I'd done the right thing shooting through." Nobody laughed.

Aristotle nodded at Hamish. "And you Hamish? You ever been home?"

Higgins slammed the jug on the table. "Will you whingers stop moaning? I live here remember? I'm a bloody Australian and proud of it. For better or for worse here I am and here I stay. I can't figure anything that bad I'd want to leave this country." Aristotle reddened high up on his cheeks. Irons clapped, cheering Bruce on. "You blokes felt bad about something back there, so here you are. Now either stay or go and give me peace to drink my bloody beer."

Hamish stood up, lifting the empty jug. "That's the stuff me old cobber, me old blue. I'll get the beer in."

At the bar Hamish ordered a refill and a fresh schooner for McGuire, who pushed his empty glass toward the barman. Banjo Dilley only refilled the jug. "I reckon he's had enough."

"I reckon he's had too much; but another one of your beers isn't going to make much difference."

"It's not my fault he's here. I never asked him to stay."

This was true. Banjo preferred him not to be in the hotel, getting drunk and singing those weird noises. McGuire the Songman, the leader of a troupe of ritual performers, the musical memory man, the choreographer and maker of new songs and dances. McGuire had been a star, in great demand. Years ago he had withdrawn to a cave in the cliffs to dream up new songs and steps for a local tribe's corroboree, but on the way back to the troupe, through the hole in the window of the Happy Rock Hotel, McGuire had seen a country and western group performing. He saw and was fascinated by the fringes on the buckskin, so McGuire had hung around while his angry troupe moved on. McGuire had lost his authority and found the beer and Banjo Dilley was not to blame. Now he clutched a greasy raincoat as his most treasured possession and waggled his toes at men who bought him beer. Hamish Creese moved and stopped McGuire lifting the glass the reluctant barman had conceded to him.

That was easy; simple. There was no strength in McGuire's fingers. Taking away the beer was easy; McGuire just looking with eyes that filled with water. Hamish Creese stood, uncomfortable, taking in the man whose toes now turned in, tensely, tightly.

Hamish Creese stepped out of his shoes, picked one up and held it out to McGuire. The shoes were the white suede; high arched slip-ons; the ones that were worn to the meetings. McGuire tried to free the laces of his own shoes, fumbled and fell from the stool. He jerked one off and pushed it into a baggy pocket. The white suede fitted. Hamish Creese picked up the round of beer and walked on stocking soles back to his seat.

"What did he do to deserve your shoes?" asked Aristotle.

"Nothing you'd notice. I just got fed up looking at his toes waggling."

Higgins rubbed at a long strand of tobacco which clung to his lip. "His feet'll never breathe in those things, mate."

Irons pulled the fresh beer over. "I think you're tuppence off the shilling."

"That's as maybe, but it's my business. Why don't you give it a bye?"

The doors banged open and a man fell in; all heads turned to view him. "They're coming, they're coming, they're on their way." The girls were coming. Chairs were pushed back, beer was slopped from jug to glass, and drinks were taken on the run. The girls were coming. Everybody moved for the door. Hamish and Aristotle waited till last. McGuire sidled over and swopped his empty for a fullish one left behind. Hamish fell in behind Aristotle and moved out the door.

Men jostled and pushed till the porch of the Shark Bite Hotel at Happy Rock was jammed from post to post. Late-comers pushed through, collected their beer and selected what spots were left for them. Some men sat in the dust of the street, some knelt on the ground, some knelt on the porch; the blokes at the back all stood. The man who had breathlessly brought the message balanced on an old cane chair. All had to have a clear view.

"There they are," shouted the man on the chair. Happy Rock was having a parade; the motorcade was on its way.

The front policeman on his motorcycle grew larger; clear now, but faceless under the safety helmet. Other cyclists rode outside the three cars, one riding at the rear, wearing a scarf to keep out the dust. Straight upright escorts who looked to their fronts through darkened glasses. The watchers watched; some silent, some whistling derision, some shouting abuse that made the riders rev their engines. Level with the hotel porch there was movement from inside the last of the three cars. The female passengers were struggling in the back. There was an almighty cheer as a bare backside was pushed against a rear window. A vocal eruption that lifted off on a stamping of feet, a slapping of thighs and a spilling of beer. The policeman behind lowered his head and adjusted his scarf.

"They're hitting us below the belt now, Hamish," said Billy, "I think they're trying to starve us out."

"It'll be the first strike that fell through night starvation."

A man ran out waving a large hat, lips pursed, trying to catch up with the last car. The car spurted, blowing blue exhaust in his face; the motorcyclist lifted a leg up and kicked out. The man fell. The onlookers surged forward but the cars, the motorcycles, the blue-shirted chaperones and all the dirt behind them, all faded, disappeared. The shouts became excited talk became a buzz became separate conversations became singular curses. The girls were away.

Hamish left the hotel to pad back up the path for a pair of shoes. The serious men from the city would probably doubt his integrity if he appeared to negotiate in red socks. There would be little to negotiate. The blokes were cheesed off, the novelty was fading. If Bollerone had put some pressure on Bernard he would have conceded it all away; for Bernard knew only Hamish Creese the mad Scotsman was tying them together. Another try at surrender? Perhaps. Time to hurry, there was the little silver plane in the sky, coming in from the east and bearing the wise men. Hamish hurried up into the barracks, past the solitary reader who lay on his bed, dictionary in front of his face. Wordless, Hamish put on the first pair of shoes that came to his feet and made off, out and down, to be with Aristotle as the craft landed.

Eagleson came first, pausing presidentially as he made his presidential half a wave. Bernard came behind, followed by Seaton who pushed and patted at the black hair streaked silver that was all out of place. Two little men talked to each other all the way across the dirt strip. These ancillaries had lots to say to themselves. But this was Bernard and Seaton's show. Or it had been. Hamish Creese tucked in behind Aristotle, for Aristotle was the chairman. False greetings were exchanged and insincere enquiries made about each other's health. Bernard walked with Hamish. He looked happy. "We've done it, Hamish. This mob has given us nearly what we asked for. We elect our own safety supervisors who can stop the job, and we increase the first aid men on the site. And Hamish, me old son, they are going to replace all the site management. They're off the site."

"Sounds good, Bernard. But what about our claim for payment while we've been out on strike? That's work time lost for us, you know."

"Exactly half Hamish. The men will be paid for half the time they've been out; if they've not been working elsewhere."

"Like where?"

"Who knows? Anyway, nobody's going to admit it even if they did work."

That would be good enough. Four and a half weeks' pay for fishing and lying under the sun fighting for a principle. The bears would accept. The other four weeks could be made up by overtime or would be added on to the schedule. The production of a building site was not lost, only delayed; once started somebody usually needed it finished. The bears would accept, just as soon as they could be rounded up into the church for a meeting.

The bears accepted. There was no need for oratory from the officials in the chancel. Aristotle stood on the steps and asked for any questions. Hamish looked at the hymn board: Psalm No. 39. Number thirty-nine.

> I will watch my ways
>   and keep my ways from sin;
> I will put a muzzle on my mouth
>   as long as the wicked are in my presence.

No one asked any questions. Here was four weeks pay to pay off Banjo Dilley and make a return to work, to work away the boredom of Happy Rock. The vote was taken; all for, with only one abstention. Carried away, Seaton announced there would be an extra plane a month to Adelaide for their week's leave, and tonight's beer was on the firm. After the cheer Seaton asked for volunteers to unload the extra casks from the plane. "Without pay, of course."

The meeting broke up. The beer was unloaded, set up, and made to flow to a full house in the Shark Bite Hotel. The early dark brought the fishing boats and their crews home to port and the squeeze for a place at the bar. Hamish stood up and waved Gerry over. Gerry pushed his way through the crowd who encircled the long corner, relief oozing from their faces.

"This isn't fair, mate. We're out there risking life and limb for Sweet Fanny Adams and you lot are in here getting pissed on Bollerone's cash. And no bastard told us about no bloody meeting."

Bruce Higgins pushed a glass over. "We sent out the smoke-o boy for you but the sharks got him. Here, get y'self behind this."

"Christ. That beer's as warm as hell. What's Banjo doing over there? Fanning it?" Gerry gave the glass to Higgins who moved to the bar. "Tell him to blow a little harder on it Brucie." Warm beer. The only thing worse than warm beer was no beer. Hamish Creese was happy to see the young Gerry.

"What do you want for nothing?"

"The Snowy," shouted Billy Irons.

The circle of beery faces was laughing. Hamish Creese has a red face. The beer, the excitement, the crowd; all flushed out embarrassment. Gerry took the signal from Irons.

"Into the white gin now are you Hamish?" The circle linked up.

"I think she fancies old Hamish."

"Hamish always wanted a native tart in bed."

"Too costly for him, he's a bloody Scotsman."

"Do you want us to have a whip round?"

"Na, Hamish? He don't need no whips."

"Too right. Reckon he must have the biggest little willie on the site the way he keeps hiding the bloody thing."

"Reckon he's got poetry tattooed all over it. That would be a new one for the Snowy." Bernard's voice came.

"Hamish, could you come over here?" The bears gave a last laugh as Hamish stood up, gave them all two fingers up, and walked over to where Bernard sat with Seaton.

Seaton extended a hand. The hand was wet. It slid down the palm of Hamish Creese, slid along the fingers, stopped; to begin pressing and pulling on the last joint of the index finger. Hamish Creese remembered a handshake like that: in the Clyde Vaults, a drunk man, one hand on the shoulder forcing the young man to shake hands. Two double whiskies followed as the drunk docker mistook the patronising shake for something dark and mysterious. Then there was anger; Hamish didn't know the age of his mother.

"My mother is dead."

Seaton laughed and sat down.

"Hamish, Hamish. I just wanted to see you before I went away." The voice was half-educated Scots, picked up from the Home

Service and mixing with one's betters. And teachers like Miss Martin. Seaton pushed a chair to Hamish. "Hamish, my job is not just resolving disputes like our little tiff here, most of my job is man management. I have to ensure that Bollerone have the best management material available to them." The black hair and silver streaks were combed through by manicured fingers, the eyes stared right in front. Something was coming. "Hamish, you have impressed me in this dispute. You know, it really is a nonsense that a Clyde-built tradesman like yourself should be stuck out here; Bollerone can make more use of you in the yard." Something had come; but it wasn't much. "Since Jacky Conroy left we've needed someone with a bit of knowledge in there, who is also a good co-ordinator. In short, I propose to transfer you to the yard. You will be in complete control of it, of course." Of course.

"But I don't work for you — that's to say I don't work for Bollerone."

"The subbie you work for more or less belongs to us. The job in the yard is yours. You'll enjoy it." Back to the yard with the arse-lickers and the wankers and the long-service pricks, to be castrated, neutered, and bumped off. Hamish Creese in exchange for the deal and the site managers. Bernard the Fox.

"Bernard, he can't do this, can he? This is a set-up."

"Nothing to stop him, Hamish."

"Bullshit. The subbies are distinct employers. You're trying it on."

Seaton and Bernard lifted and drank from their glasses at the same time.

"You put that to the men, Bernard. See what they have to say."

"There is nothing to put to them."

"Then Aristotle will do it."

"Ari isn't such a great believer in democracy as you are, mate. He'll do what the executive tell him."

"Of course he will. Always. And you know he will."

"Then I'll tell them my bloody self."

"You'll tell them what, mate? Your day is over here. Think about it. They're going back to a month's pay and increased overtime. They might think this arrangement is shonky, but there is no way they'll strike for somebody who is just being moved to another job; especially if you're being promoted with more cash." Seaton nodded. "They've made their use of you, Hamish old son, and now it's over. You're yesterday's man." Seaton smiled and extended a palm.

"Hamish. You and I are fellow Scots, we're really quite alike, you know, and I'd like to see you get on. With the right attitude you might go far with Bollerone. And if you wanted to go to night school it's never too late, Bollerone would be glad to pay any fees for your education."

"Education? Education? I think you two are giving me one right now. Listen you bastards, I've got more education in my pinkie than you fuckers have in your whole body." Hamish rose to go. "Is this Bollerone calling one in for those teak planks on your boat, Bernard? Do a good job did they?"

"Ace, mate, ace. Ask Aristotle, he supervised the job. As a matter of fact, he's on the boat more than I am."

Hamish Creese stood. There should be a remark here. One that would bring shame. One that would touch some spark somewhere. One that would leave Hamish Creese the heroic winner. There was one. There, somewhere. Someone had said it someplace, sometime. Who said it? What was it? It wasn't fair. That was for the weans. Where was it? Where was it? Where the fuck was it?

"You're a pair of right bastards. Seaton, you can take your job and stick it right up your arse." Shelley and Coleridge would not have approved. It was weak. Piss weak. The bastards in life had won again. Their organisations were too big to hit. They were smiling, waiting for more. It was time to walk away. Seaton stopped smiling.

"Hamish, just be clear. You don't work here anymore."

Seaton came up easily with his necktie, straight, horizontal across the table, head bent up from the neck.

"You are a piece of shite that has floated across here, Seaton. What were you in Scotland? What sewer did you float out of? Shite there, and shite here, shite is shite anywhere." Seaton landed back in his chair. He tidied his tie.

"I told you, Creese, we really are quite like one another."

A hand came on the shoulder of Hamish Creese. Gerry's fingers held hard. The faces round the room were watching, waiting for the bear to fight. Waiting for Hamish Creese to go off his rocker and be tonight's cabaret: the performing bear. Hamish lifted Gerry's arm away, wiped his forehead with the back of his hand then walked off, out of the Shark Bite Hotel. Gerry followed.

"Where you heading?"

"A swim. For a swim. I need to cool off and wipe the stink of those bastards off me."

"What did they say? Hey, Hamish, wait up a minute, this is me, your mate. Just hold it a second."

Gerry turned and run back into the Shark Bite Hotel. When he caught up with Hamish he carried two bottles of wine and a bottle of brandy.

"Best I could do. No stubbies left, just this cheapo plonk and the Aussie paint stripper."

At the bottom of the line of stores they veered right, walking, walking, walking and talking and drinking. Gerry asked questions as Hamish slugged the brandy and Hamish answered as Gerry slugged the wine. The sun was going out, disappearing into the sea without a sizzle. Three figures were silhouetted on the road ahead, arms linked like paper cut-out dolls. Two women were talking across the shape of a man who was watching Gerry, and Hamish Creese. Gerry waved a wine bottle by the neck.

"G'day Josiah. G'day ladies."

The Snowy was white even in this light. The younger aborigine girl was reaching for the Snowy's hand across the man's front. The women giggled. The Snowy's teeth were whiter than her skin. Whiter than albino. Whiter than white. What is white? The Snowy was a coloured white, with black tight curls. None of the bears had ever found out if it was a wig. The young Snowy had been tested by the medicos in Sydney, her skin pricked and pulled at by the clinical medical men who visited her tribe and ate witchetty grubs with her people while they interrogated her family. An aborigine girl, a Very Important Person. Until they had discovered her grandmother had known an American Negro seaman. Now she was a white black woman of the Pitjandjara tribe, with their thin face and slanting forehead. A Greek statue come alive with high breasts sloping out at a perfect forty-five degrees from the vertical. A woman filthy men joked about. Hamish Creese wanted to hold her. It was time to move on. Hamish rubbed his hand over his lips; the words to stop Gerry prattling on could not get past the lump in his throat.

"Where you off to, Josiah?"

"The day I've had, I need a drink. I'm taking what remains of my stock for a drink. No business tonight."

"We've got the cash, we got some drink." Gerry winked at the young girl.

"No. No business tonight. Why don't you come and see me at the shop. During the week maybe. Besides, The Snowy, she is out of action. Honestly."

"Look, Josiah, you know me, and this is Hamish the poet, you know what like he is, he just wants to take the Snowy down the beach and tell her some poetry stuff. He just needs some company." Gerry pulled Josiah's head over and whispered in his ear. Overhead a small plane buzzed back to Adelaide. Josiah considered.

"Double the rate, only till twelve, and you do not touch The Snowy. She is mine for now. No wrestling games and she can go."

"OK sport. How much is that?"

"Make it a hundred."

"A hundred? Here? Now?"

"I'll pay."

Hamish passed over a bill from the wallet. Josiah continued on his way.

"What did you tell him, Gerry?"

"I told him you were a poofter, sport."

Josiah called back. "Remember, no nonsense with The Snowy."

Hamish nodded, lifting his eyes up to look at his charge. Gerry placed one arm around the giggling girl's waist.

"What's your name sweetheart?"

"Kaurma."

"Well, Kaurma, let's get to the beach."

The dirt road became sand and took a dip down the steep-sided gully that led to the beach. Gerry ran, Kaurma ran behind, squealing, happy to be on loan to a young man. The Snowy slipped an arm into Hamish's. The walk took longer. They reached the beach in time to see the two naked bodies splash out into the surf. Hamish stripped to his pants for the cleansing swim.

"You come along swim?"

"No thank you. I find it quite pleasant here. Could you pass me the brandy?"

Hamish walked over and retrieved the bottle from under the pile of clothes Gerry and Kaurma had left behind. A slug for himself before passing it to the woman, who raised it high in acknowledgement. He ran slow, then fast, then faster, then galloped into the sea.

Up from under Hamish swam in a straight line pushing everything into each slicing cleave of the water, thrashing out thought, faces, blowing away insults with every turn of the head for a gasp of air, setting aggression free, kicking and punching water, to push the body machine through the waves. At the end of a fizzing line, becalmed, the arms were spread out. He floated, still. The stars said nothing. Hamish turned for the beach. The arms went forward, back, slow, in a soothing breaststroke, propelling Hamish Creese easily, until his belly scraped a shingle in the low water.

Gerry and Kaurma had finished with their games in the water; they lay facing each other. Hamish sat down beside that night's companion. The night was a warm navy blue. He turned to call to Gerry, but now Gerry's buttocks were rising and falling between the knees of Kaurma. The impetuousness of youth. And lust. Hamish Creese was cool; sober now, hands clasped, arms on knees. Words were failing Hamish Creese again. The woman was a prostitute. A cow. An exploited woman. An exploited Aborigine woman. Hamish Creese should know better. This woman had no tribe, was a misfit, she had no one, only Josiah. She was a bad woman. The kind ma said must be avoided. But it was not her fault. If she had met Hamish Creese earlier she would've been right. Hamish Creese could've been a shepherd, taking care of the lost white lamb. She could've walked tall on the crook of his arm and been given a proper name, given comfort and shelter. The breasts were moving under the woolly top, large and symmetrically perfect. A cow, a prostitute. The breasts were perfect. Perfect as against what? Hamish Creese wanted to see those breasts, touch them, feel them, kiss them, try a set-square on them between spine and nipple. She's a bad woman. Hard Hamish Creese wanted The Snowy.

The Snowy stood up. Her arms crossed over and pulled the tight top slowly up, forcing it past the extreme points of her breasts. Her hands cupped under them. She stepped forward. She was bending over Hamish Creese. Hamish Creese clasped tight hands tighter, finger gripping finger, and made no move. The Snowy stepped forward between his knees, forcing his hands apart, pressing the folds of her dress into the face of Hamish Creese.

"Do you want to see my pussy too?"

Long white fingers reached down and pulled the peasant skirt up from the hem, past the calves, the knees, and the thighs, until the frock was gathered in her arms. Hamish Creese followed the revelations. The thighs were straight, muscular, and there was the pubic hair, there, all around the SCABS. Crusty weeping scabs. Scabs flaking crusts.

"NO FUCK NO. No no no Jesus no aach go away. GO AWAY."

Hamish Creese scrambled away; up the dune gully he had just come down, past the high dune grasses. Reeds. Reedy. Reedy Reedy he's to blame Reedy. Snowy was pure, Reedy made her dirty. Dirty. Scabby. Scabby; scabby, she's a scabby Aggie. And Hamish Creese had touched her. Scabby, scabby. Reedy done this, Reedy had taken money for this. Money to make her scabby. Hamish Creese's money. The Shark Bite, The Shark Bite, Reedy's at the Shark bite. Stay there stay there till Hamish gets there.

The edges of the doors slapped each other to a close and settled quiet. Creese stood looking through the tables and along the length of the bar. McGuire made to go past him but turned to stand in the corner. The bears had left a space for Reedy. He drank alone. Hamish Creese moved up the bar through the tables. Laughs and coughs spluttered to a silence.

"You owe me money, Josiah."

"Not me sir. You are mistaken."

"You fucking owe me money. That Snowy is riddled with scabs."

"I told you she was out of action. That was OK by you. You must have tried to get something you did not pay for."

Thick fingers grabbed Josiah's jaw, pressing and digging through to the teeth.

"Where's the cash?"

Sounds forced their way out without forming words.

"Where's the cash?"

Josiah fumbled inside his jacket bringing out a wallet. Creese took the wallet and kneed Josiah in the crotch, bending with him as he fell, holding on to the jaw. The head was banged on the floor. Creese extracted money from the wallet, held it, looked down, and began shoving it into the mouth of the man on the floor, shoving and poking till dollar bills spilled out in an overflow. There. There was the final poke.

"You're right, Josiah. The Snowy's yours. You keep it."

Creese left the hotel. Behind the doors opened. Reedy was shouting at him from the porch.

"Creese you bastard. You'll pay, you'll fucking pay for this. Do you think I am alone here? Your name is in the book Creese."

THE jolly fat bear in the red waistcoat and yellow kipper tie took the young boy by the hand. Together they skipped across the screen. They stooped at either side of the mongoloid child in the wheelchair. The bear twiddled and twirled his tie. The bear pushed his face into the face of the child in the wheelchair, rubbing it playfully. This made the child smile. A separation of teeth in an open mouth. The child's head lay at an angle so the slavers ran down onto the neck. The boy smiled with perfect teeth and made an appeal to the onlooking viewers to help make the marathon-night's money rise. The bear wheeled the mongoloid off.

All through the night they had flickered in the corner, voices trembling out sadder story after sad sad story, with shaky chins and eyes which closed to dam the tears. The bear and the boy and a blonde-haired woman, aided by famous nonentities and nonentities who would never be known, who sang and danced under promise of payment from alert telephone contributors sitting watching on their televisions. Now a kilted piper had come in, pledged a payment of twenty dollars if he would play 'The Northern Lights of Old Aberdeen' for the Adelaide Glasgow Society. Hamish Creese belted the button. The piper disappeared in a slice of white light.

No television prattle prattling left the flat empty of sound. Hamish was alone. Alone. Breeze-brick walls were bare. Grey blocks with the cold breeze pointed up by vanilla-coloured concrete. This flat had nothing but the barest of essentials. Nothing here belonged to Hamish Creese. Not the blind one-eyed television, the humming refrigerator that shivered its way off with a thump and kicked its way on with a bump, not the thin hard bed, the fruit bowl nor the dead spider-plant turning brown. Not the venetian blinds which kept out the sun, the cheap chairs or the coffee-stained sofa, and not the plastic chandeleir overhead. Only the whisky the food and the beer. And the tartan holdall made in China stuffed full of shirts, socks, shoes, vests and pants and throwaway shavers. The collected works of Hamish Creese wrapped around the complete Coleridge and Shelley. The television was switched on again. The piper was grinning his way off under an eagle feather which must have come from an albatross. Hamish opened the thirty-one slats of the blind. It was time for the tools to be put to use.

Righteous Adelaide was trying to move after twenty-four hours of having the emotions ripped. Monday, Monday. Three days since Gerry had dropped Hamish Creese at that corner; down there. Just a cheery wave and a puff of smoke from the primrose-coloured van with the lightning stickers. Gerry was away. Home to Victoria. Home to his family. Home to the harvest and people who knew him. Away from South Australia, Adelaide, and Hamish Creese. The supermarket was opening, a tall young man in white coat and white box cap with a red stripe was piling cartons on the pavement. The first cars were arriving in the car park. The sun was already shining, again, colourlessly clear and hot. Today was the day to be out. Not just to the off-licence that knew the order by heart, and further than the fast-food store of the sweet Vietnamese girl with the sour New Zealander husband. John Knox would never have approved this slothfulness. John Knox's people never got the blues; because they worked. Work. Work. Work is the answer. The God of Scotland and of Zion is the God of Work. And the God of Australia isn't much different. Work wasn't there for the taking. Work wouldn't walk in the door. Work was out there, somewhere; out there. And blacked Hamish Creese would have the devil's own job finding any. But first a shower, a shave and a shirt.

The delicatessen provided the bread, milk, eggs, sausages, bacon, juice; and potato scones made by the old Irish lady in number twenty-seven. The last can of beer to wash it all down was found under the sofa. Greasy dishes were wiped and stacked to drain their drips into the steel canals until dry. Shoes were wire-brushed, hard and gentle, till the scuffs disappeared. Hamish Creese was off, out to meet the day, people, and look for salvation through industry. LABOR OMNIA VINCIT.

"G'day."

"G'day. Advertiser, please."

"There you go, mate, forty cents please."

"Here you are; forty."

"Thanks, mate. See ya."

There was no clack of a reluctant clapped-out bell from behind the shop door. There was no large jar with dark brown lollies on a stick. There was no smell of paraffin and firelighters. It was just a shop that sold newspapers and hot pies and all types of drinks. And g'day and see ya goodbye.

The grey bus was drawing in at the stop and the doors were opening. A run and an easy jump and Hamish Creese was on the platform. It was him.

"Victoria Square, please."

"Wozzat?"

"Victoria Square."

"Come again, mate. Try spelling it."

"I want to go to Vic Toe Ria Squaare, please."

"Oh, Victoria Square. Right you are, sixty cents."

Always the same ritual, always the same lines. All people with different accents made to stand and repeat their destination, for the driver was Australian and spoke only the English. He was a bad driver to boot. Hamish sat down beside a fat lady who hugged a raffia basket to her middle. Now he was on the bus. There had been no plan to go to Victoria Square, but the bus had been there and was going somewhere. The city it would be. Hamish tried to open the paper but his elbow was jamming against the woman. The front page and the sports page at the back could be read twice. Read twice, it was time for four-letter words from seven-letter words. Perhaps the front page could supply a starter. A commission was looking into industrial safety in the State. How many four-letter words were in industrial safety? The newspaper made easier reading on the bench in Victoria Square. The fountains gurgled, the sun was warm but there were no jobs advertised in the Advertiser. There were jobs; little jobs, shuttering squads, christ, these were shit jobs. Queen Victoria was looking down disapprovingly. Any Labor Omnia Vincit. The pubs were open. It was time to leave the Queen and her bronze frown in the sun. The Sign Post was the place to go, right on King William, where any bear on a city job went for the pie and the pint or pie and pints and never went back but stayed to shoot pool till too pissed to pot. Maybe the grapevine would carry some news.

"Pint, please."

"Ritchar."

The bar was already crowded; check shirts, black vests, bare chests and hairy thighs; broad hats, cotton caps, black bags and laughing lies. Hamish turned too late. The change was a silver archipelago in a puddle of beer on the bar. Not a face in the crowd was one to be recognised. A bald head looked like, turned, and wasn't. But the time was still before dinner. There was time to finish the paper and have another pint before somebody came in. Cricker Brothers crane was high over the GPO building; some of the lads would be in. Crazy Chris worked for them. Maybe he was on that job. He would come in if anybody came in.

The old mirrors behind the bar reflected the face. Hamish Creese's face was still quite young, though the crack in the gold letter C split through the forehead. The Old Toll Bar in Glasgow had mirrors like these. 'Fifty Shilling Ale' all written in gold. The glass gantry and the pewter jugs, they were just the same too. An Olde Worlde shipyard haunt and a New World den for the bears.

Somebody had come in. Just one man, just a labourer. Definitely a labourer; fresh grits of concrete stuck in his hair, on his vest and streaked on his legs with blobs of the stuff still caught in the soles of his boots. His face was red. He was early; the pour must have been job and finish; pour the stuff quick, wash down the tools, hose out the skip and brush it with oil and fuck off, to leave the chippies to square up the job. The lad was ordering four pints. More would be coming. And here they were; nearly pushing the door off its hinges. They all looked the part, yakking and yelling, still on a high from shovelling concrete over steel grids and into deep columns, under the sun which only got hotter. It was over, complete, and now they were due the pint to chase away the thirst. They were due the pint. They yakked too loud. Too loud for who? Too loud for whom? Hamish Creese standing at a bar pretending to read a newspaper.

People were coming in; both doors; each end of the bar; the one near and the one at the far end. The dinner rush was on. The tall skinny man in the black and white check shirt looked familiar and the man with the bent nose looked like the guy who had worked on that university job. It wasn't him; unless he'd changed a bit. The doors weren't opening. Time for a pee. A pee into white slabs of tiles with arches of brown stains and green copper piping that dripped water from the joints through a white frothy powder. Running water splayed out to meet the brown stains and slide down the slab to splash in the gutter and agitate the cigarette stubs that floated free their unwanted strands of shag. A strong yellow urine which splattered onto silver paper.

"Gawd, I need this, mate."

The familiar man with the black and white check shirt.

"Too right. Nothing worse than being caught short."

"My word."

The faces at the bar were just the same; maybe a few more, but no one to know.

"Fresh one please."

"Right with you mate."

Two were leaving, the seat under the window was empty.

"Pint?"

"Yes. Thanks."

This skinny man with the broad-rimmed hat and the brown Guernsey and battered little bag was determined to get into the table. There was room for two, just, a squeeze, but there was room, just. Down the hatch goes the beer and up the nostrils goes the smell. Reeking up from under the table; unmistakeable horrible smelly feet. They smelled vile. This joker had no socks on. Fair enough; but here, under this table. The smell was rising up, hitting the underside of the table, running along, over the top, up the arm and right up both nostrils.

"Jesus."

"Sorry, mate?"

"Nothing."

It was best to leave the pint half-finished. Last night's whisky was reawakening anyway. Crazy Chris had not appeared, neither had anyone else. The smell was too much.

Outside the streets were clearing, the men and women who peopled the desks, the cubicles, the kiosks and the coffee machines of the city's nervous centre were leaving the streets to the bargain hunters and those like Hamish Creese with only labour to sell and nowhere to sell it. Hamish Creese did not want a camera, a cane chair, a colour TV or a video player, a Chinese meal, a Kentucky fry, or a fondue set. Hamish Creese needed a job and wanted someone to talk to. Or wanted a job and need someone to talk to. Danny. Danny might be in. He was due getting squared up anyway. He should have had an apology long ago. Long ago. Anyway, Danny never took things serious. Always laughing, that was Danny. And Maggie was a good spud; if Danny wasn't in Maggie was always good for a chat.

"Glenelg, please."

A shoogle was a shoogle. The tram might be broader, fatter and just the one storey, but the shoogle was the same. The gallop to Glenelg was more scenic than the tenemental run from the Toll to the Cross, but a tram shake was a tramshake. Coachwork, perfection; crying out its class; but the driver didn't wear yellow gauntlets. Yellow gauntlets, spelling out wisdom in all things mechanical and power over the blue mysterious flashes from the box below the long brass handle. Uncle Willie on Lord John's side had been a driver. Uncle Willie gave the wee Hamish Creese two bent pennies from off the tracks and laughed when Hamish threw them in the fireplace. But the gloves were warm and made the fingers big and saved half of the arms from any burning rays the Mekon might fire. There was no bulky green coat to fill up the platform. This driver was looking over a clean white shirt. His tram was clean and clinical with never many passengers and no cigarette ends stuck down the slats.

"As far as we go, mate."

"Oh. Sorry. Thanks a lot."

Glenelg by the sea. Where the end of the world had never come. There was the hotel balcony where two jokers had sat in a dinghy in full scuba gear to await a crazy man's prophesied tidal wave. The state premier came down and bid the waves back while sipping a beer and eating a pie and the seer ran away to the north. Two blocks down Danny had held a barbecue and passed round the photo of the Liverpool football team to be kissed; just in case.

Danny grew his roses high. High enough to deliver up a bit of England into the nostrils when a man came home. Everybody except Danny laughed when Jacky said England got up his nose too. There was no movement of water today and the roses didn't smell. Flagstones led up to the door where an open-mouthed lion waited to be battered upon the door. The lion had no teeth.

"Hello, Maggie. Danny home?"

"No. He isn't."

"Oh. I just thought I'd come and see him. I mean I think he's, I think you're both, both due a wee apology for the last time."

"He's not here. Danny went away yesterday to start at Happy Rock."

"Oh. I see. Will you tell him I called anyway?"

The door was not for opening another inch. No chat here about jobs, their holidays in Fiji, the new car, or the price of land. No tea, no cream crackers, no nothing. No Danny.

"Sure." The door closed.

Glenelg was at the edge of the city and coming here was silly, but at least the hotel sold good beer.

"Pie and a pint please."

"Dollar seventy, mate."

"Thanks. Do you think there will be a tidal wave today?"

"Sorry, mate. Come again?"

"Nothing. Nothing. It's all right."

This pie was cold and the pub was empty; only the cleaning man rattling his mop in a pail and sploshing it down so the wet spanned out to seek out any dirt.

"G'day old-timer." At least the beer was cold. "I said G'DAY OLD-TIMER."

"He's stone bloody deaf, mate." The barman's voice shouting from a back room.

Horses were running, going at it full tilt in the moving coloured glass. A jockey fell off, somebody won. There was no sound. Sound was off. Turned right down. Danny liked this pub. this was his local. Everybody here knew Danny who stayed just down the road. Nobody here knew Hamish Creese. There was nobody here to know Hamish Creese. Just an old deaf man who was squeezing a mop into a pail. An old man. Jacky. Jacky would be in. Jacky was sure to be in; the old bastard was retired. Liz would be in too. Even a roast would be quite acceptable. No use shouting at the mopper-upper and a wave would be just as useless. There was nobody there to hear, or see. Hamish Creese was leaving.

Taxi or train. One was quicker, but rather expensive. The station was not too far and a new machine spat out a ticket once it had been choked with twenty-cent pieces. The stay for the train was short. The train was slow; pulling hard, up, away from the plains of Glenelg to the bluffs of Port Noarlunga, along clifftops sheering away to a wavy blue sea. Waves here were not as high as the Bight, no huge rollers for crazy bears to surf and play in on old scrap plywood. Not as big and just too calm.

The stores were near the station. Stores where Jacky and Liz could be bought a peace offering.

"G'day, sir. Can I help you?"

"Can I have a box of plain dark chocolates and an ounce of Virginia, please? Make the chocolates your most expensive."

"Certainly, sir."

A woman was approaching, smiling through too much make-up, holding out a carton.

"Sorry. I don't smoke."

"Here we are, sir. Will you pay over there please. Thank you. Have a good day."

Click, click, click click click. Cluck.

"Thank you, sir. Do you have the five cents? Thank you. Thank you. Have a good day."

Have a good day. Yes and you too little madame.

The branches of the trees weren't moving and on the beach an

Afghan hound loped along, chased by a fat man who stumbled, shouted, ran and stumbled as the dog held its head high and trotted along. The tide was out; on the reef a white-shirted man was holding a yellow plastic bucket up to the sky. Jacky's wall felt warm to the hand and it was high time for Jacky to cut his grass. Under the carport Hamish stopped and pulled at the heavy tarpaulin, trying to cover the outboard motor. The door opened and Liz was there.

"Hello Hamish."

"Hello Liz. You're looking good."

Liz unfolded her hands from across the front of her black dress. "Come in, Hamish. Come in."

"Sure. That's what I came for."

There was no smell of tobacco smoke, the living-room was very tidy but the magazine rack was full and Jacky's glasses lay beside the brass claw hammer. Hamish placed the chocolates and tobacco on the table. "Jacky up the pub?"

"Jacky is dead, Hamish."

"Jacky? Jacky? Jacky is dead?"

"Sit down Hamish. Please. Jacky died last Wednesday. We buried him on Friday."

"Last week? Last week? Liz how, I mean, how? Liz I didn't know a thing, not a thing. Liz you must be — I don't know, I'm beat for words."

"Please sit down, Hamish. I'll get you a drink. Would you like something stronger than beer?"

"Please Liz, I'm choked off with beer. Do you have a whisky?"

Wednesday. Wednesday. Travelling with Gerry, sleeping in the van, cooking cornflakes with the beans and Jacky had died. Down to Streaky Bay and camping under the flocks of Port Lincoln parrots. Laughing, free as you please and Jacky Conroy was dead. On to Port Augasta where Hamish Creese the poet had made Gerry get out of the van and consider the irony of Salvation Jane; pretty, purple, yet pursued: a Wordsworthian flower, a Greek tragedy of a flower and Jacky Conroy was dead. In; past the soulless bitumen and bricks of Elizabeth, to a few beers in Adelaide, on Friday, while Jacky Conroy was dead and laid to rest.

"Here you are Hamish."

"Thanks. How did it happen, Liz?"

"It was a stroke, Hamish. He took it on Tuesday cutting the grass and died on Wednesday morning. The doctors said he was a battler to the end."

"A battler. He would have liked that."

"Yes, it's just a pity he couldn't be around to hear them say it."

"I'm sorry, Liz. I don't know what to say. Is there anything to be done? Is there anything Hamish Creese can do for you?"

"There is nothing to be done, Hamish. It's all been taken care of."

The whisky was raw and went down the wrong side. It was too quiet. This silence was too much.

"Will you be all right?"

"I shall be fine, fine. I'm off to Sydney for a while. A niece of mine is due a baby soon; I quite fancy being a substitute granny."

"Why not? No kid could have a better granny, you've a lot to give."

"I've something to give you Hamish. Jacky didn't forget you."

"Me? Don't follow Liz."

Liz walked over to the bookcase. She lifted up the brass claw hammer.

"Do you remember this? He really was quite touched by it you know."

"Yes, I remember it." A gift from the boys and Hamish Creese had made no contribution.

Liz replaced it and opened up one side of the bookcase. From the bottom she pulled out something wrapped in a red square cloth decorated with green tadpole blobs in a Paisley pattern.

"Jacky used to say that when it was all over for him, to give this to you. He said you were the only man capable of understanding what it represented." She passed it over. "This is for you Hamish."

There was no mistaking it. Even under the square cloth the round knob end gave it away. The cloth fell away. It was the Mathieson brace; from the Saracen Toolworks in Glasgow. Round ivory knob, drilled and dimpled till it was a white marigold;

ebony wood; turned and planed, every flat the same; exactly; a grip that defied anyone not to use it and all decked out with silver mountings. And there it was, on the ivory crescent insert, proclaimed in scroll, 'A. Mathieson, Glasgow and Edinburgh'. In a tented city Jacky's grandfather had bet his toolkit against the brace on the toss and turn of the pennies. Two heads were up and the young aristocrat shook his hand. It was never used. A workman's artefact made highest order art by craftsmen of the tools and put in a glass case.

"Hamish, the very first day he came home after working with you, he couldn't believe he had met a man from Glasgow with a Mathieson hammer. And a man who knew it was an 'Edinburgh'. Hamish, he knew then where this tool was going."

"Liz. I want to keep it. But I'm a travelling man, I'd probably lose it or have it nicked. I can't take it."

"You will take it. It will be something in your life you must take responsibility for. Here, give me your glass."

"Liz, I have to confess. I feel rotten about not making the funeral."

Liz returned with another whisky and sat on the sofa.

"It was our fault. We didn't have your address. All we knew was you were either working at Happy Rock or living somewhere in Edwardstown. Don't fret about it."

"I can't help it. I was in Adelaide too. I was back on Friday. I could've made it."

"Don't worry about it. It's past now. I did phone the union but the girl wouldn't give me your address. Maybe she thought I was going to nail you for maintenance."

"Couldn't you get Bernard, or Paul even?"

"I asked for Bernard, but he was on holiday in his boat, or so she said. I don't know this Paul, but she spoke to someone."

"Did she? Who?"

"Hamish, it's not important. Look, she put the phone down and went away to speak to someone then came back and said the union didn't know anything about a Mr Creese. So, it's not your fault. I tried to contact you but couldn't. That's all."

"Did you tell them what it was for?"

"Of course. But I don't think that meant anything. She kept saying it was a union rule not to divulge information on members. She did say there was no Creese on the computer."

"Bullshit." The girl usually wasn't allowed to tell anything over the phone. Members shot through, wives wanted cash for the kids, and furniture stores and loan sharks wanted to be led to their money. But somebody must have recognised the name Jacky Conroy. Somebody up there did know Hamish Creese. Somebody there must have known Conroy and Creese went together. Especially one to the other's funeral. Somebody there was a bastard.

"How's the time, Liz?"

"Four-fifteen. Why?"

"I have to go see somebody."

Hamish stood up to go. Four-fifteen. He could make it. There was a taxi-rank at the shopping mall.

"Liz, I need to be off. I'll see you soon."

"Take the brace with you, Hamish. I'll be away for a while."

Hamish Creese kissed her and brushed her spiky wisps of hair back into place at the sides and back of her head.

"I will be seeing you, Liz?"

"I hope so, Hamish. Take care."

The fly-screen door shut with a bang.

HAMISH Creese paid the driver in the taxi and made up the long close without shutting the car door behind him. Up the stairs, through the doors marked Push and Pull right to the counter. Behind the counter the woman stood at a coat tree pushing her arm into a white-coloured jacket. A hat hung lopsidedly on a branch of the tree.

"I'm sorry. We're closed. Is it important?"

"Depends on which side of the counter you're standing."

The girl finished putting her jacket on and came over.

"Sorry? Come again?"

"A friend of mine phoned here last Friday and asked where I could be contacted, and you wouldn't tell her. Because of that I missed an old mate's funeral. That's important. Bloody important."

"Oh. Yes. Mr Thomas, isn't it?"

"Never mind the bullshit. Creese is the name. Hamish Creese."

"Oh."

The woman was fidgeting, pulling at her cuffs, fixing up the artificial rose in her lapel.

"You wouldn't tell her where I was even though it was for a funeral. A bloody funeral."

"Mr Creese, she could have been anybody trying it on. The union rules are quite clear. I am not allowed to disclose information over the phone."

"Just over your computer, is that it?"

"Mr Creese I keep to the rules. I'm sorry but that's it. Now if you'll excuse me, I at least have a home to go to."

"I'm sure you have. In the hills is it? The boys get it built for you, did they?"

"Mr Creese, you have no right to speak to me this way. You are not even a member of this union anymore. You've been deleted."

"Deleted? What're you giving us? Who said? Who the fuck said so?"

Deleted. Wiped out. Rubbed out. No more. Definitely on the dead file.

"WHO THE FUCK SAID SO?"

"Moira. What's the matter here?"

"This man, he won't go. I think he's drunk. He's definitely drunk."

Paul and Dudley. Ready to go. But they had to pass Hamish Creese and one of them was a somebody.

"I'll tell you what's up, Paul. One of you jokers is a bad bastard who wouldn't help Jacky Conroy's widow, or me. And I'm angry 'cos all of you bastards refused to recognise the name of Jacky Conroy. Jacky Conroy was fighting to build this union when you bastards still had the shit running out of your trousers." Paul put down the briefcase. "That's right Paul. C'mon."

"Creese, you don't belong to this union anymore, and do you want to know something? You never ever did. You're finished Creese. You're of no use to anybody. And you really shouldn't abuse Moira."

That gorilla Dudley, moving round the back. Get the back to the counter, back to the counter. Dudley moved. It was too late. Dudley put on the bear hug from the back. Paul's punch was solid, Hamish was too slow drawing the knees up. The next brought the pain and sick together. Dudley and Paul rammed the head of Hamish Creese through the doors. Paul gave a last kick. Hamish Creese was tumbling, tripping, down the small series of steps, holding tight to the brace wrapped in the red cloth. At the bottom he sat on the last step. "Piss off Creese."

Piss off. Or wait till the bastards came down. The close was narrow. Closes were made for the one on one. But at least one should be unsuspecting. Time for Hamish Creese to go home. Where? Hamish stood up, tucked the shirt-tail in, and moved out the close.

Behind his glass the bookman was arranging; shuffling the books. Several copies of a new addition to the collection were being arranged along the front. A book in a grey cover with bold black lettering: *Poems From Prison*. Poetry from a prison. The bookman placed the last three strategically, the author's face staring out at any onlooker from all sides, all angles.

"GAFFNEY YOU BASTARD!"

The Mathieson brace from Glasgow shattered the window. Hamish fell to his knees. His hands hung helplessly at his sides. Hamish cried.

☆
☆
☆
☆
☆☆☆☆☆

THERE was no laughter. The face tried to smile, revealing gaps between broken teeth, and folding the shiny scrubbed skin into deep creases which interrupted the broken blood vessels and cut across the sparse flesh of the face. She was familiar. A man come back, looking at a woman who had been nowhere, yet understanding her without knowing her non-traveller's tales. But the traveller Hamish Creese was on the doorstep and the woman was at home.

"Mrs Munn?" Two arms went across her chest and the nod was exaggerated. "I've come about the room you have to let."

"Who told you about it?"

"I seen it advertised in that shop window back there. Could I see it, if it's not let?"

"Oh it's not let, and you can see it. If I decide to let you. Are you working?"

"Not really. I've just arrived from Australia. I've not had time to look yet."

"Will you get the unemployment?"

"Broo money? I don't know, maybe, I suppose I might, I don't really need it just now."

"If you're staying you will." The eyes were travelling; up and down Hamish Creese; pricing the gear. "Are you maybe on holiday? Or what?"

"I'm not really sure yet. I'll see how it goes."

The upper lip was covered by a lower which was pale blue in front and red at the back. A frown tried to force its way down

149

through the gap between her eyebrows. "Do you come from round about here?"

Her head was poked further out and turned left, then right, then a sweep, up the street, down the street, around the street. The street was empty. Whatever might have been there, was not there. Brown, greasy fish and chip wrappers on the pavement and crushed aluminium cans in the gutter suggested a form of life had recently been there; but not this damp morning. An orange bus with a black band of rain-dropped windows swished past; wet. The bus was empty. It was an empty Glasgow Sunday morning. Everyone under covers hiding from Knox and Calvin who had died years ago but still could be seen travelling on empty buses through empty streets on an empty Sunday, looking out with the eyes of the spirits on the unwanted excess of the Saturday night out. Under covers the people would be preparing to drag themselves through another Sunday to pay for the pleasure of a dark night's sex. When the landlady's head stopped, it was time to answer.

"Not really; more up a bit, just down from the Cross."

"What was the name?"

"Creese. Hamish Creese."

"Creese. Creese. Was your mother Martha Creese? A wee buddy? Black hair and a limp?"

"That's right."

The face was eager. A connection had been made. It was enough. This woman had known the mother of Hamish Creese.

"And your Da. I knew your Da. He was a fine man, a gentleman, a real gent until the drink got him. So you're the boy. Come in, come in."

The house was in the same road and was the same style as the one Angela had lived in all those years ago. The long hall, the stairs, the doors to the left, and the single door to the right. The door of the single room on the right closed quietly. Mrs Munn stuck out her tongue at it.

"Ignore him. He doesn't mean anything by it. He's been with us a long time. He's a nightwatchman in a factory up the road. Sleeps on the boss's couch all night then pads about here all day." She tapped her head. "On a Saturday he sits in there sipping at a half-bottle and talks to a stuffed bear he took out the boss's skip."

The house smelled of furniture polish, Brasso and frying bacon. All around, the varnish on the walls, the glass of the doors, the brass plaques on the walls, reflected light. Sizzling bacon was not easy to dismiss. She opened the door of the bigger room to the left. The room was light. The wallpaper, the decor; clean, light, modern. Clear and uncluttered lines. Everything in it was a complement to something else, in colour and in style. The carpet to the chairs, to the curtains, to the bed cover, all existing independently but touching physically in abstract colour and making the room whole. Mrs Munn walked over to the far wall.

"My daughter did this room up and then got married. She's a teacher, you know. But Hughie and I have been letting it since he retired. This is a built-in wardrobe my man put up." She pulled at the recessed handle. The door came away at the bottom and fell out. Prospective lodger Creese caught and held it away from her shoulders. "Well, he never was much of a joiner. I'll try and get him to fix it."

"That's all right, honest. I'll fix it. That's my trade. Really."

"Are you taking the room then? It's fourteen a week. We keep it dear to keep away the riff-raff."

"I'll take it."

She moved away from the wardrobe and talked on as Hamish tried to fit the edge back into the runners.

"Gave me a wee turn that. It's two weeks in advance, by the way. I've got to be careful you see, I've got a sound at my heart. They don't really know what it is, but I've got to take it easy. Are you managing? Bessie Smith had a haemorrhage last week and it nearly killed her. I certainly wouldn't like my sound to turn into a haemorrhage, if you know what I mean. Him down the stairs would be clueless without me. So I just take it easy. Mind you, I'm trying to get my daughter to move back in here. She married a right rascal you know. He left her as well, left her. He's living up at that university; he's found himself an extra-mural teacher or something. I'll extra-mural her if I clap eyes on her." The door fell into place. "Is that it? That's awful good. Have you had any breakfast yet? Look, just come down and eat whatever he's made. He's really quite a good cook. Do you want to pay me now?" Two big brown ones and two blue notes were fished from the wallet.

"That's two your owed Mr Creese." Outside, the door was locked and the key handed over. Hamish Creese and his holdall had found new lodgings. Tools to follow. Maybe.

Cooking breakfast smells grew stronger as the winding descent down the stairs was made. In the room next to the small kitchen a white cloth covered the table. Plates were laid; a cruet set waited; empty cups expected and knifes and forks stood by. The brown sauce bottle had no dobs under its white cap. A man in a maroon sleeveless pullover and white shirt was tucking the teapot under the cosy.

"Hughie, do you remember Martha Creese? Remember. Her and I used to go to the steamie on the same night for years."

Hughie shifted a knife not out of place to a better place, and shook his head.

"You do so remember. She was the wee woman that had a limp."

Hughie's mouth opened, his eyes widened and his index finger pointed to something or someone in space. "Oh, aye."

"See. I knew you'd remember. Well, this is her boy. Remember the wee toff that used to come and help her hurl her washing home in her fancy pram. You used to talk about him because he wore a school blazer and thon funny wee cap. Do you remember him now that I tell you?"

"Ah, well, he was only a boy then. But I knew the face."

A hand was stretched over the table. Hamish Creese, boy and man, held out his. Mr Munn smiled, took the hand, held it, shook it, looking at the face above. "Aye, I knew the face."

"Hughie. Set out another place. Hamish is here from Australia and he's taking the empty room."

Hughie clattered out some cutlery, a saucer, plate and cup. Mrs Munn pulled out a chair.

"Sit down, Hamish. Tell us all about Australia. How long were you there?"

"Oh, about sixteen, seventeen years I suppose."

"Did you enjoy it? Did you have a good flight back? I've got a brother in Perth, Jimmy Munn, I don't suppose you bumped into him? Ach well it's a big country, isn't it it? What did you do over there?"

Hamish told them the outline of a tale as Hughie shuffled around the table, flipping out eggs and bacon from a pan to the plates. Mrs Munn placed a hand on Hamish's chest.

"Sorry to interrupt you, Hamish. Hughie. Put all of the potato scones on. I'm sure Hamish didn't get a Scottish potato scone in Australia. Did you Hamish?"

"Not quite, no." She looked pleased. It was the time for the toothless stupid grin and the head to do a noddy.

"Now, you were saying, Hamish? How did you find the heat over there? I don't think that heat would help this sound at my heart. I don't really think so. Mind you, the winters must be nice. The summers here are getting better, but the winters are as bad as ever they were. Or maybe worse. So what made you come back? Were you homesick for old Scotland, eh?"

"That's about the size of it, Mrs Munn. So here I am. But I must say, this is very kind of you."

"Och, we just like our lodgers to feel at home here. Anyway, you're going to fix that door for us."

Hughie manoeuvred a scone from his fish lifter to the plate. "What door?" He gestured with his utensil; twice down, twice up. Hamish cut a piece of scone and lifted it to his mouth.

"Hughie. Watch what you're doing. The door on that wardrobe in our Marianne's room. I warned you I would get a man in to fix it." She laughed.

Hughie finished adorning the plates with the speckled potato scones. "Does anybody want beans?"

Nobody wanted beans. Hughie brought out brown bread and a tub of margarine. Mrs Munn lifted the tub over to Hamish.

"That's a special margarine Hughie gets. It's got a lot of poly-unsaturates in it. Never used to get them. I think they just came on the market recently. Hughie's awful careful about what he eats. Aren't you, Hughie? He's a jogger you know. He's away out there, never mind the weather, jogging away for hours. Runs in the marathons and everything. Don't you Hughie?"

Hughie was eating. With his mouth full. Hughie was eating with his mouth full and open. Hamish poured tea into a cup. Hughie was eating with his open mouth full and looking at Hamish Creese, jaws working round the open mouthful of breakfast. The mixture was being mashed into wet multi-coloured paste joined to his tongue by strings of saliva. "You Lord John's boy?" Some of the mixture escaped the jaws to bounce off the upturned chin into the entangling wool of the jersey.

"That's right. Why? Did you know him?"

"I worked beside him in Brown's and a couple of other places. Good tradesman your old man. A good man wasted there. You're the one that beetled off to Australia then?"

"I don't know about beetled off, but I'm the one that went there."

Somebody remembered. Somebody remembered Hamish Creese. Maybe somebody else would. Given time somebody else would.

"I thought that. It's a far place over there. You wouldn't get home for your dinner."

"No, but they sell hot pies anyway."

Mrs Munn slapped the table and poured more tea into her husband's cup, then some for Hamish, then some for herself. The rest of the meal was eaten without any more question and answer. There was only the slurp of Hughie's mouth and throat, the punt of air through the nostrils and the occasional scrape as grinding molars met to clean each other and be polished by a searching tongue. The breakfast was well cooked. Hamish stood up as Mrs Munn collected the dishes.

"Can I help wash or anything?"

"Don't be silly. You go in the other room with Hughie."

"Thanks, but if you don't mind I think I would rather go up and get unpacked."

"Oh I'm forgetting. Hughie. Show Hamish where the bathroom is. You can have a bath or a shower if you like Hamish, there's plenty of hot water there, just help yourself."

"Right you are, Mrs Munn. I'll see you later then."

Silent Hughie led the way back up, to the bathroom, waving a hand first at the stool then the shower and bath. The place smelled like a pine forest. Hughie stopped down at the bend in the stairs and held his face into a space between two wooden banister rails. He was watching. Hamish made along and placed and turned the key in the lock of the bedroom door. Hughie was watching every turn.

"Have you seen your old man since you got back?"

"No. I haven't. I haven't had time. I was just off the train this morning. Why? Have you seen him?"

"Oh, I've seen him around. But I'll see you later. Do you take a pint?"

"I've been known to sink a few."

"Maybe have one later then. Once you've had a kip,eh? That's if you fancy it."

Come for a pint and Hughie will tell all about Lord John if Hughie is told all about Hamish Creese.

"Sure. Sounds a good idea. See you later then."

The gas popped into action at the turn of a chromium tap. The jacket was hung in the wardrobe after the door was opened warily. The shoes were taken off and toes dug into the shag pile of the carpet. On the road outside a parade of boys tramped after a tuneless brass band. Church parade. Up and out in the wet morning with shoes all shiny and leaky to march through puddles for the Lord, and fill up an empty church where a minister would bade them be sure and steadfast in order to play up and play the game, the rules of which would never be known to them. They would still be singing about anchors keeping their souls. An anchor holding the soul. Maybe Hamish Creese needed the anchor his young lungs had sung about. An anchor to keep the soul while the billows rolled and his face touched scabby pussy.

The carpet was soft to lie on, in front of the fire, elbow under hand, hand under chin, till the heat made the eyes blink; close, open, close; and the head follow the hair, in jerks, down the forearm, until the mind imploded in a jumble of brown-gloved officers, anchors and Brasso, haversacks and blanco, hymns and white-ribboned ministers, psalms and Miss Martin, smiling at a young believer who read so loud, so proud, for he did not even have to look at the book most times. A sleep.

I lie down and sleep;

The victim commits himself to you;
you are the helper of the fatherless.

All who see me mock me;
they hurl insults, shaking their heads.

to him who led his people through the desert
His love endures forever.
The earth trembled and quaked,
and the foundation of the mountains shook;
they trembled because he was angry.

A sleep.

THE door was shaking. The knock was getting louder. Somebody was at the door. There was only an outline through the glass panel. The key. The key was still in the lock. It was only Hughie.

"Sorry for disturbing you Hamish, but I thought I'd better waken you or you'll never sleep the night. I know a wee bit about that jet lag, I was in Burma during the war. Anyway; thought you might like a look at the day's papers. You still for a pint after?"

"Sure, but I'll have to eat first."

"Don't worry about it. You're eating with us. The boss said so." Hughie the emissary held up a hand demanding no reply. "You won't know whether you're coming or going for a wee while yet. I know. Just take it easy. Dinner will be in about half an hour. It's a lamb roast. Come down whenever you are ready."

The newspapers were almost as remembered. The names were changed but nothing else to protect the innocent. The royals, the strikes, the quads and a spiky-haired kid who still skelped his arse to gallop his horse away from the jolly old bobby who had never even seen a two-way radio. The only gun he had seen was the finger and thumb the kid held up to him. Grass-cutter shots and goalkeepers daring to save them. Rock-solid full backs sent off for flying tackles and no fool rebel wingers who knew their future lay only in playing their very best out there on the park. Medical illnesses and miracle cures, fly-by-night salesmen adjudged to be shysters, couthy wee sermons all nice for nice people who read crazy world politics in one whole half column. A woman was standing by the still-open door. The suit was tweed and the jacket fell away from high in front to low at the back. The lines of the jacket and skirt were clean, uncluttered. This was the woman who had decorated this room.

"Excuse me. My mother wants to know if you would like roast potatoes?"

"Roast potatoes. Sure. I mean, yes, thank you. That is if there is enough."

"I'll tell her then. By the way, it's ready. She's putting it out now."

A fresh shirt and the toilet bag were fished from the holdall. There would be no time for a shower. A quick body wash and extra splashes of deodorant would have to do. Someone was in. A return to the room to put on fresh socks over feet really needing a wash. The door opposite was opening. It closed as Hamish stepped out again along the hall to the bathroom. It closed as he came out, and again as he locked the bedroom door and went down to dinner.

The table was set for four. In the corner a small child in blue dungarees was strapped into a high chair and was using a teaspoon to paste food over his face. Hughie was filling a kettle in the kitchen, the water rushing from the tap and resounding in the bottom of the kettle. The younger woman was screwing the lid on the salt service. Mrs Munn was delivering roast potatoes from the oven tray to the plates.

"Hamish. Just in time. Could you open the wine, please? Marianne. Pass the wine bottle. Hamish have you met Marianne? This is my daughter Marianne. Hughie. Where did you put the corkscrew?"

The corkscrew was on the edge of the table. Hamish reached and picked it up. "OK. I've got it." The cork was removed, looked at, sniffed at, a small glass poured and pushed to Marianne. She picked it up, smiling.

"Do you know your way around a cheeky little red, then?"

"No. Not really. I just used to live near a wine-making area."

Marianne sniffed the glass. "Is this one good?"

"Well, that's tricky. If I don't say it's the best, I insult whoever bought it."

"But if you say it's the best you appear a fool."

"In such circumstances madame, I obfuscate."

"You what?"

"I just say it's a fruity little piece with a bouquet that is reminiscent of a sleep in the meadow on a summer's day. One may sleep in a meadow with one's nose in a buttercup; or a cowpat."

She laughed her back into the chair. Hughie came over and stuck up his glass. "Lot of rubbish if you ask me. Marianne gets it, and she gets the cheapest she sees."

Marianne closed her eyes to sip the wine. Her lids were long, drawn down, but they did not quite cover the lower lash. "Here's to a sleep in the meadow on a summer's day."

Mrs Munn joined them when the plates were full. The Munns were all interested in Australia. The weather, the wages, the working conditions, the houses, the prices, the sun, the sand the sea and the sharks. Mrs Munn related Marianne's trip to Greece when she was sixteen. Marianne was a girl of the world. She had sailed the Aegean, visited palaces and seen mountains. Marianne was Mrs Munn's daughter. Marianne was becoming embarrassed.

"Mum tells me you come from around here, Hamish. I don't suppose you've had a chance to see much yet, but I think you'll find it's changed a bit."

"No, I've not really had a chance to go walkabout yet, but I couldn't help noticing the motorways and the buildings all being cleaned up. I never knew there was as much scaffolding in the world."

Mrs Munn gulped down a mouthful. She had something to say. "That's the rehabilitation. We're all rehabilitated people round here. Except for that next block; I think there's a couple of doors up number ninety-six that don't want to be. We were one of the first rehabs in this road."

"Mum. I've told you before; it's the buildings; the buildings are rehabilitated, not the people."

"Oh, what's the difference? I'm sure people know what I mean. Are the buildings clean in Australia, Hamish?"

"Some."

Mrs Munn wanted information on Sydney Harbour and aborigines, the big red boulder in the desert and little snaky things that lifted themselves up on two legs and ran across the hot sand.

159

Hughie wanted to know why it was everybody hated Englishmen and loved the Scots. You could travel the world in a kilt and everybody would give you a lift. The wine was cold. The meal finished on Hughie's note of nationalist fervour. Mrs Munn refused the lodger's help with the dishes. Hughie pulled him by the elbow through to the living-room, put him in a chair then disappeared. He returned with two pint glasses and two red cans of beer.

"Might make good wine, but I bet you didn't get this stuff in Australia. I tried that lagery stuff they send over here. Kangaroo beer. I hopped back and forth to the lavatory all blooming night. There you go."

The glass was handed over. In London, on a train through England, a drink had never been thought about. But this was Scotland and this was Scotland's export. "Cheers.."

"Good stuff, Hughie. Some things never change."

"Don't let them kid you, son. It's changed all right; but when it happens over years and years you forget what like it was at the beginning. But the effect is just the same. That's all that counts."

Marianne was pushing the door open with her backside, tightening the skirt along the length of her thigh. She managed through unaided and turned, balancing two cups in their saucers. "Oh Dad. Did you have to? I thought you two were going for a pint or something later?"

"I didn't realise you would be so quick."

"Well you'd better take this coffee or Mum will go through you. And that goes for you, Hamish Creese."

Hamish Creese. Hamish Creese. Hamish Creese spoken quietly, softly. A rebuke with gentleness in it. Mrs Munn will go through Hamish Creese. But Mrs Munn did not know Hamish Creese well enough to rebuke him with a joke. Mrs Munn only knew Mrs Creese from the steamie. And Hughie only knew John Creese from the work. The Munns knew Hamish Creese. Hamish Creese knew the Munns.

"I'll finish this quick then. There's not much to go."

The beer flowed through the foam to the bottom of the glass. Glass and can were place discretely at the far side of the armchair.

Mrs Munn came in and the two women whispered at the door. Marianne left and Mrs Munn eased into the chair opposite with her coffee.

"Couldn't wait Hughie, could you? Take that coffee and go on up and tell the wean a story. Marianne's leaving Daniel here for a few days."

Hughie poured a giant slurp of coffee down his open throat, nodded to Hamish and left. Hamish Creese was alone with the landlady Mrs Munn who had a lovely daughter.

"I see he got you on the beer too, Hamish. You going out with him after? He'll like that."

Her sips at the cup were slow and her eyes never left the brim. It was time for Mrs Munn's lodger to prepare himself.

"I won't mind a pint myself, Mrs Munn."

"Your Da liked his pint, didn't he?"

"Too much maybe."

"Have you seen him since you got back? Are you wanting to see him?"

"Well he is my old man. I was intending seeing him and my sister. I've really lost touch with both of them."

Mrs Munn placed the cup and saucer at her feet. "Hamish, I've got to be honest with you. Your father went downhill over the years. He's one of those winey people now. Sometimes our Hughie meets him in the street and gets pestered for money for the drink." She rubbed her right wrist around in her left hand. This was a struggle. "All I want to say, Hamish, is this: if you see him don't let on where you're staying. Marianne's wee boy stays with us quite often and I don't want him to see things like that." Things like that. Now Lord John was a that. Relief had come; the wrist was let go and the cup and saucer picked up. "It's nothing to do with you, Hamish, you understand; it's just, you know what I mean."

"Sure." Lord John was not fit for human consumption. Unless one was called Creese. Creese could mix with Creese. "I'll not let on. I take it he's staying local then?"

"I don't know Hamish. I've only seen him on the streets. To be honest I've crossed over in case he recognises me, may God forgive me."

"Don't worry Mrs Munn. I'll keep my business from your door."

The triangle of envelope with Angela's address on it. Leave it in the wallet. The street directory would be a more objective place to find out its whereabouts.

"Would you like another coffee?"

"No thank you, Mrs Munn. I've had enough."

Hughie's face stuck in the door. "Are you for that pint, then?"

"Sure. I think I need one."

Mrs Munn had got her message through. The house was tighter already. Tighter and less cosy. Hughie waited till the jacket was fetched and the door locked, then he led the way out to the street. "Did you ever go to this pub when you were here before?"

"Which one is that?"

"The Two and a Half. Oh, that's right. It's changed. It used to be The Three wishes."

"I remember the Three Wishes. But I never drank in it much."

The building was being rehabilitated.

"It used to be a Catholic shop this, but it's changed hands now."

The way to the doors lay through and under scaffolding. The supports for the kick-boards pointed up at forty-five degrees, all neat, parallel to the inch. The post box was wrapped in a green dust cover and tied with a fraying rope. Just above head height a sign had been hung: MIND YOUR DEAD. Hughie had opened the door and was standing back like some under-dressed flunkey. Noises and exploding lights came from the two machines in the corner; apparently in protest at little green and purple gremlins which threatened to take over the world by scurrying off the edge of the screen onto the floor and up everyone's trouser leg. Pool balls clacked and cue ends thumped on the floor while some players screwed and some players caressed the tips of their weapons with blue squares of sure contact chalk. A blue face read out the news above the customers' heads. Hughie had found a seat.

"It's quiet in here at this time. I don't go it when it's mobbed. I'll get the pints up."

The red leather in the seat was ripped right through a

depression. The barman poured two pints, pulling at the pump handles with a podgy pinky. Hughie began to bring the beer over, but had to pause, holding it high over the pointed behind of a pot-bellied man who was pursuing a tricky piece of pool. The man missed. Hughie moved past quickly.

"Some place this, isn't it? It's the only one round here open on a Sunday, that's the reason I come here. If they get any more games in the drinkers will be out on the pavement and they'll have to pass it out to us. Christ knows what like it'll be if they lower the drinking age. Cheers."

"Cheers."

"Mrs Munn tell you about your old man then?"

"More or less. Have you seen him lately?"

Hughie pulled a beer mat over and rested his pint. "I've seen him round about the Toll now and again. But not for a while. He might be at the skippering games. If that's the case he could be anywhere. At this time of the year he's probably in the Model but."

The Model. The deedle-dawdle. Whose model anyway? Model for what? The model that had already been rejected maybe.

"Which one, do you know?" The pint was slow in coming down from Hughie's mouth.

"Listen. I don't want to upset you Hamish, but your old boy is in a bit of a mess. He's in that much of a state I don't think they would even let him into that new one they've made out of the Old Toll library."

"What does that mean?"

"It means if he is in any model, he'll be in Bellpark Street."

"Is that place still there?"

"Aye. But not for long. They're pulling it down to build new private flats nobody could swing a cat in. It's just new slums for old. But that is where he might be."

"I'll look for him there then. You for another pint?"

"Certainly. Heavy thanks."

The barman shook the glasses into a sink of grey water, churning up the greasy spots to the surface, and began to pour the pints. He was a big man. The pot-bellied pool player came to the bar. The barman took Hamish's cash, slapped down the change and turned away quickly. Two men came over from the door. Each pulled at an arm of the pool player slamming him head down onto the bar while each jammed a foot into the fat man's instep.

One man bumped Hamish and beer spilled. The beer fell on trouser bottoms and shoes. The trousers would wash. In the seat with Hughie there was nothing to be done but drink the pint and stare directly across at the pint opposite as it was being drunk. The gulps were long. The space missiles were louder. Or everything else was quieter. The man with the pot-belly was jabbering incoherently. The door opened again. A leaning man stumbled forward at an angle. He angled the half-dozen steps to the bar as if drunk. His head fell and jerked up repeatedly. Worse than he used to. The shakes of the head could not disguise the unsteadiness of his large square head. The Goalkeeper was still at his games. The pool player began crying. The jerking head was over him, strands of oily hair touching the back of his neck with each downward jerk.

"Are you, are you, are you for paying, sonny boy?"

The prisoner's chin tried to come up from the bar. The interrogator had to lean on him to maintain balance. "Are you for, for paying me?" A hand reached around the belly of the fat man, down to his body and unzipped his fly. A large flat hand moved into the trousers. The balls were being grabbed. The cry was a scream, then another. "Next week, next week, or else you're done. Right? Is that right?" The screaming and crying mixed. The trousers were ripped from the legs rendering the thighs bare. The Goalkeeper followed the jerks of his head round, turning, moving till he had squiggled a squint at everyone in the bar, then he turned and stumbled to the door, banging it open with an angled shoulder. The two helpers flung the man they were holding to the floor and walked out, looking at no one. The crying man's sidekicks went to his aid when the noise of the car receded and the noise of the television and the space invaders could be noticed again. The Goalkeeper and his kicked head from one daring save too many, was gone.

"Jesus Christ, what's the score here, Hughie? Is that him still lending out cash?"

Hughie was white. The pint was picked up, put down, pushed away, pulled back.

"Aye. He's still at the same old scrappy games. There was a big kick-up about them years ago, but it's back to business as usual now. The only thing they've changed is how you pay them. You don't have to know Napier's logarithms anymore, it's just a straight percent they add on."

"The bastards are still doing it then?"

"Aye. Round here they'd have you believe it's another branch of the Social Services. I went to his benefit match as well. I'm really sorry about this, son."

"Och, that's nothing to do with you. I wanted to get out anyway."

"Oh fuck . . . we should have got out before this lot came in."

A crowd of young men were in; noisy, pushing, jostling their way to the bar. One jumped up and pushed a button on the television set. "C'mon squire, give us the right stuff. Never mind this fucking crap." The barman stretched up to a shelf and took down a thin carton. From the carton he withdrew a video-tape and placed it into a machine under the bar. The TV screen scrambled; snow dots, faces, electric guitars, the news symbol whirling; then it settled down. People were gathering under a banner. The Orange Walk. The impatient man reached up and turned up the volume. "Go on ya beauty. Give us the Cry."

Hughie tugged at Hamish's sleeve. "That's it, come on. Every week they come in and watch that bloody tape of the walk in Belfast. C'mon out, let's go."

The air had a nip of frost. Over the road the trees in the little park were shedding redundant leaves.

"I think I'll go for a walk, Hughie. By myself, if you don't mind."

"I don't mind. I would've thought you'd have seen enough by now."

"Ach well. I'm not too tired; the air will do me good. I just want to see the street we used to all run about."

"Please yourself. I don't see what there is to see."

☆☆☆

THE church stood beside the gates of the park; closed up, locked, barred. Weeds covered the bottom steps and threatened to run up all of the stairs and crawl in under the doors. Black paint peeled from the twists of wrought iron palisades, revealing rust underneath. Metal grilles had been placed over the windows of the church hall. The wee hall; tacked onto the side of the church, just an adjunct, an appendage; the wee hall. The Drill Hall where all the action happened. The hall where tiny Hamish Creese had huddled round a radiator to watch older boys consecrate themselves to Jesus, and had envied the leader of the maze marching who needed no orders but knew every turn and step of the way for his followers. The hall where little Hamish Creese had led the maze marchers and won the Best Boy of the Year and Lord John hadn't come to see. No one had come to see. Mammy and Angela had stayed home with their only tatty dresses. No one saw the Best Boy march out in front of everybody else's Ma and Da, salute the Skipper, take the flag, run it up, tie it up without a falter, step back smartly, look up, salute. And cry. The hall where Hamish Creese had won another bible. Wee Bible Hamish from the street at the Cross.

The rails of the padlocked park gates hurt a face pressed against them. Divots had been dug up out of the abandoned bowling green where the older men had tossed up the jack and threw over wisdom to the half-drunk young bucks on the next rink, who only wanted to play for a laugh and to pass the time until the Vaults opened for the evening session. Scraggly grass smothered over what was once the trickiest putting surface on the South Side. A properly aimed hit could find the rutted tramlines to the pin and win two bob, or fly over to the next hole where the dollies were playing. The park-keeper's home was derelict. Old McCarthur. Old McCarthur; he flew the Scottish Lion above an upside down Union Jack every Queen's birthday, and chased the Black-Hand Gang out of the shrubbery. Weans who only wanted to steal the earth to build Garden Cities on top of their dykes and their middens. Garden Cities where the three-wheeled Dinky cars were not allowed to leave their own roads in case somebody was knocked over and killed. Old McCarthur. Probably dead now. The motorway slashed the skyline. Giant concrete columns encamped on half of the park. Resolutely. Striding across the spaces left. That space was the pitches; and that was where the Big Jumps were. The Big Jumps that were the rites of passage from being a wee man on the wee jumps to being a big yin who could defy the glass-panelled danger of the subway roof. The subway looked as if it was still there. Not the pink-tiled grand draughty entrance; only an apologetic sign, poked up from a hole in the ground. But if the subway was still there, the street must still be there. A train shuddered the ground underfoot. A cross-timber fell into McCarthur's living-room. Dust escaped out the space where the door had been. A walk round the long way would bring Hamish Creese back to his street.

The walk was past the Medicine Man who had the best pint of Guinness in Britain; although Murphy's had the best in Glasgow. Round and up past the cinema where a white sink hung out of the projectionist's window, hanging on an umbilical cord of copper piping. Slabs of corrugated tin passed a rattle from one to the other across the space which had once been a marble foyer with a kiosk; where the man would keep the queue in suspense by dallying, and talking to the ticket woman, before coming out and ushering the hordes in, counting with his eyes, till his railway signal arm fell across a wet disappointed chest. Over the pits in the street; beyond the school that kidded on it was the Blackboard Jungle because that lot were all the 11+ mediocrity who needed fame. Thirty-three was where Rab's Auntie Jean lived and gave out her broken biscuits from the biscuit work. And now the phone box at the corner was only a battered frame; no glass, no phone. Round the corner was the street. Round this corner. Round here.

Round. Nothing. On the left-hand side nothing was where something should be. It, the place, the places, nothing was there. Corners of red brick poking through glass and gravel, stone, dust and impacted dirt. No reference points. No café, no fruit shop, no bookies, no co-operative store. A body inside the body of Hamish Creese was trying to leave its container, stricken onto panic. A Hamish Creese wanted out. This Hamish Creese could stay, but this Hamish Creese was away. Off. Out. Out to move away, find a landmark, a benchmark. But there was a benchmark. The flat of the streets formed a cross on the rubble. On the right-hand side, at the junction, held in the arms of the apex, lost and forgotten, one tenement block stood, ragged blinds flapping through square holes which once were windows in somebody's home. A tenement not even allowed to tumble down and die, but held up by a rank of grey wooden struts; eight-by-threes clamped together and jammed between the gable wall and the raised steps of concrete on the ground. The bulge in the wall was held. For what? Under the diagonal timber props, under the blacker holes in the black sandstone, The Clyde Vaults. The Clyde Vaults. Still standing. Frosted glass holed, broken; plaster chipped and crumbling; but standing still and full of memory. The iron strap across the doors hung down, loose.

A push on the wooden outer doors made them open. The split doors inside opened easily, swung back, and came to rest behind Hamish Creese. The old brass fire surround, bent, buckled and sagging, stood before the fireplace where bums had jostled to be heated in winter. There were no mirrors in the gantry; broken shelving lay at all angles behind the long bar. Three sections of rubber tyre outlined the place on the wall where the dartboard had been. There was nothing to mark the spot where the points of two nails had entered the floor. The only mark was in the mind of Hamish Creese. Gaffney's green green spittle covered the top lip and ran down into the mouth. Hamish Creese saw Hamish Creese in the Clyde Vaults.

Hamish Creese standing in the Clyde Vaults felt the pain for the Hamish Creese lying there, the Hamish Creese who cried in the pain of pointed nails and pished-upon impotence. Hamish

Creese standing there felt the pain with him in screwed-tight eyes and stretching bending neck. Hamish Creese wiping three fingers through the muck on the floor felt the pain and knew the only cure. The poor bastard lying there must be helped to his due. This young man was due better.

He had read his bible, tried to please his parents, listened to his teachers, and stuck in at his homework with shaky pen as Lord John battered and cursed at the door. He had listened to his journeyman, learned the ways of the tools and the meanings of the drawings till his time was out and the yard gates closed. He had worked hard, been polite to women, a peacemaker amongst his friends and Eddie Gaffney had blessed him with his due. There never was any merit award in the South Side for good working people. Ham actors got Oscars and juvenile idols got Emmys. Welders got cancer. But people like Hamish Creese must have their due. That was only justice. And people must not get more than that. Now Hamish Creese would help Hamish Creese to his due. Free him from the pains of that injustice. The poor bastard must have his due. Hamish Creese would help Hamish Creese who merited better than to have his humanity stripped to a raw animal state. Until then Hamish Creese could not be the total Hamish Creese. Being the incomplete Hamish Creese was too painful. Hamish Creese made Hamish Creese angry and tearful.

The subway ran its course under the street. Grit and pieces of shelving fell. A rat scampered from the grate of the fire. Some soot shook out onto the broken bricks of the hearth.

The brass fingerplates were grimy, sticky, and left a greasy film on the fingers. The doors swung easily together behind. Hamish pulled the outer doors together. Along the road a small woman in black stood looking up at the sign for the subway. She stood looking. A yellowing face turned and looked at Hamish Creese. A black shawl was pulled over her head and she disappeared into the Underground. The echo of a train's hoot came up as Hamish passed.

The streets were stranger on the way back to Mrs Munn's. Stranger streets, gaps between blocks, made the walk a hurry back. A hurry back to an already familiar door clicking, closing, and to the soft shaggy carpet under the feet.

"Hamish? Are you back? Can you let me in please?"

The door was opened. Marianne stood with a small portable television and some cable. "Mother thought you might like to have this television in your room. It's not the best of pictures you get on it, but it's good enough if you've nothing else."

"Here, give it to me. I'll get it."

"Not a bit of it. I can manage, thank you. Look, you clear that stuff off the wee table. If I remember correctly that's the only place the thing gets a picture."

Hamish began clearing the table. He paused to study the bronze statuette of an ape seated on the Book of Darwin in front of an open bible. The ape was studying a human skull.

"I like your sense of humour." He waved it before stowing it under the table.

"Do you like it? I'd forgotten all about that. It is quite good, isn't it?" Marianne plugged in the set and inserted the aerial.

Hamish ran his fingers down the line of buttons. "Which one is ON?"

"The one with O-N on it."

"That wasn't easy."

The screen filled with a woman's head in three sections. Marianne picked up the round piece of metal with two prongs sticking from it. "This is the aerial. You'll have to manoeuvre it about a bit. Here, come and see what you can do, I'll go and make some tea."

"Tea? Tea? Marianne, I'm only renting the room here. Already I've had breakfast and dinner, now you're for making tea."

"So? You're not paying us for our hospitality, Mr Hamish Creese. We don't rent that, we give it. Or would you rather pay cash for it? Because if you insist upon paying for everything, you'll have tea and no conversation. You take sugar don't you?"

"No, just milk, thanks."

"Right. Here take this and see what you can do."

Hamish took the aerial from her, moving the prongs through all the angles and variations from 180 degrees through to 90. The picture disappeared, came back, bent, flattened, shouted, whispered. Aerial upside down; the face came together, but the jaw leaned to the right, stretching, attempting to break off from the rest of the head. Aerial on the floor; on the chair; on the mantelpiece, and slung over the set itself; all ways there was little visible result. With the prongs closed and the right arm stretched at thirty-three-and-a-half degrees the picture was excellent, though it still had a tendency to move to the right.

"Are you relaying a message in semaphore, Hamish?"

"Looks like it, doesn't it? I think I'd need to be desperate for news to keep this up."

Marianne placed the tray in front of the fire. "I've just remembered where I used to put it." She took the aerial and crossed over to the wardrobe and pulled one door slightly open. The cable was jammed at the top in the space between the doors. The aerial swung down. The picture settled with the aerial. The picture was clear. The face on the screen was happy. "There we are. How's that?"

"Oh that's smashing. I'll just hang myself up at night along with the jacket. Is that the idea?"

Marianne stuck out her tongue, bent down and pulled the tray over. She bent to lift the milk jug, stopped, kicked off her shoes and sat; crossing and stretching her legs along the floor. A big toe had escaped from the stocking. "Shall I be Mother?"

Hamish sat down; back against an armchair; legs drawn up, arms balanced on the knees, fingers interlocked, but not tight. "Why not?"

"Dad says you went for a walk. Did you see anybody you knew?"

"Not really. I just went walkabout over by the park and the street I grew up in. But it's all away now. At least most of it is."

"I know; depressing isn't it? Especially if you can remember what it was like before. I stay in Partick; apart from the posh areas it's about the only district in Glasgow that's anything like what it used to be."

"Do you like living in the past then?" Marianne wiped her lips.

"I didn't mean it to sound like that. I'm not a nostalgia freak altogether. No; I think I'm just like most people, I remember happy times and forget the sad buildings. What about you, you're the one who's just come back."

Three spots of white milk were coagulating in the tea. "Oh, the same I suppose. I hadn't really thought about it much until recently. I can still feel the shock I got today when I turned that corner and the old street was down. It was physical, as if someone was reaching in and tearing out a piece of my mind. I was frightened."

"I know what you mean. Oh look. There's Eddie Gaffney."

Gaffney. Eddie Gaffney. Where? There he was. On the television screen. Behind the glass, in a tube, safe. Leg over leg, arms resting on a chair which had no arms, leaning back, relaxed, smiling. Smiling at an interviewer who was askew and almost falling over the side of an armchair which had no arms. Spectacles were below the questioner's eyes, resting on the bridge of his enquiring nose, and threatening to slide completely onto the floor. The interviewer was smiling back. Both smiles were meeting halfway.

"Do you remember him, Hamish? He was one of those gang leader types. Maybe it was while you were away; they got him anyway and put him in the jail and now he's out and quite famous. I can't make my mind up about him. He did some terrible things, you know. But he seems genuine enough. It's hard to say." Marianne looked away to her tea.

The voices were talking poetry. Gaffney's poetry. Poetry full of pain, now bound up and issued in a new volume, hardback. The wise interviewer said the critics had understood the meaning of it all.

"I remember him well. He's a poet now isn't he?"

"Yes, yes he is. His first book was quite good, actually."

"Do you like poetry."

"As long as I can understand it. That's what I liked about Gaffney's poetry, you didn't have to look for hidden meanings."

The interviewer was smiling even more broadly and nodding even more wisely. More wisdom must have come his way. Marianne was making to speak; a finger on the lips shooshed her. The new work was to be launched at the Poets of Scotia evening

172

in the City Gallery. Gaffney would be reading from the work. Gaffney would be there. Hamish Creese would be there.

"I think I'd like to go and hear him. Would you like to come with me, Marianne?"

"Love to. But these things are usually invitation only, aren't they?"

"Don't worry; as long as you look rich enough to be able to buy the book, they'll let you in.Anyway, it's an evening with poetry, not strictly a launch; and I'm a poet too, you know."

"You? Are you? Really? I mean, why shouldn't you be?"

Her eyes were blue and she was red with embarrassment.

"Exactly. Actually I've contributed to some journals in Australia. I've been quite widely read from Queensland to South Australia." A finger was plunged through the blob of turned milk on the top of the tea. "There was considerable interest in Gaffney over there. Anyway; you fancy the idea?"

"I look forward to it."

Gaffney had vanished from the screen, the bookish programme faded to an advertisement for washing powder. There was nothing to be said about washing powder. A knock came from the door. "Come in."

Hughie entered, but stayed at the door, holding the handle. "I was just thinking we'll maybe need to get going, Marianne. I'd like to get you over the road so I can be back in time for the late-night picture. If that's all right I mean. I'll take you later if you like."

"No; that's all right Dad." She gathered up the tray. "Till next week then, Hamish?"

Hamish extended both palms and lowered his head to his chest. "Next week."

☆☆

THE smell was of damp, dried, and drying urine. Daylight was either closed out by the thick, tight-fitting doors which slammed shut, or it deliberately passed on by, not caring to go where no one cared for illumination. Two men were behind a front of little square glass panels. The weight and thrust of the door had rushed it back to close in the slam, but these two hadn't moved. A bare bulb hung. Hung above a bald head dropped down studying a book of long white pages, thin red lines, and squiggly writing. A man in a brown faded pinstripe double-breasted jacket stood behind and peered over the head of the man who pored. But neither was peering, neither was poring. Hamish Creese was waiting. A back-heel kicked the door three times. The bald head lifted. The nose skewed to the left. Narrow eyes almost disappeared in a squint.

"What's the matter with you, son? The door do you some harm did it?"

"Do you run this place?"

The biro was jerked over the shoulder. "He's the boss, but I run it. What's your problem?"

"I'm looking for John Creese. I heard he might be staying here."

"John Creese? I don't know; I'll need to look and see if he's in the book."

"People used to call him Lord John."

"Oh, Christ, you mean Lord John?"

"Sure. That's what I said."

What do you want with Lord John? Who wants him? That's if he's here."

"I do."

"And who are you? You look a bit prosperous to know Lord John. Are you some kind of social worker? Or maybe the polis?"

"I'm his son. Now stop the bullshit; is he here or isn't he?"

The ledger was slammed shut. "Aye, he's here, and you're fucking lucky he's in one of his good spells. I hope you're no for setting him off, cause he's a carnapcious wee bastard when he starts. And I don't give a fuck if you are his boy, he'll be right out that door."

The man in the brown jacket leaned over and rapped the glass. A finger with a dirty cracked nail signalled Hamish down the passage. Wooden wet floorboards felt loose underfoot and the creaks echoed. The passage ran off left past thin round pillars, down in a steep slope, down into a dark the eyes were not used to. A series of iron bars from floor to ceiling barred the way. On the other side of the bars the bossman was searching through a ring of keys, looking for one to fit the large square lock. The key was found, the lock was turned, the gate pulled open, swung open, held open until Hamish Creese stepped through. The gate was closed, the lock rammed home, the key replaced. Hamish Creese was in the model. The boss spoke; the voice coming from beneath white eyes, and eyebrows staining blond spots on the dark.

"You must excuse the warden, Mr Creese. Today, is the day, the residents receive their cheques, from their distant relatives at the social security. Giro day, always gives us, more problems, than all of the rest put together. But your violence, toward the door, was just a little unwarranted. We were, actually, engrossed, in checking our bookings."

"Fair enough. Sorry. Where can I find Lord John?"

"Lord John's room, is on the fourth floor, number fifty-six. But, today, being what it is, you may find him in the basement, cooking. On Tuesdays, I believe, he likes to cook a hotpot, while the Giro lasts. May I leave you to it? Just bang on the gate when you want to go."

The visitor was in a square hall. Some captured light ran round on random pillars, catching a ride on the spiral motif. Between the pillars, trestle tables and wooden chairs were scattered in two rows. Men sat at the tables, shuffled among the tables, slept with their heads on the table. A fat television sat on a triangular shelf set high in a far corner, sounding out its message to rebound from the walls. Colours moved from side to side, up and down, and flitted on and off the screen. Its light fell over the silhouettes at the tables; moving, sleeping, sitting still; all miming the act of living.

A stairway ran off from the right of the hall. The choice was the stairs or the basement. The basement was probably here, somewhere, wherever; but the stairs were here, to the right, running up till gradually the light made the steps visible and clear to the curious. Hamish started the climb. Curious.

On the second floor an old man wrapped in a grey blanket sat blocking the corridor. His head poked through a hole in the blanket, and his hair was matted and stuck out horizontal as the wing tips on the crow.

"Are you the man from the television? Are you keeping the thirty-bob to yourself? Where's my share?"

Hamish moved on up the flats to the fourth. Numbers were stencilled on the doors. Doors across the pigeon-holes for men who couldn't handle being pigeon-holed. Number fifty-six. Lord John's berth. There was no noise behind the door. Snores and blubbers came up from some securely asleep under their own little section of the wire mesh coverings above the cubicles. Curses came from someone still fighting the toss, and another cried for mercy from Mother Mary. But no sound came from behind number fifty-six. The thin plywood door trembled under the knock. There was no answer from the place where Lord John lived. All behind the partition, in the cubicle, jammed between cubicles, was quiet. Humanity wasn't in today. Lord John was not in his bunk. Hamish Creese's father was not at home. Hamish Creese's father had no home.

The man in the grey blanket yelled as he crawled along to stop the visitor going down. "You can stick the thirty-bob up your arse, ya bastard."

Another voice told the man to wrap it.

Lord John didn't appear to be in the tableau in the square hall below. A man carrying a large silvery tin disappeared into the corner by the television. Perhaps the route to the basement lay that way. Over past the tables, past the chairs, beyond the faces that turned and looked and those that didn't. Hollowing faces, bruised faces, empty faces and questioning faces; and a lone face that lifted, looked, and lay down closing the eyes over. Chipped concrete stepped the way down to a basement brightly lit by fluorescent tubes hung between strips of filled-up flypaper and greasy cloth-covered cable which once had lit up conventional bulbs. Bodies queued at a rightly made partitioned kiosk, buying things from a woman in a pale green overall who pushed their change back with the tips of her fingers. Lord John was not in the queue. Bodies sat at tables; eating. Some with knifes and forks, some with knives, some with forks and some with dabbling fingers. Some sipped tea from mugs or chipped cups or wire-handled cans which once had held syrups. Lord John was not at the tables. At the side, to the back, bodies hunched over steaming pots and pans which were set on a thick scries of black rough ironstone slabs set on white-tiled bricks to form a large rectangular hotplate. A broad-backed man, with freckles on his shoulders and a damp patch on a khaki singlet, was bent over, throwing old shoes and bits of wood into a grate and pushing them further into the fire with an iron cleat that rattled on its long handle. He was cursing and talking to himself. Lord John was there. At the back, stooped over, looking down into a pot, right hand gripping his left arm. The bald patch was bigger.

Lord John looked up. A black patch covered the eye. He had lost it. The eye was gone. He had lost the eye and no one had mentioned it. As though everybody knew he had only one eye. As though he'd always had only the one eye. But once he'd had two. Two. Two good eyes. Now there was only one. But Gaffney still had two.

Down from the steps, moving across; the bodies were standing aside. Lord John's lips were stretching under that ginger moustache. The head was back into the quick jerk and turn, and the face angled into the same mixture; a mixture of sad surprise and cynical disbelief. The homework is done Da. Can I go? Can I go? Please? And then the disbelieving smile.

"Hail fellow. Well met."

Hail fellow, well met. Fourteen thousand miles and all the years. Years of no son. Years of no Da. Years of nothing but hail fellow well met. And now hail fellow. Well met.

"Hello. Hello Da. How are you going?" How are you going. That wasn't much better. In this place. The place shrieks. "Fine place you have here."

"Now, now, Hamish. Don't let the man hear you. In any case it's coming down."

"Not before time."

"Ah, that's as maybe. But where do we go from here? Some of us will end up out in the cold, cold snow. Including your humble. Unless you're here to take me away from all this?"

Lord John looked down into the pot. The pot was filled with water. Bubbles were forming; on the bottom, on the sides, fighting free and foolishly trying to follow the steam. "I shall be with you anon, my son. I have a little operation to perform here." He took off the rough tweed jacket and handed it to Hamish. The cuff he rolled up once had been white. A mound of red, blue and black skin came to a green and yellow pointed head across his wrist below a hand of ingrained dirt. The question was read. "A slight altercation with an ageing pugilist who nowadays prefers rather blunt kitchen knives. Misery makes a man acquaint with such strange bedfellows." From a pocket he brought out a small wooden-handled knife with some string tied around the handle, edge scraped to a sharpness. He dipped it into the water. "Not the best of implements, but, needs must when the devil drives, eh Hamish?" The blade slit the wound open. A release of pressure pushed the pus free. Lord John held the seeping wrist above the gash, folded his fingers over, tensed the palm back up and back, then slowly brought the wound down to meet the water. He dipped it in, pulled it out. Sweat drops burst out among the thin hairs above his forehead. The wrist was dipped again. Held longer. Pus was coming forth in strings. Miniature thin green spaghetti. Attached to the wrist but coming. Out. In again. Strands of pus stretched and struggled in the water. The wrist was pushed, pulled, screwed, twisted tight, as the gash was dipped in, pulled out. Under the pullover and under the shirt, the skinny frame of an old man was holding on. Blood began to mix with the pus. The rubbing and gripping grew faster. The one eye was screwed shut. This time the hand was held, and held; held until it was pulled free and held high. "Dear Jesus, dear Jesus. Hamish. Quick. Quick, in the pocket there, there's a bandage. Get it out will you?" The bandage looked like a strip torn from a sheet, but at least it was clean. "Don't examine it, c'mon, get on with it, son. C'mon, do your stuff." He held out the wrist. The strip had been measured well. Enough for decent cover and not too much to make it awkward. The wrist and arm were thin. They used to be thick, with the big muscle that ran from the base of his thumb to way past his wrist. The knife. The knife cut the last eighteen inches into two strips for tying. The reef knot to stop the rip continuing, and two to tie but not too tight, but tight enough. "Hamish, I always knew that Boys Brigade stuff would come in handy someday." Lord John approved. Hamish had done well. He helped his father on with his jacket. Lord John lifted the pot over to a deep enamel sink and ran water into it from the dull brass tap.

Coloured mixture frothed, spilled over down the outside of the pot until the water ran clear. He slunged the last slunge around the sink. The stoker with the khaki vest cursed. Lord John gave that jerk of the head. A full pot was brought back over and replaced upon its spot on the hotplate. "Keep your eye on this and I'll get the tea."

Hamish looked down into the pot. The water looked clean enough. Lord John had moved over to a rank of battered lockers and given one a hit just below the lock. The door sprung open. A little white paper bag was brought out. He was calling over. "Do you take sugar, sir?" Hamish shook his head. The bag was brought over and shook over the pot. Black and brown dusty dry tea was tipped in. At once leaves floated up and darkly covered the surface of the water in the pot, becoming darker as they absorbed the water. "The cup that cheers, is that right Hamish? Come, regale me with news. Am I the father of good news?"

All that could be managed was a shrug of the shoulders. "News? I don't know what you mean, news."

"News, sir, what news? Are the colonies at peace? How fares Australia?"

179

Hamish smiled. "It's all right, as far as I know. At least it was still floating when I left."

"Good show, sir. Give those abos a touch of the old what's what, did you?"

Plops of steam and water were forcing their way through the brown mat of tea-leaves which was holding the brew back. "I think the tea's ready." A bandaged arm was up in front of Hamish's face. Lord John's eye peeked from behind the space made by hand and thumb. The pot handle was too hot. A handkerchief was needed to wrap around the handle. Lord John waited. "This way, my man."

The way was over to the end of a table adjacent to the rank of lockers. Another hit opened the door. Grains of sugar and flecks of dry tea covered the floor inside and stuck to the greasepaper wrapped around a square of margarine.

"Are you sure you don't want sugar?"

"No thanks. I'm not sure I even want tea."

An enamel mug with two black gouges rusting red near its bottom was placed in front. A gold-coloured syrup tin was hit on the side of the table before being placed beside it. "You have the mug."

Tea missed the mug; Lord John's pour was shaky. Maroon black tea. In a chipped enamel mug at a long table beside men who shovelled stewy mixtures into toothless mouths beside a man who called himself Lord John. In a bare bulb basement under a hall filled with empty men watched over by a faded brown suit. Hamish Creese had come to tea. And this hunched-over little man with the flapping tweed jacket was dishing it out.

Lord John sat down, patting the bandage. "I do believe you missed your vocation, sir."

"Isn't your arm louping?"

"Stoicism, sir. No pleasure, no pain. But how now, is this you finished with your antipodean adventures? Or are you just slumming to find out how the poor are doing?"

Maroon black tea in a mug and tea-leaves floating on the top, pulling themselves together into the middle, away from the sides. "I just thought I'd come and see you, see how life was treating you."

"That's today, sir. But what has brought you back. Surely you didn't miss your old father?"

"Maybe I did. Do you think it's impossible?"

"Not at a distance, no. Did you have some sort of, how shall I say, misadventure with one of our dear ladies of the opposite sex?"

"Your tea's lousy."

"The same sex maybe? I believe it's rife in Australia."

"You're not funny." A tea-leaf was picked off the tip of the tongue. "It was just time for me to come, see you, Angela, and anybody else that's left."

"Well, here I am. I don't know where your beloved sister is, but here I am. What's new sir?"

Nothing was new. Nothing. Not even the feeling of deference that forced the eyes to move around, come to rest, seek out things to look at; things on the table, anywhere; in the mug, at the hotplate, up and down the rank of lockers; away from under the eye of Lord John. This wasn't deference. This was guilt.

"Nothing much, I don't suppose. How're you?"

"Oh no sir, no. How are you? My circumstances are easily read and understood. Age, ache, penury and imprisonment. All in equal measure." Tea was running down a stubbly chin, slipping out past the recess on the top of the tin. "What brings you back? There can't be anything much for you here."

That was not a statement, that was a question, with a big question mark.

"I'm not sure. I just felt like coming back to Scotland, seeing how things were. I was beginning to miss the place."

"And me? Were you missing me? I don't think so, Hamish. You hardly missed me when you were here."

"Look, I just wanted to get a few things sorted out in my head. I've come back, I've come to see you, can we leave it at that?"

"Fair enough. Where are you staying?"

Mrs Munn was shaking hear head. "I've a room over in Partick. I think I've been quite lucky. It's as clean as a whistle. In fact, the landlady gave me in a TV."

A piece of red and silver foil had been pressed into service as an ashtray. "You got a smoke?"

The red foil spun when the finger was turned in the centre of it. "No. I seen Gaffney on it the other night."

"Gaffney? Well, he's a nearly famous man now, son. He's been punished; but not for this." The eye patch was tapped. "The pity is the bastard left me one to see the shit that I live amongst."

"Da, I'm really sorry about your eye and everything, I mean, I didn't even know you had lost it."

"Really sorry? Sorry? But what have you to be sorry for Hamish? You did your best at the time, didn't you? I just wish you had the build then you have now. Anyway; I have no way and therefore no need of eyes. Have you not even got the makings?"

"No. I don't smoke. I never have."

"Ah, but you forget, I haven't seen you for a large part of your never."

"OK. Look Da, I'm just trying to talk to you."

"Why? What for? To help who — I beg your pardon — whom? You, or me? I don't think it's for me you've come back and I don't think it's for me you want to talk.

A man with cropped white hair and tiny round spectacles came between the tables; stopped; then sat on a seat beside Lord John. His baggy coat, open, fell to the side. A Glasgow University tie held his trousers up. His mouth was closed, but champing, moving little muscles high on his cheekbone. A piece of orange peel slipped out and was pulled back into the mouth. Orange peel to cover up the smell of surgical spirits in the urine. The stink that flowed from the lavatories, round the bars, and put men off their pints, and made landlords apoplectic.

"Ah, William, come and see. This is my boy. My boy."

The man leaned over the table, hands still in deep pockets, pulling his lids together, trying to focus. His eyes had yellow lumps and technicolour bumps on the retina. Still leaning over he palmed a small bottle of milky white liquid to Lord John. "Here, Jock, have a go at this. Is this your boy then? The one you were saying was in Australia? He certainly looks too healthy to come from round this way."

Lord John screwed the cap from the bottle, looked around, lifted the liquid to his lips and drunk quickly, gasping to a finish.

"Finish it, Jock." Lord Jock finished it. The benefactor pushed him over a long strip of orange peel, rose, and nodded at Lord Jock's boy. "Nice meeting you, son. Will you get rid of the doings, Jock?"

"Of course, friend William, of course. My esteemed thanks to you. I shall see you anon."

Lord John licked the ragged wet hair edges of his moustache. Hamish watched as he bit off a piece off the peel and began flicking it round, back and forth in his mouth. "Do you have to drink that stuff?"

"Ah, Hamish, this stuff is the stuff dreams are made on." The two teeth came up to bite the upper lip. That smile was almost a snarl. "But you never needed such a stuff, did you Hamish? You were always the dreamer. My unhappy wee dreamer looking for his land of holy men and shining cities and playful jolly japes where boys and girls were always chums and didn't feel each other's dirty bits." The eye was fixed; there was nowhere else to look. "And always dreaming for a holier father. But you only had me." A curse from the man with the iron cleat sounded loud. The cleat rang as he threw it onto the hotplate. A bang came from the left. The kiosk window was being shut. somebody sneezed. That eye was bright enough for two. "As soon as your time was out you got rid of me, remember? You and that other one; as soon as you were into the big wages. I was the embarrassment. Now you and your wee life come and make statements about what I drink. Did you bring me any duty free?"

"No. I brought a couple for — for Angela. That's all."

"See? See what I mean?"

"See what? What're you on about?"

"You don't try and think what I need. And you never have son. Did you never think your Da needed something from his son?"

"Look, do you want a drink?"

"Oh no, you keep it son. It's a bit late. That's not what I need. I just wanted a son that I could talk to about books, or go for a pint and play some dominoes with. But you believed the books, and I couldn't be your hero. You know the best thing you ever did for me was stand up to Gaffney. I was quite proud of you; and then you threw it away, didn't you?" He was away. There was no stopping him. He was away. And that eye wouldn't let go. "After Gaffney done you, you didn't give two fucks about me. You were over there on the North Side making plans to join our refugees in the colonies while I was lying there with this." The patch was tapped and tapped and tapped tapped. "I could've lost this fucking thing there and then, and you, you wouldn't have come. Now you're back and you offer me a drink. Sorry, son, you keep it. I'd rather have William's. He just thought I might need a charge."

The woman of the kiosk passed by, dressed in a fur-collared coat, and swinging a black handbag. Bodies were squealing chairs back. The man with the khaki vest had a shirt on, left open. One old man was at the plate hypnotised by whatever was in the pot. The basement was closing up.

"I'm sorry you see it that way, Pop, I'm not going to try to defend it. Is there nothing I can do for you now?"

Lord John's head was shaking. The mouth with the two teeth fell open.

"Naa. You carry on, son. Whatever you're going to do you do it for yourself. It's you that needs it. On your way. I'll see you again."

It was time to go. It was over. "Thanks for the tea. I'll probably see you about. Take care of yourself."

"That's right, Hamish. Maybe we'll meet in heaven."

No use standing. There was nothing here. A positive act had been made negative by Gaffney. Gaffney hadn't been content. He had come again. And Lord John had lost a new found son. And Hamish Creese had lost both ends up.

Half-turned, ready to move, but Lord John's mouth was moving. "Hamish, I'll take the price of one, if you have it."

"Sure." Ten was too much. Five would be enough for Lord Jock and William to get some good stuff. For a night.

There was no looking back; to the bald head and the skinny frame, and the bandaged arm above the bony hand that gripped the money. Just get clear of this place where bodies of men shuffled and slept beneath a television that made only coloured sounds. Bang the bars; bang the bars till he comes and fishes out that key. What takes him so long? Why does he have to lock it?

184

"Why do you have to lock the door anyway?"

"I assure, you, this is only a security measure. The residents, request it. To help keep out undesirables."

IT was Angela. No doubt about it. Angela. No one else had hair that colour. She had shrunk; or maybe it was just the coat. A suede coat strained tight against the hips. Maybe dumpy is the word. The fur-fringed cuffs of the coat were halfway up her arms; the arms looked stretched, pulled by the combined weight of the four plastic carrier bags. Two pairs; each pair bumping the front and the back of a knee. Both hands were pink turning blue with the cold. Two giant steps and one step to the side brought Hamish and Angela side by side.

"Carry your bag, Mrs?"

Angela was resisting, pulling the bags, stretching the handles.

"Eh? What?" Her face was flushed and she stopped. Angela Creese was looking at Hamish Creese and did not know him. A smile to reassure.

"I'll carry it for threepence, or ginger bottles if you've got any."

"Hamish, my God, Hamish. What on earth are you doing here?" Surprised, shocked, taken aback. But also embarrassed. Embarrassed to meet her brother.

"I've come to see you, what else? Here, give me a couple of them."

Two bags were slid from the white grooves along her fingers. Hamish transferred them, left to right, adding them to the one he already carried. His free arm he slipped through Angela's free arm. The coat was soft. Leaves on the trees in the gardens were in their autumn colours. Hamish Creese and his big sister were walking home on a Scottish autumn day with the messages for the tea. Hamish was walking quickly, gently pushing, and Angela laughing to the front, looking round, catching eyes, then laughing to the front again.

"Hamish, Hamish, take it easy, it's just along here."

"I know, I was here yesterday, and twice today, but there was nobody in."

"Oh that's a shame. Yesterday was the long weekend, and I worked in the mornings. Was there nobody in at all?"

"No, but don't worry about it, I went to see our beloved father instead."

"Oh. And how is he?"

"Ach. So-so. Maybe a bit more so than he used to be. It's in here isn't it?" The gate was a bad fit and scraped open on the concrete of the path. Berries filled the two rowans, all bent and pulled over, and intertwined to keep out the bad spirits. "Did you plant the trees?"

"No. They were here when we came here."

Angela put down her bags, flicked through the coins in her purse and found the key.

The door opened onto a small tight square of a hall. Two people and five bags manoeuvred, bags to bags, smile to smile, to allow the door to close. A door inside opened. A tall young man stood, one hand on the door edge the other on the opposite jamb, framed. He had Angela's colour of hair. Angela looked up from her purse. "Are you not away? I thought this was your signing-on day?"

"No. That's next week."

He let go his pose and threw himself into an easy chair, making it move. Hamish edged the bags through the door.

"Just leave them over there, Hamish, will you? Stewart. Get up and say hello to your Uncle Hamish."

The chair moved. "Hello."

"Is that the best you can do? Uncle Hamish hasn't seen you since you were a wee boy. Can you not be just a little more sociable?"

"Hello Uncle Hamish."

The chair reached a wall. Stewart was studying the scratching of a nicotine-stained finger. Angela kicked him on the leg.

"Go on you big . . . get out of my sight."

"Angela, listen, it's OK. I mean to say, Stewart hardly knows me. Sit where you are Stewart. Can I take my coat off, Angela?"

"Of course you can. Stewart, see if you can at least hang your uncle's coat up. Put it in your wardrobe up the stairs." A smile was a waste of time. The coat was taken away. Angela called from the kitchen. "Just ignore him, Hamish. He gets like that sometimes."

Conversation could be held better from the door of the kitchen. And Hamish could watch Angela working. Her fingers were still long, though a bubble of fat was falling back over her wedding ring. Without her coat she was not so dumpy. At full stretch to slide tins into high cupboards the outline of Angela was almost the same as the outline of the memory.

"I take it he's not working then?"

"Afraid not, Hamish. Stewart hasn't worked much since he left school. He was never very bright, but I think some of the people he did work for took advantage of him. You know, promising him things when all they wanted was a big strong boy. It's a bit late for him now. Never mind that, how are you? You look terrific."

"Ah, well, thanks very much. You're not looking so bad yourself. Here, I've brought something for you. It's just some duty-free. And this."

The yellow ribbon had stayed tied around the box. At the time the yellow had seemed the nearest colour to Angela's hair, but it was really too bright. Angela wiped her palms on the thighs of her skirt.

"What's this? For me? Hamish. That was awful nice of you."

Angela pulled the ribbon out of its bow. She had kept her fingernails clean and manicured. Her fingers reached in and lifted free the small fat bottle with the square crown stopper, and pale, pale liquid. Freddie.

"Freddie. Hamish, this is the best there is. It must have cost you the earth. Hamish, you really shouldn't have."

"Well, I was behind this bloke at the duty-free and he was buying some for his sister. I remembered that I too had a sister. Anyway, I wish you the best of health to wear it."

The crown was pulled off, the bottle turned upside down onto the tip of a finger. The head half turned, dipped, and dabs were spotted on empty earlobes. "This is lovely. Here, smell it." Angela held up the miniature decanter, turned her neck and flapped her earlobe with a finger.

"No thanks. I can smell it from here. I'm glad it suits you."

"Suits me? Do you really think so? Anyway I'll make sure it does. That was awful nice of you." Angela moved forward, stepped back, "Would you like some coffee or tea?"

"I think I'll have coffee, thanks."

"Right. Sit down and I'll be right with you."

"Can I use your lavatory first?"

"Don't be silly, of course you can. Upstairs, straight facing you."

A door on the top hall was open. Heavy breaths came from inside. Hamish peeked around the door. Stewart sat upright on the far edge of a bed staring out of the window. His shoulders rose and fell with the irregular breathing. A koala bear sat on the dresser. Tufts of fur were missing showing bald spots underneath. The koala. That was sent for a birthday. A long time ago. The first year after getting there. A furry koala sent for the wee man. He had got it all right. And kept it. The coat was on the bed.

"How're you doing, Stewart? I didn't realise you were so big. In fact, you're a man now, aren't you? I just kept thinking of you as a wee boy. I see you've still got the koala. That must have been a long time ago, eh?"

Only Stewart's shoulders moved. The body was straight, the head fixed, turned to the window. No reply came. There was silence in the room. Outside rain. Dreich. "I'll maybe see you later then?" Still the silence. Dreich inside. The lavatory was empty and smelled of wet unwashed towels.

The coffee was welcome. Hot, sweet; but conversation was needed. Little triangles of sandwiches were placed down, and a thin china plate full of round chocolate biscuits, all of which leaned one on another. Angela was fussing. Everything out, one item at a time. "Oh dear, I've forgotten the salt." "That's all right, this is fine, honest." "No, I'll get it."

Conversation was being avoided. Now the clacking of the teaspoon was being overdone. It had been a long time. Angela had been the last to write.

"I'm sorry I never answered your letter about Douglas. I never got it till recently. I was sorry to hear about it. But I should have answered."

"That's all right, Hamish. Don't worry aobut it. I just thought you might want to know about it. Never mind. How was Australia?"

Australia the diversion. Away from Douglas. Away from pain. Perhaps just as well. Douglas was the link. From Des to Angela to Gaffney. Best to keep it loose. Carefree in carefully chosen subjects.

"Ach, it was OK. But I cam here to hear about you; how have you been doing? What's been happening with you?"

Just the silly face and the shake of the head. She didn't want to tell. This was a skip around, no filling in, just the verbal gloss; more about life in Scotland than the life of Angela in Scotland. This place is . . .; fill in the blank from: done   finished   all change now. People are: only out for themselves   only helping their own keeping themselves to themselves   definitely all changed now. Angela is: sad   anxious   worried   all three.

"What about young Heather, is she still at school?"

"Yes. Oh yes. She's sitting her Highers next year and then she's hoping to go on." Angela jumped up. "Thanks for reminding me Hamish. She's in a hurry out tonight and I promised to have her good skirt ironed. Why don't you make yourself a drink with that stuff you brought? I'll take one as well."

Hamish removed the plastic bag from around the bottles as Angela pulled an ironing board from a cupboard.

"There's some lemonade at the side of the fridge, if that's whisky. There's glasses in that cupboard to your left."

Hamish poured as Angela clattered a tin ironing-table onto its legs. Angela almost finished the drink in one gulp and laid the glass on the sideboard. The skirt was tucked around, the pleats folded, straightened. Silently. Fingers were licked and tried to the base of the iron. It was replaced.

"I thought you were supposed to spit on it?"

"How's that, Hamish?"

"I read somewhere that if your saliva formed into a little ball and rolled off the base of your iron, then the iron was ready."

Angela poked her tongue out and in, in and out, working up a spit. A discrete spit was managed onto the bottom of the iron. A small white ball jiggled its way off.

"There you go. That's you ready."

Angela fetched a plastic basket full of washing, raking through it for the particular garment. "How did you manage when you were on your own? You that always tried to look smart."

"Ach, I just managed. I used to read all the wee columns you see in the papers about the thousand and one uses for glycerine and starch and how to tell if your iron is ready. I'm an expert on the removal of bloodstains, grease stains, beer stains, and any other kind of stains."

"Perhaps you should have got married." Angela pulled out the skirt, held it up. "Or was looking after one enough for you?"

Looking after one. Hamish Creese looking after Hamish Creese. Angela. Angela. What was behind that question?

"Maybe. At least I never had any arguments that way." Angela was not laughing. She was serious. Pass on. "I remember one landlady I had did my laundry for me, and she did the state premier's as well. Do you know she used two pegs to hang up his underpants and only one for mine?"

"Maybe he was a bigger bum than you."

"Angela's head was down, into the ironing board, hair hiding her face. She flicked it all up over, and stared. No smile, because no joke.

"Oh, I'm a bum am I?"

"Not really. I was only joking. Don't take it so seriously. Tell me about Australia." Angela was serious and was sorry because she was serious.

Tell Angela about Australia. Again. Tell Angela about Australia, and while Hamish Creese talks of Australia, Angela Creese will iron and switch off.

The outside door opened and closed. "That'll be Heather."

Heather pulled the door open and came in. She did not look like Angela at all. There were no Creese characteristics in that face. The lassie was tall; but dark, not even reddish like Hamish Creese and Lord John. Definitely dark.

"Is that my skirt you're ironing, Mother?"

"Yes, I'm nearly finished. But don't you know who this is?"

The eyes were dark too and didn't blink. Heather made a face and shrugged her shoulders.

"This is your Uncle Hamish."

"Oh, you're Hamish. That's a coincidence. I was reading your letters to mum only the other night. Mother keeps them in a biscuit tin with all the old death and birth certificates."

"Heather you did not. Those letters are private."

"Och mum. They're only from your brother, not your lover."

"It doesn't matter, my lady, they're mine, not yours."

"I'll get them when you die anyway."

"Oh God forgive you. I made sandwiches for you. While you're in there pour another drink for your Uncle Hamish and me."

Heather replenished the glasses, stuck a flop of a sandwich in her mouth and handed them over. "I loved those letters, they were quite poetic."

"Do you do poetry at school?"

"Well, sort of. I'm not awful good at writing it, but I enjoy reading it."

"Who's your favourite?"

"I don't really have any. I just like it if it makes me feel something. There was a bloke on the telly the other night reading some poetry about his time in jail. I thought it was good, you know, sad. Mum, what was that bloke's name again?"

Angela slid the skirt along the sideboard. "I don't know; I wasn't really watching. Look your skirt's ready."

Heather lifted the skirt from the sideboard, surveyed it, chomping at the sandwich. "By the way, is the doo-lally in? He owes me a pound."

"Heather. Don't call your brother a doo-lally. Do you hear me? Don't you call anybody names in here."

"Oh for goodness sake, mum, all he ever does is sit and look out that window. He's like a racing pigeon on strike. Honestly, he's pure catatonic."

Heather ran up the stairs. Angela reddened, slammed the ironing table shut and rattled it away into its cupboard in the kitchen. "Kids, Hamish. You don't know the half of it."

"She's not what I expected."

"Is she not? What did you expect? She's just a girl like any other girl."

"I know, I know, it's just that you wrote and said she looked like you, that's all." There was agitation here. Angela was not comfortable. Her face was tight, the smile was not a smile. None of them today had been a smile. More like attempts to stop watery eyes overflowing. Angela attempting to be tough. Life for the widow must be hard. "I just meant she's lively enough, that's all."

"Meaning what?"

"Eh? Meaning nothing. Nothing. Just she's lively. She just seems to have bags of energy."

"And Stewart hasn't?"

"Stewart? I wasn't even thinking about Stewart. I definitely wasn't comparing them."

"Hamish, you're still the same. You've been comparing everything in here since you came in."

Hamish is still the same. The same as when? The same as when? Angela had never said this before.

"Angela, what're you saying? Comparing what to what?"

"Oh everything to everything. Scotland to Australia, Heather to Stewart, and me to your memories. And everything to what you think it should be. Grow up Hamish."

The telephone rang. Angela crossed the room and answered it. A man called Gavin was coming at seven. Angela had a boyfriend and the long weekend had been lovely. Her laughs on the phone were genuine. Gavin would be here at seven. The phone call finished too soon, but at least it would help change the subject.

"Is this a boyfriend you have then?"

"Yes. And he drinks and he gambles and he's unemployed. Does that suit you?"

The poison was in flood. Hamish Creese was not wanted on voyage. Not today. Maybe never.

"Listen, Angela, I think I'd better go."

"Yes, I think you'd better Hamish. Gavin and I might decide to have it off on the carpet right in front of you. Now that would really upset you. Or maybe doo-lally Stewart will do a maddie on you. He does, you know."

The head was refusing to order the legs to push the body onto

193

the feet. The door was there, but far away. There was only Angela, left foot bouncing and wedding ring rapping flat on the glass.

"Angela, what's wrong with you? What have I done?"

"Nothing Hamish. Absolutely nothing. You've just come here Hamish. Just come back and been yourself. And you forget I can read you like a book. You sit there with your tan and your fancy clothes making judgements and wondering why everybody isn't like you. Thank Christ they're not. You know since Douglas died, Hamish, I've had a chance to think about all of the rubbish I've put up with over the years. I don't cry for others now Hamish. Only me. No more playing at cowboys for some John Wayne."

A clock somewhere ticked; the tap in the kitchen dripped, the arm at least made the stretch to place the glass on the coffee table. "Angela, I'll go away and come back another time."

"But that's what you're good at Hamish, isn't it? You go away and come back when you think it's all quiet on the western front. Then you can sidle in, unblemished, and make judgements on what you see. What you see. What you see and don't like to touch."

The brain gave the order, the legs stretched, but the feet wouldn't move. "Angela, I haven't a clue what you're on about. Maybe you shouldn't have had that drink."

"Oh, it's the drink is it?" Angela deliberately opened her mouth wide and let the remainder of the whisky flow, then turned the glass upside down and shook the drips onto a spread tongue. "No, it's not the drink with me Hamish." Her snarl was the same as Lord John's. Just more teeth showing. "Look at you. You come in here with a wee bag of duty-free and think that entitles you to re-enter my life. Reclaim a family with a bottle of perfume tonight. Or drink if they prefer it. Just a pity you were not here to help them with their struggle. But as always, Hamish Creese wanting the world to suit him. I should be a mourning widow, Stewart should be a doctor and Heather, what should Heather be Hamish? A poet, do you think?"

Angela lifted the cups through to the kitchen and clattered them along the sink-top. Hamish held out the salt cellar. "It's not for me to say anything about your two. But you know if I could've helped you only had to ask."

"Ask? Ask? Couldn't you think? No, you were quite happy to be free at the far end of an air-mail letter. A card at Christmas and duty-free whenever you came back. Oh yes, you've got away with the prize. But really you owe plenty. And you'll never be able to pay it back."

Someone was padding about upstairs. Flat-footed. The bass from a record player pounded on through the floor. A piece of coffee biscuit had stuck to Angela's chin. Hamish Creese should wipe away that crumb.

"Angela, I don't know what's bothering you. If I can help, I'll help, but honestly I haven't got a clue what you're on about."

"No. You don't have. And neither did Douglas. Just me. Angela. Just another mother that had to keep things to herself. Mustn't upset the men. Even when it's them to blame. Let it go. They've enough on their plates. Says bloody who?"

"Let what go? For Christ sake stop talking in riddles. Forget it."

The water was gathering behind the bottom lash, but there was not even an attempt at a smile. The kitchen was narrow. She could not get past.

"I meant to forget it. But do you really want to know? Why don't you take a right good look at Heather, Hamish? She's not like me, you're right. And she's not like Douglas either. She's yours Hamish. I paid for her. For you. Or maybe half for you, and half for Douglas."

Two clocks ticked; one in the kitchen and one on the wall above the sideboard. Angela turned back, snatched at the tap, turned it on, turned it off.

"Angela, talk sense."

"Certainly. Heather is Gaffney's daughter. But it's thanks to you."

A sneering dark-eyed face, nails and a hammer, pain and slime and the girl with the grin was the face's daughter. No.

"No. No. What are you saying? And how is it thanks to me?"

Angela was in charge. She had turned face on. Hamish Creese was stuck, unable to move, from the kitchen, from her face. How Hamish Creese?

"Remember I pawned your tools? Remember? I pawned your precious tools to save Douglas from a hammering; and because you were too miserable to lend us the money; because it was for Douglas."

"That's not true. You could have had it."

"Oh aye. Five days too late, when you were sitting there with a walletful. You were quite happy not to bother. I pawned your tools because it was quicker, but do you know something? I felt so guilty and sorry for you I paid Gaffney behind the door."

Gaffney and Angela. Angela and Gaffney. Grunting and groping in the high-ceilinged room. Douglas and his debt. Written off for a screw at the Lord John's daughter.

"You got your money and the ticket for your tools, Gaffney got what he wanted and Douglas never got touched. Just me."

Gaffney on Angela's body; pawing, slobbering, hawking greenspit.

"Angela why? Why the fuck why?"

"There you go again asking why, but making a judgement. I suppose I loved two men. Just a pity one was Douglas and the other was you. But never again. No way."

The chair was there against the wall. Hamish Creese had to find it; sit. Angela made Hamish Creese pay. She had saved it up and let him have it. Hamish Creese had paid. For what? Miserableness? Cowardice? Blindness? Hamish Creese was paying for something. Pain after pain and woe succeeding woe. And people slid off their chairs for Gaffney.

"Does Gaffney know about Heather?"

"Don't make me sick. I was watching her watch him the other night and I felt everything about that time all come back. I could feel his nails digging into me and his teeth in my neck and she was saying 'He's a fine boy, isn't he mum?'. And today you turn up. I can turn the telly off, but what do I do about you? I could bear it easier with you away and Douglas gone. But you're not just a reminder. You're a judge. Well, make your judgement, then it'll be done. finished. But you'll carry your share."

The living-room door clicked open. Heather poked her face in the door. She saw. She saw something, but was choosing to ignore it. Now her eyes looked familiar. The grin was as wide as ever.

"I'm off now, mum. Sorry I never had a chance to talk to you,

Uncle Hamish, maybe some other time. I really loved your writing, you know. See you, mum. I won't be late.."

Hamish stood up. A room had lost its cosiness and Angela was not for being Angela. "Do you think I could have my coat Angela?"

Angela nodded, stepped over, opened the living-room door and stood in the hall and shouted for Stewart to bring down the coat and come and say cheerio to his Uncle Hamish. There was no movement, no answer. Angela ran up the stairs in tiny steps and returned with the coat.

"He really is just a big doo-lally him. I don't know what I did to deserve him." She began to cry. "Hamish, I'm sorry, I . . ."

Hamish hugged his big sister with one arm and placed one finger over her lips.

"Sh. Sh. It's all right. She'll be right."

On the doorstep Hamish turned. "The perfume does suit you, you know. Make sure you wear plenty for Gavin."

Bigger pieces of rain dripped a semi-circle from the rowans. The gate scraped shut along the concrete.

H

☆ ☆

A GIRL in a pink trouser suit came over to the man in the shiny green suit with the dull brass buttons. Hamish Creese and partner did not have a large square ticket with frilly sides and a band of gold around the edges. Her short straight hair hung perfectly, but she flicked it back from the face it was not covering. The red bow under her nose parted and words came out. "Can I help?"

"They've not got a ticket."

"Oh, I see." She bent one leg up and pushed some pink trouser down into a stiff leather boot. She was buying thinking time. Hamish spoke.

"I'm real sorry, miss, I didn't realise this was a proper launch. I thought it was a public reading."

"Yes, well, actually it is a launch for Eddie's new folio. We are having a reading with other poets, but actually this particular evening is by invitation only."

"Oh gee, that's a pity. I've come a long way. I'm over from Australia on holiday."

"Do you read Eddie? Or better still, do you know him?"

Hamish began to reach to the inside pocket of his jacket, fumbling. "I am familiar with his work. Back home I write a literary column for the Townsville Telegraph and put out a programme of poetry for Queensland Radio. The QBA? 'If you're a vulture for culture, you're OK on QBA.' That's our jingle." The girl's red mouth had drooped further open. "I just thought I could have a nice evening with my girlfriend here and pick up some material while I was here. Eddie Gaffney has a following in Australia, you know."

The man with dull brass buttons was edging them all over, inwards, to get to more tickets.

198

"Oh. Right. Yes. that's true. Well. I'm Elena and I represent the publishers. Please go through, I'll see you later. Bye for now." Her wave and eyes were on someone else.

Hamish gripped Marianne by the shoulders and pushed through, past another man who gave them a programme, into the foyer, where people were doing their milling and mingling. Tables full of multicoloured-jacketed books lay along the length of each wall. Some piled one on one and others standing for attention. Marianne started to laugh.

"Was all that strictly necessary? That girl must think you're not quite right in the head."

"Nonsense. She thinks I'm a dinkum cultured Australian. Just shows you, nothing succeeds like a little bullshit."

"If you ask me it was your tan that did the trick."

Waitresses in flat shoes tramped around, smiling. Some had trays of white wine, some had trays of red. A tray came to them, was held out to them; they hesitated, and it was gone.

"Ah well. Easy come, easy go. What is the position here, Marianne? Drinkwise, that is."

"I think we can have all the wine and fancy biscuits we like, but anything stronger has to come from the bar down there."

"Bloody cheapskates. What's your poison?"

"Vodka martini, please."

Hamish went toward the bar; arm up, touching the shoulders of people who took tiny steps forward. Side-stepping the stuck-out arses of people spilling drinks, who were shaking their fingers and licking them and laughing, to show they just didn't care. It was all fun. At the bar thin lit glass bulbs shone through narrow tubes of glass to reflect bright from the glass of the gantry mirrors to the dimples of the beer glasses and the upturned bases of wine glasses held in reserve. A girl nodded at his request for a double whisky and vodka martini. He looked up from his wallet to find another girl looking at him anxiously.

"You getting it?"

"I think so, I mean, I've still to get a vodka martini."

"Right."

The girl with the whisky returned.

"Anything else?"

"No. I don't think so, that other girl is getting me a vodka martini."

"Who is?"

"She is."

"For the same order?"

"Well, for me, yes."

"Who told her to get it? Was it you?"

"Well, I, is there something wrong?"

"You're not allowed to have two serving you at the same time."

"Oh. I thought it was all right since it's all going on the same bill."

"Aye, did you? Well for your information it's not all right."

The girl with the vodka martini returned. The whisky girl pointed at an already speared cherry. "Is this for him?"

"That's right, him."

"I was serving him as well."

"For Christ sake, another diddy."

Two heads converged beside the till. Pieces of paper were compared, placed on the ledge of the till under the green digital light and surveyed again. Pencils were applied, paper rubbed, paper scrubbed. An older lady with no white cuffs to her blouse joined them. Her head turned slowly, looked at Hamish Creese hanging onto the bar. The queue was getting longer. All three women kept tutting and pointing their sharp pencils at Hamish Creese who stood with the queue behind him. The older lady came over and presented two slips of paper at Hamish.

"I must ask you not to do that again, sir." For an old lady she had a loud voice. The queue fidgeted; a man dangling two drinks stopped, his arms in mid-air, frozen; two eyes looked over a pint pot. "It's their commission, you see. The till works it out as they go. Now they've had to half you between them."

Hamish felt suitably sliced up. She was paid; he pocketed the change, left the two slips on the bar and escaped out from the baying crowd to find Marianne.

Marianne had found a little table in the centre of three chairs whose backs leaned away. "What took you so long?"

"There was a bloke made a bit of a blue there."

"You, you mean."

Even Marianne had noticed. Hamish manoeuvred himself down. The drink was out of the reach of his hand. He leaned forward, edging his buttocks up to the edge of the seat until he found a nearly suitable position for drinking. At the next table a group of people clustered around a podgy man in a white pullover. Men stood, one hand on glass; one hand in pocket. Ladies stood, thumbs on the stem, fingers under the bottom, glass held up. Some women sat, legs bent at the knee, ankles crossed, arm to support, forty-eight degrees from the shoulder, palm spread, with only the pinkie open. The men, glass lifted up, tilted, head back. The ladies, head forward, lips to the glass, suck or sip or syphon up a sniffy nose. The podgy man was grinning and scratching his head. He lifted his spectacles off and a cluster of accented laughter erupted. Tomorrow they would remember the gesture and know they had been in the great man's company.

Blue denim moved among velour and cord among velvet. Hand-made suits escorted peasant dresses. But the shoes were all shiny leather. No man-made uppers here. Hamish took a drink. Hamish Creese had a good suit on, leather shoes and a white shirt. But the mates that laughed at the jokes of Hamish Creese were probably singing and fighting their way out of Banjo Dilley's. Although Marianne was here, tugging at his sleeve.

"Hey mister. Watch it. I think a chip is beginning to show."

"Is it that obvious?"

"You're looking at everybody in here except me and your face is getting longer by the minute. Marianne says relax."

"Sorry. It's just these places. I don't think I'm cut out for them."

Marianne reached. Marianne hugged an arm to her. "Nonsense. They're only people. They're just other people, that's all. You really can't say anything about them if you don't know them." Hamish shrugged his shoulders. Marianne pulled harder at the arm. "There couldn't be a wee bit of jealousy there, could there? You must not compare yourself with other people, you know. Especially if you only know what you see."

"Drink your drink, Mrs, and tell me how your day went..."

Marianne had no chance to begin. Elena the publishing girl was standing at the end of the foyer. She was calling for Ladies and Gentlemen and tucking trouser into boot. The reading would begin in the Govan Room and now was the time to go through and secure a table. The leg was bent higher; more pink trouser being tucked into a black boot. She was a flamingo with an itchy foot. Wine would continue to be served between readings. Marianne stood up. Hamish Creese stood up. Together they finished their drinks.

Hamish Creese was twiddling with the buttons on his jacket. Hamish Creese was lifting a hand to Marianne's elbow, more to be held than to hold. Hamish Creese was clearing a throat that was empty above a stomach that was tight. Hamish Creese was walking inside this set of clothes. Feeling them from the inside, pinpointing the position of every fibre by its touch. Over to the queue, getting in line, squeezing into the security of the crowd, looking at the carpet on the floor. Do not disturb. Hamish Creese is studying the design in the carpet. The Coat of Arms of the City of Glasgow. Miss Martin had taught them that rhyme. Banging with her pointed on the drawing on the blackboard.

There's the bird that never flew
There's the tree that never grew
There's the bell that never rang
There's the fish that never swam

THERE'S THE GAFFNEY OVER THERE
GAFFNEY THERE   GAFFNEY HERE

In the same room, breathing the same air, and perfectly at ease. Signing books at a table, between the two other poets of the evening. An older man with white hair and a long-bodied man in a rough tweed jacket. The Poets of Scotia. And Gaffney was one. Or maybe he just had the same publisher.

Marianne led to a table which sat only two. Voices were rising, babbling, agreeing, disagreeing agreeably, exclaiming too loudly. Heads were nodding, quaffing, shaking, exaggeratedly laughing. Eyes were shifting, this way that way, seeking to see who was doing the seeing. Hamish Creese would have to look at Marianne. "Well, here we are. Not a bad crowd they've got."

"Yes, quite impressive Hamish. I feel quite excited." Where was Gaffney?

"Good, then you won't go to sleep on me then?"

"No; I don't think you'll have to worry about that, Hamish."

He's still there. The human flamingo introduced a man in a black suit as the representative of the City Gallery who proclaimed himself proud to be associated with this launch for Eddie Gaffney. He waved a book in the air. A green leather-bound volume of Gaffney's first collection, *Poems From Prison*, for the man himself. Claps egged Gaffney onto the small stage. Clap clap clap.

Gaffney was fit. Denim clothes were casual, but these fitted well; no pulling, no stretching of material. Gaffney's stomach was flat. Hair was curlier; hairline receding a little, but hidden well. The grin was the same. The voice was the same. Vowels were softer, smoother, but the voice was the same. The audience clapped his small sentence of appreciation and stopped only when he regained his chair. Marianne's claps were loud. CLAP CLAP CLAP. Marianne shouldn't clap.

"He's quite a mannish man, isn't he?" Mannish man. Man pish man.

"No doubts about it. Fancy him, do you?"

"Oh definitely. But you'll do for this evening." Concentrate. Calm calm.

A tubby councillor was wiping his brow and telling everyone how the whole evening was due to him. Applause was more than polite. Hamish Creese could only look to Marianne, hold himself in her face, talk to her.

"Do you think there's actually any poets here?"

Elena finished with the explanations and asked again for drinks only to be uplifted between readings.

The old man was first with a poem; of seers and of prophets who lived on the far isles in self-imposed exile because knowing the future they had to shun their people lest they love them and in the loving fear for them and attempt to change all history. His next told the tale of a mountain complaining of the cold because he stood in a cold dark loch with his head at the cold snow clouds of heaven. The poet read first in the Gaelic and then in English. People stared at each other and into their drinks as the sounds of the Gaelic washed over them. Applause for the man was loud and was long.

Marianne signalled a waitress and lifted two white wines from a tray. Hamish saluted with the glass. "You shouldn't mix the grape and the grain, you know."

"I'm hoping it'll melt you a bit. You're looking awfully serious."

"I'm sorry. I didn't realise. Maybe the Gaelic struck an old Celtic chord in me."

"God, that's all I need. A Celtic manic-depressive."

The poems from the man in the tweedy jacket. In the preparatory explanation his head jerked from left to right as his shoulders alternately rose and fell. One up, one down. One shoulder always lay higher than the other and he appeared unsure as to which way to droop. His poems were a grey humour. Not black. Not hilarious. Grey. First person grey. Everyone clapped him off, except the podgy man in the white pullover who scratched his head till his hair stood up like a coxcomb, and the young man with his back against the wall and knees up. He was fast asleep. Gaffney was next. Hamish Creese had to pull himself away from the looks of Marianne, look round to the stage, look at Gaffney, see Gaffney, hear Gaffney. Gaffney made no explanations as to the genesis of his poems. He read them and people listened. The first two were read over while Hamish Creese was taken elsewhere. Mind pushing memory back. Mind rescuing Hamish Creese from his memory. Concentrate. This is the last. The applause for the previous set was settling down, glasses were being sipped at, bums and buttocks shifted. Gaffney was speaking.

"This last poem is called 'Run'.

> The inarticulate pain in your head
> Beats me down,
> Keeps me down,
> Till I rise,

Still here,
Alive.

The stapped-up stench of your bile
Hurts my nose,
Bursts my nose.
Till I rise,
Still here,
Alive.

Alive.
Still here,
But risen.
Affronting you
Confronting you
The trusty guardians of my time.

The tight-shut teeth of your mouth
Nip my skin,
Rip my skin.
Till I rise,
Still here,
Alive.

Alive.
Still here,
But risen.
Facing you
Chasing you
The trusty guardian of my time.

Better flee.
There's more like me."

Gaffney's voice was deep and the poem was read well. All inflections, hushes, pauses and stresses, used to the best of effects. And no need for any critical structuralist analysis. The meaning was there; staring you in the face. The meaning was known, and there was no sound from the listeners. No one smiled, and there was hesitation before the muted reserved applause. A reservation which had its genesis in the expression of the poem, the terseness of the text, and the intensity of the author. And Gaffney's stare. Gaffney had to crack jokes and they were all relieved. The accented laughter came down with the rest. Gaffney had struck gold.

"Hamish. Didn't you like that poem? I never saw you clap. I thought they were all excellent. Especially that last one; he made it kind of creepy. I kind of, I don't know, kind of felt threatened by it."

"Yes."

Gaffney had told the story with little recourse to adjective or verb. Invective in poetic staccato running. Elena called time out.

"Hamish, I'm afraid I'll have to visit the ladies." Hamish stood up. Marianne gathered her bag and left. Hamish Creese had to try not to look at her from behind. Hamish Creese had to stare at the wall. Stare at the wall, Hamish Creese. Light brown plywood panelling, veneered; fixed with darker brown $2\frac{1}{2}'' \times \frac{3}{4}''$ strapping, with $\frac{1}{2}'' \times 3''$ chamfers cut to simulate the highly desirable olde worlde that only needed the pewter pots for to hang from hooks. The ashtray; bottle green glass with white lettering. How many four-letter words in LAGER. Some of the white paint was flaking. RAGE. L was disappearing. Three little depressions to take smoking cigarettes. LARGE. Did Gaffney smoke? Marianne didn't smoke. Hamish Creese didn't smoke. Did Gaffney smoke? Never mind Gaffney. Gaffney was there; behind; somewhere; probably signing the books with his face on the cover. Looking at the wall wasn't so good. Hamish Creese had always looked out from a back to the wall. Staggered; the chamfers on the wood on the wall were staggered; one left side, one on the right side. All the way up. Staggered. Or all the way down. Gaffney was probably there behind. Gaffney the mannish man. RAGE LARGE RAGE. The mannish man. The man. The man himself. Gaffney. A man from the same gutter now sitting easy with the velvet jackets and the round vowelled accents. Sitting easy with his conscience. Something was wrong. Maybe this lot had forgotten.

Maybe they had forgotten because to them it was just a story. Maybe just a continuing serial, where the past bits didn't need to fit the latest bits. Only what was happening the now was important. REGAL. Who keeps continuity, when to be careless is easier on the brain. LARGE REGAL RAGE. Hamish Creese was part of a forgotten storyline. Hamish Creese was a forgotten episode. A blank in the rhymer's verse. A dissonance in the rhyme. Leave it out. The story should be made complete. An epic simile for the epic poem of Gaffney. Hamish Creese. Gaffney and Hamish Creese. A tale, tales, to be told, but not finished with words. Words were for rationalisation, as well as poems. For analysing. Above and outside of feeling. Rational words were the beginnings of sedentary understanding and forgiveness which all added up to a forgetting. Words could be devious bastards. Words could be useless bastards. She'll be right. There's more than words to come. A hand, female, patting the shoulder.

Elena's smile, set in its glossy parenthesis, was being aimed down. Gaffney was at her back. But this was not the place. Not the time. But it was coming.

"Hello again. Are you enjoying it? I've brought Eddie over to see you. Thought perhaps you might like to do a piece for your journal." Now the smile was aimed at Gaffney. "Eddie, I promised that little man from the BBC a word, but I'll catch up with you before the discussion starts."

She kissed Gaffney on the side of the mouth. That mouth. That mouth and Angela's mouth. Gaffney sat down on Marianne's chair. Two tartan-sleeved arms came out of loose blue denim sleeves and turned the green ashtray around in pale fingers. He broke the silence. "Elena tells me you're an Australian poetry buff; I'm afraid I don't really know much about their stuff myself. What was the name, by the way?" You should know the name.

"Lawson. Harry Lawson."

"Hey. There's an accent in there, isn't there? You're not Australian, are you?" Where? How?

"Afraid not. I'm as Scots as you are. Glasgow, actually. South Side."

"Is that right?" The ashtray turned in the opposite direction.

Gaffney did not want to remain on the South Side. "How come you do radio in Australia?"

"Oh, I just kept writing wee pieces and sending them in until they all of a sudden asked me." How was easy? Where? Where?

"Elena reckons my stuff sells very well in Australia. How is that?"

"Australians buy an awful lot of books. But as far as your stuff's concerned I reckon it's because your story relates to their own early background. You know, the convict legacy, and all of that stuff. Overcoming hard times and authority. Nothing an Aussie likes better than a battler."

"So I'm a battler am I? Well, if that's a compliment, you'll need to say thanks for me if you're writing a piece."

"Sure. In fact I've got a better idea, just listening to you; why don't you say it yourself?" This where was correct.

A waitress proffered a tray of drinks. Hamish lifted off two glasses. Gaffney waved a palm. One was replaced. "What's your idea?"

"Well, it's not original really, but I'd like to do one of those hometown interviews. You know the type of thing: walk along with you where you were brought up, ask you some questions, all the usual stuff. Maybe just a walk from the Toll to the Cross, giving it memory lane, that kind of thing."

"It's not my cup of tea."

"It wouldn't take long. When I go back I can edit the stuff and intersperse it with your poetry. In fact I might even read it myself. In my best Glasgow accent, of course." The wine had been lying long and was bitter. The stare was quizzical. The base of the glass could be hid behind. Gaffney laid the ashtray to rest.

"Sounds good. But I don't go back there, there's nothing there. I've never been back. Not once."

"There's always a first time. And let's face it, this is the only kind of way Eddie Gaffney is going to be able to promote his stuff in Australia. And you'll be giving another wee Glasgow boy a national scoop."

Gaffney shoved the ashtray away, shoved the chair away but didn't rise. "How long will this take? I'll tell you why, I've to be in the city on Friday, at some bookshop or other. You might give me an excuse to get away."

"It won't take long. I know what I'm about."

Gaffney rapped his fingers on the table and pushed a lower lip out over an upper. "I don't know. It's really not my cup of tea. The idea's OK, but, ach, I don't see myself in it somehow. I don't fancy it."

Gaffney was preparing to go, to wherever he goes, to his friends and fellow poets. Catch him. "Can we leave it loose? If you fancied doing it I could meet you at the Park subway. Would that suit you? The whole thing will last about an hour."

"Look, this thing doesn't finish till the back of three, I couldn't be down there before four. That's if I come at all."

"Four would be fine. And if you don't turn up, you don't turn up. I'll maybe get you some other time."

Gaffney rose. Hamish Creese stood up. Hamish Creese took the hand of the evening's *cause célèbre*; Gaffney: poet, media figure. And here was Marianne rushing.

Marianne was pushing through the chairs, around the tables, pushing past the people coming and going or simply standing; she was rushing all the way up to stand shiny-eyed between Hamish Creese and Gaffney. "Oh. I'm out of breath." She placed a hand on Gaffney's forearm. "Oh." Fingers spread, hardly disturbing the material of the jacket. The other hand was rubbing her chest. "Goodness, I think I've overdone it, but I wanted to catch this man here. C'mon, aren't you going to introduce us?"

"Mr Gaffney, this is Miss Marianne Munn. She's a keen fan of yours."

Marianne had to transfer a book from her left to her right to shake the outstretched hand. "I don't know about a fan, well I suppose I must be, I've just queued to buy your book. Would you autograph it for me?"

Gaffney took a pen from his breast pocket, silver with a black heart design on the clip, took the book and opened the cover. "What shall I put?" The pen was stuck between pursed lips, brought out and put to paper. "There. I hope that's OK. Now I'll really have to go or my friends will think I've deserted them."

Gaffney stepped away, stopped, faced backwards. "I'll see you Friday then?" Hamish pointed a finger and thumb.

"Look forward to it." Marianne cried thank you after the receding back.

"See what he put Hamish. 'To Marianne. Hope it was worth the wait.' He really is very nice, isn't he?" Her head never rose. All she could do was read and read that message on the page. She closed the book. "What was that about you meeting him on Friday? Are you really?"

"Yes. It seems we have a lot in common."

"Really? You and him? Is that why you're meeting him? Where are you meeting him?"

"I'm not sure. We're thinking of going for a pub lunch round about the Toll, or the Cross maybe. It's only for a wee talk about old times. Marianne, do you mind if we skip the discussion? I'm feeling hungry. How do you fancy a vindaloo? A sitty-doon one I mean."

"I think I would prefer Italian. I'm all gone just now. One poet writes in a book for me, and another offers me out to dinner. 'A loaf of bread, a jug of wine, and thou.' I think I'm getting quite romantic. Definitely make it Italian, all this poetry is rushing to my head."

"Mine too."

The man with the dull brass buttons opened the door for them. Beside him a white chipped enamel bucket was filled with large square tickets with frilly sides and gold around the edges. All torn up.

☆☆

THE stairway was tiled; rectangular cream tiles with a border of dark green bevelled tiling. The wood on the banister was polished smooth with shiny brass studs sticking up every yard of its length. Book title: *Nail on the Banister* by R. Stornoway. No arse had ever slid down this banister. No happy paper-boy or over-anxious tick-man had ever used this one as a get-away. Half-landing windows were of stained glass: golden yellow and red and blue panels; straight stretching lines of an art nouveau that stemmed from Charlie Rennie Mackintosh, who made latticework tea-rooms full of secret space and narrow tight boxes that shut in the cash girl. Doors on the landings were solid, with large brass handles set in star-shaped fingerplates. This stairway had made little concession to time; all the way up; somehow it had stuck. No change of tenant here had brought change here. Each new tenant was probably happy to wallow in the inherited solidity and put on airs of a long dead time. Tiles, stained glass, brass handles, polished banisters with shiny brass studs; silly things to feel inferior about. But Hamish Creese did. The Creese's close had been flaking brown paint and chipped plaster, and it mattered.

"You should have told me you were up the three flights."

"Oh, come on, a big man like you. I'm sure you're only pretending."

Marianne's door was a panel of frosted glass. Marianne inserted her key, swung the door open, stretched her hand in, put on a light. She stepped inside and held the door open. It was as expected. Modern. Bold reds cooled only slightly by tinted whites. The piano in the hall was out of place. An upright black, old, completely out of tune with all this colour.

"Can you play this thing?"

Marianne lifted the lid and played some notes with one hand.

"Of course I can. My father was a great man for the piano when he was younger. This was his."

"Hughie?"

"Yes, Hughie. Why not Hughie?" Hamish shrugged. Marianne sat sidesaddle on the stool. "What would you like?"

"Can you play far away?"

"Is that the best a man of the world like you can do?"

Marianne began to play. The tune was 'Autumn Leaves'. Melody was interspersed with long runs, tinkling slow runs and leaves were falling. "C'mon, what's your pleasure?"

"Do you know 'John Brown's Body'?"

Marianne dropped a hand toward him. "You sing it and I'll put the coats away."

Hamish took his coat off, singing, "Solidarity Forever, Solidarity Forever, Solidarity Forever, and the union makes us strong."

Marianne reappeared from a room. "Hamish. That is not quite what I had in mind. Neither am I quite in the mood for any more jingles. Surely you know something better than that?"

Marianne sat on the stool. She had changed into little woollen slippers. Marianne Munn was at home and Hamish Creese was with her.

"Well, the only piano thing I know is something that goes la di da di da di da dee dum."

Marianne was giggling. Trying not too hard not to. Spluttering. Hamish laughed. Loud. Open. Hamish Creese the bear couldn't sing. So he laughed at himself with a woman who laughed and laughed and shook her head at Hamish Creese. Hamish Creese was having fun. Marianne checked herself by biting her top lip. "I think I know what you mean, believe it or not." Small fingers moved the keys. Right hand played the la di da di da di da dee dum. Left hand stretched over to pick out stronger more definite notes. Melody came. Notes ran to support. Her back was straight. Marianne was lost in the melody. She was part of the melody. Hamish Creese had overdone the wine. The hands played and finished; held above the keyboard, not moving lest the sound waves be disturbed. Hamish clapped.

"What's it called?"

"Für Elise."

"That's right. I don't know why it is but that tune stuck in my brain. I listened to a bloke play it on a piano in a bar right out in the Bush. I don't know how they got the piano there in the first place, but this young labourer spotted it and began to play it. It was really weird; he played this tune and cried his eyes out. Everybody just standing there with the dirty vests and getting into the beer, nobody bothered about him. But when he started to cry, everybody shut up. Nobody looked at him, but we all shut up." Marianne closed the lid.

"It's a nice piece. But go through to the living-room and I'll get the coffee on."

Living-room the same as the rest. Modern. Standard lamps, table lamps; all with the droopy head of an early snowdrop. Prints in aluminium frames of sharp-featured girls with flying red hair and silver-haloed knights with plume, helmet and lance. Black glass tables on chromium legs and narrow high bookshelves with very few books. *William Morris: A Spirit Lives On; The Scottish Renaissance: Fact or Fiction?* Gaffney's book would go there; in the middle.

Coffee was brought through and she sat as she had sat that other evening in the room. This time there was no hole in the foot of her stocking. Marianne skimmed a spread across a digestive and bit through it.

"I don't know about you, Hamish, but I've had a really nice night. That meal just finished it off."

"Well, you chose the place; I would never have known it. There's an awful lot of restaurants in this area, isn't there? I would never have known which one to go to."

"Just depends on the mood you're in, doesn't it? Tonight I felt Italian."

"Can't say as I've ever felt Italian. Or like a Chinese or an Indian either for that matter." Hamish was trying to scrape the last of the spread from the knife to the biscuit. The biscuit broke. Crumbs were picked up from trouser legs as the fingers tried daintily to hold the two main pieces together. "I must be honest,

I'm not exactly a bon viveur. I'm afraid I'm too used to the cardboard carton and the can of beer."

"That's only because you're too lazy."

Picking biscuit crumbs into the mouth was like feeding a budgie. "Lazy?" How do you mean lazy?"

Marianne folded an arm across her middle, waited till she had finished chewing. "Well, in that restaurant. You let me do the ordering while you did your boy from the sticks act. And it is just an act. You're simply too lazy to be bothered taking an interest. Either that or you're afraid your bear pals might get to hear about it, in case they laugh at you. Hamish. There are bigger bears than you can carry themselves off in any particular place." Marianne tapped her head. "I think you're just a touch silly about it."

The two main pieces fell. Slippy side down; right on the kneecap. "Silly? I didn't do anything silly did I?"

"No. Of course not. What I mean is you don't want to learn; you don't want to change your ways. It's almost as if you're afraid some other people will disapprove of the changes. You must carry your judges about with you." She was bending over, placing her cup into its saucer, but looking, checking for reaction. "Hamish, this is the nineteen-eighties. If you want to do something, you do it. Never mind what other people think."

What other people think of Hamish Creese. Lord John. Hamish Creese didn't give two fucks for his Da. Angela. Hamish Creese liked to hide at the far end of an airmail letter. Hamish Creese. Hamish Creese. Hamish Creese had Hamish Creese up to the eyeballs.

"I think I preferred you playing the piano."

Marianne shook her head. Shook her head till her hair shook.

"There you go. 'Drink your drink, Mrs.' 'I think I preferred you playing the piano.' Getting too near Hamish Creese, so let's be macho."

"You seem to have me worked out for somebody that hardly knows me."

"Oh I know you all right, I know you."

Marianne stood up and lifted the tray. She held the tray steady as fingertips of crumbled biscuit were rubbed on the the tray. She talked as she walked. "Hamish, I'm a primary teacher. I've seen young kids with their ideas already fixed at the age of twelve. Good teachers are good and all bad teachers are nasty. I always hope their ideas change when they get older and realise the world is just full of fallible human beings." Hamish followed her into the kitchen, but stood, unsure what to do. "I think you're a wee bit like that Hamish. I think a lot of your ideas are fixed. Fixed from another time, while you've grown up holding onto them. You can lock yourself out of a lot of what is going on if you're like that."

"Am I like that? Really?"

Marianne switched off the light as they left the kitchen. Halfway across the living-room floor she stopped, turned and lifted his hand in her fingers. "Poor Hamish. I'm afraid so, just a little. Look, do you dance? I bet you've never learned to dance."

A cassette tape was selected from a plastic file, placed into a music centre. Buttons were clicked until Marianne was happy. The final button pressed, she swung round on a flourish of skirt. The music was featureless; slow, a string orchestra stringing along on the clack of a drummer's beat. Left foot was lined up to right and right foot to left foot. Hamish was drawn in. In her stocking soles she was a little smaller. Not much, but enough that her eyes had to look up. Brown. One arm was lifted up, held up, the other placed around her waist. With the hand on his waist she began to push; backwards, backwards. A squeeze of the hand in hers to stop, turn. Space was confined. A narrow strip of carpet between table and chairs and the window on the wall. Steps were small. Back, back, pause, forward, into the turn, turn turn, backwards go. Marianne's hair was rubbing on the cheek of Hamish Creese.

"Why are you so tense, Hamish? Oh Christ, Christ, mind my toe. My toe."

She hopped to a chair and sat down, placing the injured foot on the opposite knee, and working the toe between fingers and thumb. Hamish stood.

"Oh don't just stand there, do something."

Do something. Do something. Do something for a toe that had been flattened.

"Do you want a cold compress?"

215

"I'll compress your blooming head." The toe was being rubbed more vigorously. A concerned Hamish sat down opposite. Marianne laughed again. "Oh don't look so bloody helpless, it's me that's got the sore toe." Marianne inclined into a chair, at an angle, but the body almost straight; stretching her legs, wriggling her toes. "It's all right, Hamish. There is nothing broken. And I think I know the cure for you."

The cure. Hamish Creese must be ill. Must be sick. Maybe people will come and visit and bring chocolate. Orange Cream.

"What's that?"

"TLC."

TLC. TLC. Sounded like the stuff Mammy dished out on the first day of the holidays. Drink up, it's for the change in the water.

"TLC eh? What on earth is TLC?"

"Tender Loving Care."

Tender Loving Care for Hamish Creese. Hamish Creese approves. Give Hamish Creese TLC and he'll become suave and know his way around a cheeky wee head waiter. A hand was reaching across, taking a hand. "Don't worry. I'm not after your body. Well not yet, anyway. You're far too intense, Hamish." She kissed the hand, picked up the other and held the two palms together. She picked at the finger ends. "Honestly, you're far too intense." The hands were moved apart and she slid off the chair to kneel between the legs of Hamish Creese. La di da di da di da dee dum.

"Why are you tense, Hamish?"

"I didn't know I was until you mentioned it."

"You are. Constantly wound up. Watching, taking note of everything that goes on around you."

"I'm sorry. I hope it didn't spoil your evening."

"It didn't." She reached; both hands clasped around Hamish's neck. Hamish's head was brought forward; gently. He was kissed. On the mouth. Suffocatingly soft. Marianne jumped up.

"I think maybe we'd better let that be enough of TLC for this evening. I don't want those judges you carry around in your head to disapprove of me, do I?"

"Whatever you say. I'm completely in your hands, doctor." Hamish stood up.

"You don't have to go right now; I can make more coffee."

Conversation might come with the coffee. Conversation that would surely wind round to the subject of a tense Hamish Creese. Enough had been said for one night.

"No thanks, Marianne. Anyway, your old mother will be watching the clock on the wall."

Marianne didn't argue. She recovered the coat from the room, held it open for him to slip into. She turned Hamish around, and dusted non-existent flecks from the grey wool. Her last kiss was quick; softer.

Hamish Creese turned for the door. She watched as he went down the stairs, looking back, looking up. She called.

"Hamish, I'll maybe see you Friday. I'm coming over to collect baby Daniel. If I leave him over there much longer, they'll steal him off me."

Hamish nodded, waved. Near the bottom he felt like sliding down the banister. Then he remembered R. Stornoway.

☆　☆
☆☆
☆

☆

THE doors of the orange train closed together: black rubber to black silent rubber; acting on a release of air from somewhere, triggered off by someone, someone up at the nose tip of the train, sight unseen. The train rattled away and was gone, off into the tunnel, bumping sideways on the tracks which circled the city. Off to lay down more people, pick up more people, carry more people round the underground system. All from, to and at their stations, and continuing around. Two tracks: clockwise and anti-clockwise, and sometimes the lights of the train on the opposite track could be seen passing as a quick blur through maintenance gaps in the tunnel wall. Only sometimes they arrived at the stations together. There was only one train arrived at Park station. Only one person got off at Park station; only Hamish Creese. An empty platform and it was already four o'clock on a Friday.

New narrow platform and new narrow stairway, finished off with little steel barriers to filter people through with a click, for their own safety. No need for width; not anymore. There was nothing left here at Park. Or very little. The forge, the crane-works, the jam factory; all gone. Gone with the buildings of the people who had made hammers bounce on anvils, put rivets along the gantries and sweetened the preserve for the shopkeepers. There would be no rush, crush of bodies here anymore. No last horn would be blown to set off the bolt from the gate, the stampede of tackety boots, the familiar yells and insistent bicycle bells. No need for a wide entrance, passage and stairs, to funnel the crowds. Funnel them to the trains standing ready to funnel them to stations further up the track, where they would be jostled by another mass being funnelled to the station left behind. No mass here. Only a solitary individual; Hamish Creese. Stepped off a train modern and empty, at a station modern and empty, into the old district, dead and empty. Empty but for the Clyde Vaults and the tenement shell above; standing, propped up, waiting. Waiting for Gaffney and it was five-past four.

Six-past four; no one on the outline of the streets that was traced out by broken pavements and tarmacadam which merged into dust at the edges. Never noticed before; the jaggy coronets of the university could be seen now, away down there, over, right across the empty Clyde where a ferry used to chug and smoke and cross. The university only seen now the tenements were flattened. Whole streets away, whole tribes away. Away. Thirteen families to a close, unable to see beyond the tenement in front, the tenement to the back. Hang out the window they could all see the comings and goings against the backdrop of the tenement block across the road, up the road, down the road; or the wall of the church or the boilermakers' yard. At night little Hamish Creese had tiptoed across the floor past Angela's bed to watch the blue white light come and go through the glass panels of the boilermakers' roof. Sharp straight-edged light cutting through glass panels which were still streaked black from the nights of the blackouts. Brilliant illumination from something a man was doing. A welder tacking and running out strength. Flashlight disappearing somewhere between the chimneys and the stars. Nobody here now to see, nothing much to see. An empty oil tanker was riding high on the river. Only Hamish Creese. And maybe Gaffney. And even he would have to be reminded.

Thirteen-past four. Another subway underfoot and no Gaffney. No; Gaffney wasn't coming. Perhaps the chance had gone. The chance had been at the City Gallery, in front of Gaffney's own kind. Own kind. Were those Gaffney's own kind? Serious but laid back with it, tensely standing, one leg crossed over the other, nodding rapidly rapidly and letting out embarrassed laughter with an accent and swallowing slices of culture whole. Soft hands, loud voices. Was Gaffney in with them now? Rebuilt. A new man. Maybe. Maybe a new man built on the old. A rehabilitated man. A man who had been rehabbed. A poet. A polished coarse speaker of the words. Aggression only in rhyme. Violence only in staggered stanzas. Hamish Creese I fling a word at you. Do what you like to me and I'll answer you with a poem. A reformed man. The pen is mightier than the hammer. Rehabilitated; nearly brand new. Lord John's eye, Angela who? That guy? All in the past. Maybe. From another time, another place, under other conditions, caused by another man. A man alive before the struggles written in the poetry gave birth to the new. A man now dead, but never to be buried. Cancelled out, erased, but with traces that would show.

Or maybe he's positively brand new. A man now without crime. All that was another Gaffney. Some other man had driven in the nails, dropped the bag, hawked the spit and pished the piss upon the clothes that were Hamish Creese. Overalls were not the definitive Hamish Creese. Working boots were not Hamish Creese. Hamish Creese was his clothes, his style. Everybody knew Hamish Creese by his style. Good suits, good jackets, the best of footwear; these were Hamish Creese. Clothes that had to be the best to combat any traces of the poverty that used to be, and give confidence where there was none. The clothes declared Hamish Creese, a man who had had his struggles. Now there was only one struggle left to make Hamish Creese complete. At one with the Then and the Now. Gaffney was needed.

Gaffney was needed. Gaffney would learn that the pain of the other past people had to be the pain of Gaffney. The pain of Hamish Creese had to be made known to this new man. Gaffney needed to know the pain of an ordinary man, ripped from his roots and sent spinning, loose and lost. Torn from his track never knowing the whys or the wherefores. Gaffney would learn and if he became truly repentant Hamish Creese might forgive and be absolutely at peace. But he must feel the pain.

Gaffney would fight back. He would. He definitely would.

Twenty-past four. Another subway rumbled under and no

Gaffney. The game was a bogie. Gaffney was not coming and the Clyde Vaults had a droopy look. A walk along for another look inside; hear the click and clack of the dominoes, the cheers and shouts for the winners' beer, the thud of the darts, the exclamations of the thirsty. Just to remember. The Clyde Vaults was a good shop. Everybody knew everybody. Everybody knew Hamish. Bonzo, Den, Jake and Jacky Johnstone and his mate from up the butcher's close. The steel strap still hung down. Hamish Creese stood back, one hand angled into the slit which served as a pocket, the other gripping the small black leather case slung round the shoulder. The varnish on the door had worn well. Ernie, Pie, Matt and Henry. Not one had moved as the nails went in.

"Bastards. The whole fucking lot."

The door was kicked open. It flew back and the steel strap fell flat with a couple of clangs that were hardly heard. "Bastards."

"Lawson. Lawson." The voice was from behind. "Harry Lawson."

A faint shout, but there. Hamish Creese turned round, but stayed under the damp wooden props. Gaffney was running from the subway, waving, calling out that name. He was here. And he was coming to Hamish Creese. Wait. Let the running man come on. Let him come here to the Clyde Vaults. Let Gaffney come to meet Hamish Creese.

Gaffney avoided a brick on the pavement, kicked it to the side. "I'm glad I caught you. I took a chance you might be waiting."

"That's OK; I was just taking a trip down memory lane here."

"Aye, well, that's what I came down for. I've only come to say I can't help you today, but if you and your girlfriend fancy coming out for a meal tomorrow I'll give you whatever you're looking for. But right now I've got to rush."

Hamish Creese stood, nodded. Creese placed a hand on Gaffney's arm, gripped it, beckoned with a finger and backed off past the outer door. Nearly in already. "Come in here a minute. I just want to see what you make of this."

"Look I don't go this kind of caper at all, and I've got people waiting." But Gaffney followed on, as Creese's back pushed apart the swing doors. "Look pal, will you let the arm go? I'm afraid I'll have to leave you to it." But Gaffney was in, as Creese looked and engaged the eyes. "Is there something not quite right about you? Look, if you come out with us tomorrow I'll give you all the nostalgia crap you want. And we can be a bit civilised about it." Through. In.

Creese let the arm go and walked through the dirt and the grime to the other end of the bar. Gaffney stood, watching. Creese pointed to a spot on the floor beside the buckled brass fireguard.

"Do you remember this bar, Gaffney? Do you remember this bit here?"

Gaffney frowned, hesitated, walked down and stopped, face to face with Creese. A glance at the area the finger was pointing to, then he spoke.

"I don't know what you think you're on, but this man's not playing. Don't bother coming for that dinner; you've had your lot."

Creese moved slowly. He slipped the black leather case from his shoulder and placed it on the bar. He turned his back on Gaffney, leaned on the bar, clasped his hands, and looked straight ahead. Gaffney stood, silent.

"Do you remember crucifying a guy here?"

"Crucifying? What're you talking about, crucifying? I never crucified anybody." Creese opened his palms turned them to Gaffney. Each palm had a circle of white in the centre.

"That right? Do you remember an old guy getting some tumbler in his eye?"

"What's the score here? What are you trying to say? Get to the point, whoever the fuck you are."

"Creese. Hamish Creese. That's who the fuck I am."

Gaffney shrugged his shoulders. "And what's this to be then? Are you working something out here? Wee bit revenge maybe? Is that what this is all about?"

"You tell me, Gaffney. You're the educated man here. All those books you get in jail and the wee letters after your name. You tell me."

"Well, if you're trying to make me have a go at you, you're not on. I'm not doing any more time for anybody, if that's the way your mind's working."

Gaffney stood still.

"You might have done time Gaffney, but you weren't punished for what you did to me, and my old man, and and, and maybe some others. Do you know what I mean? Did the one punishment wipe the slate clean? Tell me Gaffney."

"Listen pal, you don't need to talk to me about punishment. I lived my punishment, every day was a punishment." Gaffney turned, leaned on the bar clasped his hands. "I could write a book about punishment."

Creese turned his head to look at Gaffney. "Well, tell me this, how do you know when somebody's had enough punishment?"

"What kind of crap is that to come away with? I know I had more than enough."

"You reckon? I'll tell you what I reckon Gaffney." The black leather strap was lifted, flicked clear off the case. It fell in a loop of dust across the bar. "I think a man's only been punished when he realises the full consequences of his actions and is sorry, genuinely sorry."

"Sure, put him in a wee black hole till he sees the light. That's really good."

"That's not what I meant Gaffney. That treatment only hardens the man. And it might even make him think that the brutality cancels out his own, then he'll never be sorry for anything. No, that's not the answer."

The chromium clasp on the leather case was snapped open, the top hung loose.

"So that's it? If you're after a wee bit of the old eye for an eye stuff, then that'll only make you as bad as me. If that's what's in your mind."

"Up to a point I agree with you. But you see Gaffney, the point about it all is that folk like you should know they've not been like other men."

"And are you for making me like other men? If it helps you any I'll promise never to steal another bar of chocolate in my life."

The lid of the case was flipped open.

"You misunderstand me Gaffney. You can't just act like other men, you have to feel for them, understand them. Realise they're just like you. Sympathy, Gaffney, but even that is just a bit of it. It's the sympathy that leads to conscience Gaffney, and I didn't hear any of it in your poetry."

"Sorry about that. Look, there were lots of reasons for me doing what I did, but what's done is done: I've exchanged lots of present time for my past, and that's about all there is to it.."

An Edinburgh hammer and two long nails were taken from the case and placed upon the bar. Even in the gloom the nails shone and the handle of the hammer reflected light. Gaffney made no move, but looked.

"That's my problem, Gaffney. You see, I have to know that you are genuinely sorry. And you're only going to be that when you're able to feel what I felt."

A finger pointed. "You nailed me here, Gaffney, my old man ended up with one eye because of what you did here, but do you know what was the worst, Gaffney? A big green goggle brought out from up your nose and spat into my mouth and the pish of strange people in my shoes. You did that to me Gaffney and I want to know if you've any kind of conscience about it."

"And if no, you're going to hammer me into the deck, is that it?" Gaffney straightened up. "Fuck off."

Gaffney turned, walked away toward the door. Creese stepped, reached, jumped and grabbed the collar of Gaffney's jacket. Gaffney was pulled in close; the collar was held by the right hand; the left hand was pushed through under Gaffney's crutch. Gaffney was lifted, swung round, let go. His head met the fireplace and his body stretched up behind him with one leg hanging over the fire surround. Two hands reached over, pulled him up, straight, and battered him down again. The hands lifted again, but this time held him in, eye to eye, face to face. Gaffney butted the face. The face recoiled, blood flew, but the grip remained. Gaffney dropped down on one knee. Creese was skewed, his legs were grabbed, and he was over sideways. Gaffney pulled away, rising and running in one movement. A hand pulled at his ankle, pulling his body along the floor, scraping his face along the canal made for spit. Creese sat on Gaffney's back, digging his knees into Gaffney's biceps. He gripped a handful of hair and banged a battered Gaffney's head off the floor. One hand was slid round Gaffney's jaw and the head was pulled up and slowly round. Creese wanted Gaffney on his back, flat. The knees had to open slightly to allow the turn. Gaffney revolved himself quickly, leaned forward from the stomach and sunk teeth into Creese's thigh. There was no scream, but a reflex movement to clutch the thigh set Gaffney free. Gaffney wriggled out, set to run, but heard Creese move. He turned and the boot swung up to the face, and it connected. Creese was over flat on his back. The second kick was grabbed and Gaffney was pulled down on top. The struggle was close now. Two times two arms, two legs and the two heads rolling tight together along the bar floor. Twisting, turning, rolling, holding on, biting, rolling, stopping, punching and rolling away from the blows, but not letting go.

Dust from the floor was in the air, rising to the ceiling. A subway ran under, rumbled under, and dust from the ceiling joined dust from the floor. Plaster from the ceiling fell on the men on the floor. Thin wooden straps sprung through holes that were new, or old and getting bigger. More plaster fell on the men on the floor. Two men rolled on the floor and the building shook. A wooden prop burst through the window above two men who struggled on the floor. A wall moved to the side and wide cracks widened. Sandstone blocks appeared behind the plaster like a stairway. And two men fought along the floor of the bar. Plaster piled in, wooden strapping, beams and floorboards from the house up above surrendered and fell through the gaps in the ceiling. Stones, bricks, sandstone blocks, crumbled, fell down, and down. And the plaster and the wood and the stones and the blocks fell over the two men fighting each other on the floor of the bar. And they were continually covered until the shaking of the building ceased and there was only the dust of the air between the ceiling and the floor.

Even before the last stone had stopped falling, Gaffney had dug himself free. He huddled in a corner, head buried in his arms, and waited for the rain of brick and boulder to pass. Another last chip fell. He scanned the remains of the bar that was the Clyde Vaults. Gaffney was looking for Hamish Creese. There was only a pile of sand and stone and crazily pointing sticks and boards. The building groaned and more loose chippings fell. One of the swing doors was four inches higher than the other. The building was collapsing, little bit by little bit. And there was no Hamish Creese. Hamish Creese was under that mound, somewhere near this end of the bar. He was under there and Gaffney was here, and this building was only waiting on the next subway to pass.

"No no no no no no no no."

Gaffney eased to his feet. The struggle had taken them nearer to the door. They had been somewhere there toward the end of the bar. He guessed a spot, crawled over and began digging. digging digging digging faster, clearing away dirt, pushing rubble behind and heaving away stones.

"Creese. Creese you bastard can you hear me? Creese for fuck sake Creese."

His nails were broken, the fingers bled and stiffened into claws. He saw the hammer at the end of the bar. Gaffney went for it, bent over stiff, unable to straighten up. The hammer was used to dig harder, scrape away the stuff from under the big blocks, keep it coming out and make enough room for the fingers to get in, get a grip. To get a grip under this one, a big one. Gaffney heaved; moved it, held it while strength ran from his thighs through his back to his shoulders and down to his arms. It moved. Held up then pushed to slide away down the other side of the mound. And Hamish Creese was there. He was there. There. Gaffney dusted the eyes and cleared the nostrils. The eyes opened. "Creese? Can you hear me? Creese." The chin fell but the mouth never opened. Gaffney dug. The shoulders were clear now but one long block lay across the chest. Gaffney took up the hammer again and began to scrape away underneath. Scrape, scraping out a channel for his fingers. This block was too heavy. It would not move. Move. Hamish Creese was forcing words out.

"Gaffney, Gaffney, you're wasting your time."

Gaffney tried. His whole body was put into a heave and a push at the sandstone slab. It was jammed and it never moved. It stayed on the chest of Hamish Creese. Stuck. "Gaffney, don't bother, it's done." The voice was a whisper now. "The good die first."

Gaffney reversed the hammer, using the handle to push and pull and rapidly paddle away under the stone. His wet lips formed a hole in the dust of his face. "The good die first?" He dug. He dug again and did not stop but spoke as he breathed.

"The good die first, eh? That's right. That's right. And those whose hearts are dry as summer dust burn to the socket, is that it?" He dug. "They'd like us to believe that wouldn't they?" He dug harder. Gaffney dug and the eyelids of Hamish Creese closed over. Gaffney noticed, stopped, leaned over, listened. Nothing. Hamish Creese was dead. Eddie Gaffney cried.